My Lady

Sincerely,

Joyce Wheeler

My Lady

a novel

JOYCE WHEELER

Pleasant Word
A Division of WinePress Group

Pleasant Word (a division of WinePress Publishing, PO Box 428, Enumclaw, WA 98022) functions only as book publisher. As such, the ultimate design, content, editorial accuracy, and views expressed or implied in this work are those of the author.

Unless otherwise noted, all Scriptures are taken from the *New King James Version*, © 1979, 1980, 1982 by Thomas Nelson, Inc., Publishers. Used by permission.

ISBN 13: 978-1-4141-1384-5
ISBN 10: 1-4141-1384-6
Library of Congress Catalog Card Number: 2009901046

Contents

Prologue

*J*OLENE WATCHED THE parched Wyoming scenery flash by in a dreary sense of brownness as she straddled the back of Dexter's Harley. The hot August sun beat mercilessly on her black pants and shirt and ran tiny rivulets of sweat down her back. Even with the helmet and earphones, the drone of the motorcycles all around them was deafening and she only caught a small part of what Dexter was saying to her.

She wondered again why anyone so immersed in comfort as Dexter DeLange would even consider taking a motorcycle the four hundred miles from Denver to the rallies in Sturgis. And why would anyone who valued the quiet life as much as she did even consider going on such a noisy, crowded, hot journey as this was proving to be?

She sighed and slumped a little more into the muscular back of the man who talked her into such nonsense.

"Jolena?" His voice purred into her earphones. "Only a couple more hours. Do you want to stop for a while?"

Looking at the mass of humanity barreling down Interstate 25 she couldn't imagine anyplace being quiet and cool and private. Better to get to the motel in Sturgis and relax under a cold shower than to stop along the way.

"Why do these bikers think this is fun?" she muttered into her mike. Dexter took his hand off the handlebars and squeezed her knee. She heard his low chuckle.

"It's a chance to be bad boys and girls for a week … dress the part, roar around, and be big spenders. Then go back home and into the old routine."

"Is that why you wanted to come, Dexter, for us to be a bad boy and girl?"

Once again she heard his low laughter. "Sometimes your virtue is overpowering. I need to shake you up a little."

Only Dexter could say such a thing to me, she mused as they sped along. When he had first mentioned going into the South Dakota Black Hills for a photo session, she had visions of a quaint lodge somewhere in the mountains. Only the day before they left had he informed her of the Harley and Sturgis. She had argued vehemently against the plan, suspicious of his planning to dress her like the biker women she had seen on TV whenever August and the Sturgis rally rolled around. She frowned suddenly. How did Dexter always manage to get his own way with her lately?

She sat up a little straighter and pulled away from him. Once again she felt a gentle squeeze on her knee. He knew her every move. That was the trouble, she realized. He studied her every action and knew by the expression on her face what she was thinking. If he didn't know, he made it his business to find out. Dexter was the most complex, handsome, and exciting man she had ever known, and she loved him with abandon. However, there were moments she was suspicious of his motives, and even a little scared of his obsession with her.

CHAPTER 1

Life's Changing Moments

SPRINGTIME ON THE rolling sand hills of Nebraska can be a panorama of sunny days and green grass, baby calves, and wildflowers. Jolene O'Neil sat easily on her horse, Tango, and watched her parents ride across the calving pasture with their usual careful supervision of their cattle herd. She felt overwhelming gratitude as the balmy breeze ruffled her horse's mane.

Ah, dear God, thank You. Thank You for springtime and ranches and parents. She could have added many other things to the list but Tango was ready to join the others, and she relaxed the reins and let the horse lope across the short distance. Spencer and Barbara O'Neil had raised their only child with the love of the land and the O'Neil cattle heritage in her blood. Jolene knew they were as proud of that fact as they were of their sixteen-year-old daughter's riding ability.

"How many calves born today?" she asked them as they ambled toward the barn. She noted her dad had his saddlebag crammed with ear tags, and the ever-present calving book was in his pocket. He seemed slow in answering her, and she was surprised to see her mother give him a concerned glance. The moment passed quickly, however, and he replied in his soft drawl that they had marked over fourteen little rascals. He added that Jolene's mother was as graceful being chased by a mama cow as she was at everything else. They all laughed at that bit of humor, and as the twilight shadows lengthened Jolene felt her usual contentment that all was well in her world.

She appreciated the gentle hues and soft colors that were woven into her life's tapestry. Her parents had taught her about the great love the Master Weaver had for all His children and how each trial was His way of making a beautiful masterpiece. Yet when the vibrant, dark colors of sorrow started in her own life, she was unprepared for the grief they represented.

Jolene's dark threads began the day Uncle Walt and Aunt Arlene came in with grim faces and in halting tones told her both her parents had been killed instantly when their horse trailer came loose on the steep road out of town. The threads became darker still when her grandmother on her mother's side insisted Jolene come and live with her. Even over vehement protests from Walt and Arlene, Grandmother Florence prevailed, and Jolene started her junior year of high school in Sterling. Expecting to stay at Florence's ranch and drive the twenty miles to school, she had another jolt when she was told with undue firmness that she would be staying at the Reverend and Mrs. Taylor's home. In a voice that boded no argument, Florence insisted that their daughter was Jolene's age and it would be good for her to be with young people in town instead of with crusty ranchers and their horses.

With great understanding and compassion Walt and Arlene gave Jolene a pickup to drive the eighty miles to the O'Neil ranch and their permission to come whenever she could. However, when winter howled in from the north, her trips back home became less frequent.

The Taylors were kind people, and their daughter, Rachel, soon became Jolene's best friend. Jolene slowly settled into their routine, joined in with other students at school, and attempted to understand the bewildering events that had brought her there. She and Rachel spent a great deal of time in Reverend Taylor's book-lined study, quizzing the gentle minister on godly matters pertaining to life after death, and tenderhearted Rachel's eyes would fill with tears that threatened to spill over and down her cheeks. She would often jump out of her chair and give Jolene a hug, as if by that act of compassion she could make life better for her friend.

It was during just such an episode in late December that the doorbell rang, and Jolene could hear Mrs. Taylor's quick steps answering the chimes. "Well, hello there!" she exclaimed and soon ushered their visitor into the study.

From her curled-up position in the winged armchair, Jolene noted Harold Taylor's delighted look as he quickly stood up. With outstretched hand he walked around his desk and exclaimed happily, "It's been a long time, you rascal!"

Jolene peered around the wing of her chair and quickly ducked back with wide eyes. This guy was one unbelievably handsome rascal.

"Uncle Dexter!" The shout Rachel gave as she rushed into the visitor's outstretched arms was one of pure delight. "I didn't know you were coming! How long can you stay?"

"A couple of days, Princess; long enough to be the family barber and see what you're giving me for Christmas." The voice seemed to purr and fill the whole room.

Jolene's young mind nimbly put the pieces together. This must be Dexter DeLange, Betty Taylor's brother and renowned hair stylist and designer from Denver. She recognized him from the many photos that graced the hallway upstairs.

"You haven't met the young lady who boards with us," Reverend Taylor said as he directed his brother-in-law toward Jolene's chair. "Dexter, this is Jolene O'Neil, Florence Johnson's granddaughter; and Jolene, this is Betty's brother, Dexter DeLange."

Jolene reluctantly uncurled herself from the shelter of the big chair and stood up. "Hello, sir," she mumbled, and realized she was only a few inches shorter than he was.

The dark eyes seemed to flicker in surprise. "Miss O'Neil." He folded his arms across his chest and studied her closely. "Were your parents"— he paused before continuing slowly—"Barbara and Spencer O'Neil?"

At her nod he reached out and clasped her cold hand in both of his warm ones. "I was very sorry to hear of their accident. Your grandmother Florence told me about it." Releasing her hand he added in an offhand voice, "You certainly resemble your mother. When I was young and just starting DeLange Designs, I asked Barbara to be my receptionist." He suddenly gave Jolene a wry grin. "She had, however, met and married your father."

Before Jolene could reply, Betty hugged her and said, "Barbara was an astute young lady. She and Spencer were perfect for each other. I think it was love at first sight."

"Grandma Florence always said she married the wrong man, but Mom would ..." Jolene faltered as she realized that very possibly she was speaking to Florence's Mr. Right.

"Yes? And what would your mother say to that?" His dark eyes seemed to be mocking her.

"She would always say that ..." Jolene paused again and looked down at her feet. She supposed only the truth would do, and, raising her chin a little defiantly, she continued. "She said the man Grandma thought she should have married dated many women, loved none of them, and she was no exception."

Jolene was relieved to see his white teeth flash in amusement. "And she was correct in thinking that, Miss O'Neil."

He turned toward Rachel and seemed to abruptly change the subject. "Now Miss Rachel"—his voice purred once more—"have you given any consideration toward the modeling profession we usually discuss?" The elder Taylors glanced at Jolene with rolled eyes. "Never mind your parents," he added with a smile. "They always look like that when we talk about your future career."

"I will be your number one model if the world wants someone with braces and a geeky look." She gave her uncle a grin that displayed the whole range of her wired teeth.

"Geeky my foot," he replied. "You'll always look like a princess to me." Once again he looked at Jolene intently. "And what about you, Jolena, have you ever thought of being a model?"

She answered rather gruffly. "It's Jolene, sir, and no, I want to be a ranch woman when I grow up."

In the evening Jolene watched as the family bustled around and got ready for the traditional hair session. With scissors in hand, Dexter proceeded to snip and fluff, and soon Betty was gazing in the mirror with a satisfied look. Harold gladly took her place and reminded Dexter that the last time the local barber cut his hair it was shorter on one side than the other. He said he was afraid to point it out for fear that by the time it was even he would be bald.

"Daddy always tells Uncle Dexter that story," Rachel whispered to Jolene, and both girls giggled. Rachel had found a picture of the way she wanted her hair to look, and now she waited patiently with drips of water trickling down her face from her shampoo at the kitchen sink.

It was while she watched Rachel's black tresses being coiffed into perfection that Jolene realized she was being studied by calculating dark eyes. It suddenly dawned on her that her own blonde hair would be considered the next project by this industrious uncle, and with that thought, Jolene panicked.

"Good heavens! Look at the time!" she blurted out. "Homework! I forgot all about my homework!" She abruptly stood up and took several steps toward the door before Rachel stopped her.

"But, Jolene, don't you want to wait until Uncle Dexter can fix your hair?"

She slowly turned and faced both of them. "I guess I'd better skip the beauty treatment tonight," she answered carefully, and while disappointment was etched on Rachel's face, an amused look crept over the uncle's features.

"There will definitely be another time, Miss O'Neil," he offered quietly, and reached for a cigarette in his shirt pocket.

As she hurried upstairs to her room Jolene wondered why the thought of a man working on her hair should be so upsetting. She showered and popped into her pajamas, and then she caught a glimpse of her damp, straggling hair and knew the answer. No man as good looking and sophisticated as Dexter DeLange, even if he was old enough to be her father, was going to see her with sopping wet hair and water running down her face.

As she slowly crawled between the sheets, a Bible verse her mother often quoted filtered through her mind: "Vanity of vanities, all is vanity." She sighed deeply and the usual ache of lonesomeness whenever she thought of her parents crept over her.

"What a day, dear Lord. What a day. Whoever would have thought Mom and Dad would have known someone like this Dexter? Vanity, Lord, I missed a chance to get my hair looking decent because of my stupid vanity. Good grief."

CHAPTER 2

Difficult Decisions

THE CHICKENS CLUCKED contentedly at Arlene's feet while she and Jolene set out their grain and brought in a pail of water. On this spring day, Arlene noticed more tears than usual filling Jolene's eyes, and her nurturing nature was trying to find a way to bring some comfort and smiles to her husband's niece.

After Spencer's and Barbara's deaths, having Jolene come live with them had seemed the only sensible solution. They were stunned when Florence insisted Jolene live with her and her son Dale on their ranch and even more indignant when Florence placed Jolene with the Taylors. Walt and Arlene had many conversations about Florence during the winter, and none of them were complimentary.

"Imagine," Arlene sputtered during breakfast one morning, "just imagine our Jolene having to live in town during the week! She is a country girl to her very core. Horses, kittens, dogs—Jolene has always had her animals. She won't be happy there one minute. What is that Florence thinking of anyway? I could just scream."

Walt looked at his normally placid wife with some alarm and slowly drank his coffee before he answered. "I can't figure it out. Florence has never fussed over Jolene much, mostly left them all to their own doings. She's always wanted everything for that selfish brother of Barbara's—what's his name?—Dale, and he's as surly as they come. Jolene don't like him one bit. Maybe that's why Florence wanted Jo to stay at the Taylors'. Maybe Dale didn't want her there."

Arlene's eyes had flashed fire to think of anyone not wanting a young girl whose parents had been killed. His only sibling's child to boot. "Well, this I know, Walt O'Neil. Come summer, Jolene is coming here, and come fall, she's a-staying here with us and going to the school she started in, and that is final. Period. No one is going to tell me this isn't where she belongs and that is that. Period."

"Amen, sister!" Walt's eyes crinkled with good humor at his gentle wife's declaration. Arlene was easygoing but when her hackles were up, she could be a formidable soldier.

They had told Jolene their intentions that morning, and she had cried with relief. Arlene knew their niece was fond of the Taylor family, but she was just as sure Jolene's heart broke every time she had to leave the ranch. She missed her old schoolmates, she missed her aunt and uncle, and on this sand-hills spring day, Arlene sensed Jolene missed her mom and dad almost more than she could endure.

Jolene nudged an inquisitive hen off her foot. "Aunt Arlene, would it be all right if I went over to the folks' place today?"

Arlene reached over the brown hens and gave Jolene a quick hug. "Honey, Walt and I were wondering if you might want to do that. There are papers that need to be found and gone over … if you're ready for all that."

The tears ran down Jolene's cheeks unchecked. "I'm not ready, but it has to be done. I'm already miserable, so we might as well do it now."

"Hmmm, guess there's a certain logic in that … I think." Arlene laughed a little ruefully while her own eyes brimmed over with tears.

The three of them rode in silence on the drive over. No doubt the others were lost in their memories as Arlene was, and the past year had made those memories even more poignant. The house had been locked, and Walt checked things regularly, yet the place had that unoccupied look that made it seem lonesome. After Spencer and Barbara's deaths, Walt and Arlene had gone through most of the papers for the ranch. They had removed an entire file cabinet with the help of their son Ben, and it was at their house. Yet the desk drawers needed clearing out and a few other items needed attention.

Before they entered the house, Arlene took Jolene's and Walt's hands in her own and looked at both of them. She loved these two people and had the uneasy feeling that the task ahead of them was going to be daunting. "I feel the need to pray." They looked at her questioningly, but both stopped on the porch steps and bowed their heads.

"Dear heavenly Father." She began without any more preamble. "Dear Father, our hearts are so heavy. Please help us. Give us the comfort today that we need. Only You can help us through times like this. Only You, Father, know what we need today to give us strength. We ask this in Your Son Jesus' name. Amen."

"Amen," Walt said softly. Jolene nodded her agreement, and Arlene heard her take a deep breath.

They walked through the rooms, noting that the beds were still made, dressers still full of clothes, dishes in the cupboard. The rooms felt hushed, as if waiting for the laughter and love that used to fill them up. Finally they entered the den. Spencer's big desk beckoned them, but it looked different from the way Arlene remembered it. All the years she had known him, Spencer kept a neat desk, but now sticky notes covered most of its surface.

Jolene sat in the swivel chair and slowly opened the big middle drawer. Walt removed a side drawer and sat on another chair to begin sorting. Arlene sat on the floor, looking through files of horse registrations. They were all silent, as if speaking would disturb the memories the room contained.

Suddenly Jolene gasped and then cried out. The color drained from her face, and her eyes stared in disbelief at the paper in her hand.

"What is it?" Walt asked sharply.

With a shaking voice Jolene repeated over and over, "Oh, no. Oh, no … is this true, Uncle Walt?" She looked at him beseechingly before she added, "I never knew—did you have any idea?" She rose quickly out of her chair and brought him a paper that bore the name of a doctor and a medical clinic.

Walt scanned the page through his reading glasses. After a few minutes he removed them and said softly, "Arlene, read this."

She took the paper, looked at the two of them, and slowly, out loud, read what it said.

My dear friend Spencer,

I have sat here for some time trying to compose this letter. You asked me to write you the results of your last test, rather than call you. Spencer, how do I tell you that you have an inoperable brain tumor? Or did you already suspect that when you came to my office?

When you told me your symptoms, I was worried. When the MRI results came in, I was devastated. Six months, Spencer, is usually the limit. Get your affairs in order. Call me as your condition worsens. I can help make the end more comfortable.

You requested that I not say anything to Barbara about your visit and, my friend, I will honor your request, but you will have to tell her eventually so she can understand the changes in your personality. Your love for each other and for the Lord will carry you through this.

With my deepest prayers,
Joseph P. Cramer

Stunned silence permeated the room after Arlene finished reading. Then once again Jolene asked, "Did you know this?" Her eyes looked imploringly from one to the other. "Did you know this?" The blank looks Walt and Arlene gave her answered her question.

Walt said, "I can't believe … I never noticed a thing. Nothing. He kept it all to himself, never let on." Walt paused then added in a shaking voice, "That was so like Spencer. He was always thinking of others, always wanting to do the right thing." Walt's voice cracked. "He must have been so worried about leaving you without a father, of leaving Barbara, the ranch, all of us. He just kept it all to himself. I just wish he would have told me … I wish he would have told me." He covered his eyes with his hands and his big shoulders shook with grief.

Jolene knelt beside him and put her head on his knee and sobbed. His callused hand patted her shoulder and Arlene's arms surrounded both of them. The realization that Spencer had carried this burden all alone was heavy on their hearts, and though the accident that so quickly took his life was grievous, they had always comforted themselves with the thought that at least he had been happy until his and Barbara's death. This new knowledge meant he knew a time bomb ticked away his life's moments until it would render him incapacitated.

"When was the letter written?" Arlene asked. She checked the date. "This was written about a month before they were killed. A month … probably before his condition was noticeable, but surely there must have been some signs. I never thought much about it at the time. Jolene, honey, can you think back? Can you think of anything?"

Jolene's nose needed a tissue and she sniffled her way to the bathroom and brought back a whole roll of toilet paper for the three of them. Walt and Arlene gratefully acknowledged her thoughtfulness and took turns pulling off wads of paper to blow their noses and dab at their eyes.

"You guys," Jolene's voice came out rather nasal. "We're all a bawling mess and I love you both for crying with me today! I don't know why I just can't seem to quit." Arlene took several more sheets off the roll and quickly handed them to her.

Jolene held it to her nose, but the tears kept coming. She took several deep breaths, and when she spoke her voice was thick. "I'm remembering something." She blew her nose again. "Last spring, when we were all out riding, I remember Dad taking a long time answering me, and Mom looked at him funny like." She sniffed and took another deep breath.

Nothing was said for several moments, then Arlene patted Jolene on the knee. "You know, your Uncle Walt sitting here sharing a roll of *toilette* paper with two women is sorta funny like too."

Jolene and Walt both threw startled looks at Arlene. She grinned at them as they shook their heads and started chuckling.

Suddenly it seemed like the spell of gloom was broken. They pulled up the shades and walked through the house, discussing what they should pack, what they should leave, and, most importantly, what they would do with the ranch.

Ben came over and together they formulated a plan. He was getting married in the summer, and he and his new bride, Sarah, would live there and rent from Jolene. Arlene was relieved to hear Jolene say she was grateful someone she cared about would be taking over her old home. It needed life and happiness. Her parents would have wanted that.

As they gathered around her folks' kitchen table, Jolene was thoughtful. "I believe, now that I think about it, there were other signs," she said. "I remember how Dad started making notes to himself. I'm sure you noticed them stuck all over his desk. He just said one day that he had so much on his mind that he was going to get it written down so he wouldn't forget. You know Mom was always a note maker, so it made sense to her."

"I think God knew Barbara would have been inconsolable without him, so in His wisdom He allowed the accident to happen." Arlene liked tidy solutions to problems.

"I never could figure out how that trailer came unhitched. Spencer was always so careful about things like that. I wonder if the tumor had something to do with that ..." Ben shook his head.

"I guess we'll never know how the accident happened," Walt said, "but I'm grateful we came here today and learned the truth about Spencer's illness." He paused and looked at Jolene. "It gives me a different feeling about their death, makes me realize that God has mercy."

Jolene rested her chin on her propped arm. "It's probably a good thing Aunt Arlene prayed before we walked in the house. I suppose it's easier knowing they went quickly instead of watching

Dad die slowly. It would have been so hard on Mom and me to see that." She sighed. "Ben and Sarah will have a good home here. I suppose we can move forward now."

Arlene thought Jolene's voice sounded far older than her seventeen years. "Well, I can tell you one thing; I feel drained and in need of a cup of coffee. Period."

Once again there was quiet laughter. Maybe it was just Arlene's imagination, but the place seemed to be a little less lonesome when they left.

CHAPTER 3

Proms and Promises

*Y*OU'LL LOVE THE prom, Jolene. Everyone gets all dressed up and there's flowers and all sorts of great things," Rachel said as the great day loomed closer. The two girls were walking home after school on a balmy spring afternoon, and Jolene had just confided to Rachel that a senior boy in her ag class had asked her to be his date at the Sterling High School annual prom and promenade. "The best part is that Uncle Dexter comes with some of his staff to one of the local salons and helps style some of the girls' hair!"

Jolene frowned. "Why in the world does he do that?" she asked. She had already decided to fix her hair herself.

"Well, he's always looking for new models, and if he sees someone here that he thinks has all the qualities plus a desire for that lifestyle, he helps them," Rachel explained. "He says he loves the world of fashion because it's as fickle and as changeable as he is, but I actually think he likes the money he gets from all those models he's discovered."

"Well, that life wouldn't be for me," Jolene declared. Then as if trying to prove how ridiculous the whole idea was, she struck an awkward pose and smiled a cheesy smile.

Rachel laughed as Jolene wobbled into a lilac bush. As the two girls began walking down the sidewalk again, she continued.

"Uncle Dexter has a good friend who's a photographer, and he and his wife have a studio at DeLange Designs. You'd enjoy seeing all his neat pictures. Sometimes Mom and I go there and get the royal treatment. Generally there's some gorgeous woman with Uncle Dexter, and she's dressed to the hilt and so is he. Don't you think he's the most handsome man you've ever seen, Jolene?"

"Rachel, just where have I ever been to see good-looking men?" They both got the giggles over that, and when they reached the Taylors' house they were ready for their usual afternoon chat with Betty before they started on their homework.

To Jolene's dismay, her grandmother Florence was sitting in the kitchen having coffee with the Taylors. Her blue hair was piled high on top of her head, and she wore her usual heels with her slacks outfit. Jolene wondered every time she saw her why Florence insisted on staying at the ranch with Dale. She obviously didn't act like the ranch women Jolene knew in the sand hills, and as far as that went, Florence wouldn't know how to staple a fence or drive a tractor. As far as Jolene knew, she never wore jeans or boots, she didn't like animals of any kind, and she was as far from being like her daughter Barbara as the north pole was from the south pole, a fact her son-in-law Spencer mentioned and gave thanks for many times.

"Jolene dear!" Her voice always grated on Jolene's nerves. "We were just talking about you and how glad Dexter was to see his old flame's daughter. Poor man. Oh, yes, he called me many times and asked about Barbara. I felt so sorry for him." Her breathless voice seemed to prattle on and on.

Jolene sighed inwardly. Grandma Florence was the only person in the world who thought Barbara had a broken hearted old flame. Jolene remembered very well the irritation on her mother's face when Florence would blat on and on about it, and on more than one occasion she had heard her mother remind Florence that such talk was only a figment of Florence's imagination.

Jolene realized that only this winter she had a name and face to go with Florence's ramblings, and Jolene seriously doubted that Rachel's Uncle Dexter had wasted any moments pining over some long-ago flirtation. She noticed the Taylors both looked a little pained, and wondered how long her grandmother had been sitting there keeping them from their work.

"That Dexter is a charmer. He's always telling me of some new fling he has, but I know he'll never find anyone like my Babs. Of course, she made the wrong choice, but, then, what can a mother do about that? He is a heartbreaker, though. Betty dear, how many times have we heard how he loved them and left them, and all the poor things still just crazy about him. You probably don't remember this, Reverend Taylor, but when he was a little boy he was so cute. When he didn't get his own way he'd stomp his little foot and those black eyes would just snap. Of course I'm sure he still wants his own way all the time, but of course now that he's grown up he probably doesn't have to stomp his foot. Oh, dear me, that would be funny.

"Jolene dear, don't just stand there, hovering over me. Sit down and tell me who you'll be going to the prom with. I might know him or at least his parents. Good heavens, at my age I might even know his grandparents." She tittered over such a preposterous idea.

Before Jolene could answer, the phone rang, and Reverend Taylor sprang up with amazing agility to go answer it in his office. Betty also stood up and asked if the girls would like some sandwiches before they tackled their homework.

"Oh, but Betty dear, I was going to take Jolene home with me this afternoon. She so misses our ranch when she's in town all week, and her uncle Dale always wants to know how she's doing. Don't you think you should come, dear?" She held out a well-manicured hand and patted Jolene's arm.

"I probably better not this time, I, uh, I have quite a bit of homework." She hedged, trying to think of a better reason and looked desperately at Rachel.

"Oh, no, Mrs. Johnson, she can't go with you today!" Rachel came to her rescue with a determined look on her face. "Not only do we have gobs of homework, but the prom committee is getting ready to decorate, and you wouldn't want her to miss that!"

"What are the decorations like this year, Rachel? Jolene never tells me anything, and since I'm so far from town I like to hear all the news the few times I get in."

Rachel tried to discuss decorations, dresses, and other prom-related subjects, but everything she said reminded Florence of some distant event in her life, and she would interrupt constantly to elaborate on a memory that would have been better forgotten.

While Rachel and Betty listened politely, Jolene groused to herself that Florence was in town every week to get her hair blued and fixed. Another figment of Florence's imagination, Jolene grumbled to herself, was the idea she missed that place. For as long as she could remember, Jolene had thought Florence's ranch was a mean and miserable place, situated in a draw with a sullen barn that had windows arranged in a perpetual frown. When she was a little girl and they came for their yearly visit, she would always cry when she saw the barn. She said it didn't want them there. She still felt that way, and her uncle Dale added to the unwelcome feeling. Her grandmother's house was a study of perfection with doilies and knickknacks everywhere. A speck of dust wouldn't dare show its dirty little face, and for that matter, neither would a child.

When Florence finally left, the Taylors and Jolene gave an audible sigh of relief. Their nerves were jangled by her constant talk. Jolene mentally thanked God that Grandmother didn't stop in every time she was in town. Yet, as Reverend Taylor remarked, Florence was lonely and he wished she would move to one of the many apartments in Sterling. She always had some excuse or another, but basically, she didn't want to leave Dale alone on the ranch.

As Rachel had predicted, Dexter and his crew came to style hair for an excited group of teenagers. There was a buzz of anticipation around school as all the girls talked about having such a highly esteemed hair stylist in their midst, and more than one asked Jolene when her appointment was. She had to keep explaining that she hadn't made one, and several girls asked her if she wasn't at least going to take her dress in to have him critique it. She looked at them, puzzled. "Why would I do that?"

They screamed with laughter at her ignorance. "Everybody has DeLange Designs tell them what looks best for their shape and coloring. Where have you been, Jolene?"

She thought the whole thing was ridiculous, and after school and all the way to the Taylors she mumbled and muttered to Rachel about dressing up and having people fuss with her hair.

"Ah, Jolene." Rachel's voice was hesitant. "Uncle Dexter is ah, well, sometimes he's pretty determined about hair and styles, and he can be quite opinionated about other people's taste. Don't feel bad if he, you know, doesn't like what you picked out."

Jolene thought mutinously that it didn't matter to her if he liked it or not. He wasn't going to fix her hair, and he wasn't going to see her little red dress.

They could smell the cigarette smoke as soon as they entered the house. In the kitchen with his feet propped on a chair sat the man himself. He was drinking a cup of coffee with his sister, and his short-sleeved, black silk shirt hung in gentle folds over his broad shoulders. Jolene noted his square jawline and olive skin and couldn't help but give a nervous shudder. Uncles should not be that handsome.

"There she is," he commented to Betty. "Well, Princess, get your hair washed and we'll get you ready for the ball." Without a backward glance at her friend, Rachel hurried upstairs to do his bidding.

Jolene started to follow, but Dexter stopped her in midflight. "And you, Miss O'Neil, when are you getting your hair fixed?" She turned to see those black eyes looking at her amusedly.

She smiled politely. "I'm just getting ready to do that now, sir. I'm going up to get my dress and ... all that ... stuff."

He took his feet off the chair and stood up. "I'll go up with you."

Her eyes widened. "Why?"

He laughed a little wickedly at her discomfort. "No one has shown me your dress, Jolena, and let's just say I'm curious to see what you picked out."

"Jolene, sir. My name is Jolene."

"Oh, sorry, I forgot again." He followed her up the stairs.

She stopped so abruptly on the landing that he almost ran into her. "Mr. DeLange." She turned to him and sighed. "I like my dress, whether you will or not, and even if it isn't right, I'll still have to wear it because I don't have anything else."

He raised an eyebrow at that and steered her into her room. Without a word he gazed at the red dress with its high collar trimmed in black piping. He fingered the cap sleeves, also trimmed in black. He stared at the black sandals, bravely standing at attention, and then, putting his fingers to his mouth, he walked around Jolene, studying her from every angle.

She twirled a pencil around her bangs, becoming more nervous by the minute. To her horror, she had entangled the dumb thing, and hard as she tried, could not dislodge it from the curl that had formed around it.

"Well, thanks, Mr. DeLange. Nice of you to take a look at the dress. I'm sure Princess is waiting downstairs for you …" He stood in front of her and gently unwound the errant pencil and tossed it on the dresser.

"Now then." His voice seemed to purr. "This color red makes you look blotchy." He turned her around to face the mirror and started rolling up the sleeves of her T-shirt. "Yes, it's as I thought; you have biceps."

His flat statement made Jolene jerk her arm out of his grasp. Then she realized what biceps were and demanded, "What's wrong with that?"

He smiled down at her. "Jolena …"

She started to correct him, and he held up his hand. "Yes, excuse me. Now then, *Jolene*, let me tell you that cap sleeves are not going to flatter your arms. Black piping is not going to help matters. Your hair is styled all wrong." Once again he held up his hand as she started to interrupt. "If you'll allow me to—and we don't have much time—if you'll cooperate with me, I can make you the belle of the ball."

"Mr. DeLange, I appreciate your offer, but even a fairy godmother couldn't pull that one off."

"No, Miss O'Neil, but I can."

Three hours later, two young men came to the Taylors' door to claim their dates. One met a vision in pink gossamer. With her black hair curling around her face and seeming to glimmer in the lights, Rachel indeed looked like a princess. The other young man had to wait a while, but when he saw his date come hesitantly down the steps, he watched in open admiration. Her green gown was modestly v-necked and sleeveless. Her blonde hair was a creation of curls piled almost recklessly on top of her head, exposing a graceful neck. Her green eyes snapped with merriment, but not at him so much as the man standing behind him in the kitchen, smoking a cigarette.

CHAPTER 4

Captain John Harris

CAPTAIN JOHN HARRIS looked up from his Air Force recruiting table at Chadron State College in Nebraska to answer the question the young lady had asked him. Dressed in jeans and a green cotton sweater, she had half perched on his table and was looking at Air Force material.

"Yes, of course you can take these brochures. Are you interested in the Air Force?"

"Oh no, no … I just have a friend who isn't here today and he wanted some info." John liked the sound of her voice and the twinkle in her eyes. Wanting to prolong the conversation, he asked her what she was interested in. He was rather taken aback when she answered with one word: "Ranching."

She must have sensed his unspoken questions and said she was studying everything in marketing and business that would help her. Then she added that this was her second year at Chadron State College, and she had gone there because it was close to her family's ranch in the sand hills.

She laughed. "Now you have the whole nine yards about my life," she said with dancing green eyes. "And that was probably more than you wanted to know." She held up a couple of brochures. "Thanks."

He watched her walk away, her long legs taking easy strides across the gym floor.

For reasons he never would understand, he rushed after her and said, "Nine yards aren't nearly enough to satisfy me."

She agreed to have a cup of coffee at the nearby café. That wasn't enough to satisfy him either, and he continued dating Jolene throughout the fall and winter. By Christmastime, he knew without a doubt he wanted to spend the rest of his life with this woman. She was everything he thought his wife should be, yet he realized there were issues that needed to be addressed between them.

John was a thoughtful young man, and he knew Jolene was infatuated with ranch life. He wondered a little sadly if his love could make up for her lost dreams.

Jolene wondered how she could have fallen in love with a man who wasn't in the cattle business. She spent soul-searching moments with God, asking over and over again what He wanted her to do. She confessed that her heart would always be on the prairie, and yet the love she felt for John always drew her away to him.

She knew she was starry eyed whenever she talked to Walt and Arlene about her captain, and one weekend morning in late January she found herself rambling on about him over breakfast coffee.

"Jolene." Walt interrupted her a little gruffly. "I think you need to stop and think about this. I don't know what your future plans are, but it looks to me like, well, like this is getting pretty serious." He took a drink of coffee before continuing. "This guy is not a cowboy. If you get hitched up to his wagon you won't be a cowgirl. I always told your dad that you were all O'Neil. No one can hold a candle to the way you sit on a horse or work cattle."

He looked down at the table and wiped an imaginary crumb off. "I don't believe in interfering with affairs of the heart, Jolene, but, well, you just need to stop and think about this." Before Jolene could reply he pushed his chair back and muttered that he had cows to feed.

"Oh, and Arlene, when the cake truck comes, tell them to unload it in the overhead bin," he added.

Walt's seriousness was unsettling to Jolene. She understood what he was saying and knew he felt it needed to be said, but this particular January morning her heart wanted to be carefree in her newfound love.

With a little laugh she said, "Talking about cake reminds me of the time John heard me saying something about caking the cows. He looked completely baffled!" She continued merrily. "I had to explain that what we call cake is a pellet with nutrients that we feed to cattle in the wintertime to supplement their feed."

Walt shook his head and headed into the porch to put his coat on.

After he left, Arlene refilled their coffee cups and sat back down. She patted Jolene's arm and said, "Walt and I are selfish, honey. We both had hoped you would find someone around here to marry. I guess we just wanted you close to us."

Jolene nodded. She had wanted that too. A ranch, a rancher, children. Those were all her dreams, and yet … "Aunt Arlene, I know. I know what both of you are saying. Especially when I'm here with you, I realize how much all this means to me." She gave a huge sigh and looked at her aunt. "But when I think of not having John in my life, somehow all those things don't seem so important anymore. He's such a good and godly man, Arlene. He knows my life will change if we get married, and he worries about that."

"Has he asked you to marry him, Jolene?"

"Not yet, but when he does, I'm going to say yes."

They set their wedding date for June 15 at the Air Force Academy chapel in Colorado Springs. Because time was limited, they planned a simple ceremony and reception, much to Florence's great dismay. She had been sharply opposed to John, stressing over and over again that she was sure he wasn't the man for Jolene. She wanted the wedding in Sterling. She wanted a big wedding. She wanted this and that, and yet Jolene knew that she would do very little to help with any of it.

Then suddenly Florence had a whole new interest and dropped all of her objections to Jolene's plans. Florence's son Dale was finally getting married, and his wedding was going to be in Sterling on May 5. Jolene wondered what woman could tolerate Dale, and when she received the wedding invitation, curiosity got the better of her and she decided to attend.

It was a cold and blustery May afternoon when she walked up the steps to Reverend Taylor's familiar church. She would have chosen to sit obscurely somewhere in the sanctuary, but the ushers escorted her close to the groom's family, and after smiling and waving at Florence, who sat a couple rows ahead of her, she slid into the pew with relatives she barely knew. She was attempting to place in her mind just who they were when an usher seated someone else next to her.

An unmistakable low voice said, "I hear the bride is wearing cap sleeves."

Amused, she turned with a smile and looked into Dexter DeLange's mocking eyes.

"I'll bet it looks darn nice too," she replied.

The look on his face told her that he would bet a large amount the opposite way. He leaned back in the pew, crossed his arms over his chest, and then looked down at her again.

"Did you ever use the gift certificate I sent you for graduation?" He critiqued her appearance in a slow appraisal that went from the top of her head to her feet.

Jolene studied him as he made his assessment. She had felt stylish enough when she entered the church with her black heels, tailored black skirt, and white v-necked sweater. She had some sparkling jewelry on, and with her darker skin, she thought she had pulled together a look that was flattering. At least there was no black piping anywhere. She was rather amused to see that he wore a white, open-necked silk shirt under his black suit, almost like they had planned to coordinate their clothes.

"No, I didn't. I just never got to Denver to take advantage of it, but I want to thank you again for the thought."

"You're welcome, Jolena, and the offer is still good, but this time we might do away with the curls."

"But I'm not old enough for a bun."

"How old are you now?"

"Twenty."

"Twenty"—he sighed theatrically—"and attending college at Chadron. You probably have found a boyfriend, and what's this?" He ended rather sharply as she held up her hand to show him her diamond.

"Florence will have another wedding in June," she happily announced. He took her wrist and ran his hand under hers to study the small diamond setting.

He scowled at her and shook his head. "This is sudden. Is there some little crying reason for the big rush?"

She jerked her hand away with indignation and gave him a withering look.

"Sorry, Jolena, bad question." She noticed he looked unrepentant.

The pianist began the prelude for the bride's attendants. Two very self-conscious, plump matrons came down the aisle, and when they reached the front of the church, Jolene noted that while she and Dexter were talking, Dale and his two groomsmen had come onto the dais. Dale looked as nervous as a cat, and the teenage boys who were about to become his stepsons looked equally uncomfortable. The striking notes of the bridal march started, and everyone rose to face the back. The bride, in stark contrast to the rest of the wedding party, strode forward with complete assurance, and by the set of her jaw, Jolene knew this woman would forevermore be in charge of Dale and maybe even Florence. That knowledge brought a smirk to her lips and a mischievous sparkle to her eyes.

Dexter stole a sideways glance at her. "You're very wicked, you know," he muttered.

She nodded apologetically, but couldn't resist the urge to wink at him.

The reception seemed to drone on as toasts were made, wedding cake was cut, and gifts were unwrapped. Before it was half over, Jolene was ready to leave. She said her farewells to Florence, congratulated Dale, and suffered his new wife's hug for "little niecie." With a sigh of relief she walked out of the church, glad once again to be in the fresh air, and shivered as a cold wind whipped through her sweater.

"You should have worn a jacket." Dexter's voice sounded behind her.

"I have one in the car," she retorted, looking over her shoulder. He sauntered beside her and placed a warm arm over her shivering shoulders.

"My car is right here." He guided her to a black Cadillac and opened the door for her to get in.

"But my car is just over there, Mr. DeLange. You don't need to drive me half a block!"

"Get in, Jolene, I'm not driving you to your car. I know a place where we can have coffee in a real cup and have a quiet visit." He tucked her into the passenger side, and then answered her inquiring look. "Yes, I want to talk to you about something."

She had no idea what the conversation could be about, and she shivered as she settled back into the leather seat. He slid under the wheel and the smoky scent of wild musk drifted over to her. She looked at him and sighed inwardly. The rascal was just too good looking she decided, wishing she were in her little car heading back to college. She wasn't uncomfortable with him, but she had to admit he unsettled her.

The feeling didn't go away after they were seated in a secluded little nook and served piping hot coffee in real cups. "Oh, this is good." She sighed, enjoying the warmth and quiet of the place. He had been studying her with careful scrutiny, and she wondered what was on his mind.

"You should be a model, Jolena. You have the right shape, face."
He held up his hand as she started to protest. "No, don't interrupt
until you've heard me out. I want you to think about this. You could
make good money. I could get you in all the right places, watch
over your career. I think you have what it takes to make it big in
the business." He looked at her with a raised eyebrow. "Jolena, there
is so much more waiting for you than being an Air Force wife in
some foreign country."

She looked at him, puzzled, and asked how he knew John was
in the Air Force and where they would be stationed. He answered
with one word: "Florence."

"Oh, bother my grandmother! She always talks too much,"
she snapped.

He sat back in his chair and stretched out his legs, took a drink
of coffee, and then summoned the waiter. "I believe this young lady
and I will be having dinner. Would you bring us a menu?"

"I'm really not hungry. I ate at the reception."

"You ate nothing at the reception—don't look so surprised. I
was watching you. One sip of coffee from a foam cup, and you set
it down and left it. You visited with Betty for a while, saw some
other friends, endured a short visit with Florence and a hug from
Dale's new master, and you were ready to leave."

"Are you always so observant of people?"

"Only the ones I'm interested in."

"I'm wondering why you're interested in me."

"I'm wondering that myself."

The waiter came back with the menus, and Dexter quickly
glanced at his and ordered for both of them, which brought a
frown to Jolene's face. When he left she said a little testily that she
usually ordered for herself. He countered by taking her hand in
both of his.

"You'll get used to it," he assured her suavely, and was given
another frown while Jolene tried unsuccessfully to pull her hand
away. "Now, Jolene, we can have a battle right here … or you can
rest your biceps and let me talk some sense into you."

She sighed in frustration. "Listen to me closely, Dexter. I do not want to be a model." She repeated that again, enunciating the last words very clearly. "I want to be John Harris's wife." She leaned closer to him over the table and said in a loud stage whisper, "I love him!"

"Love, Jolene," he scoffed, letting go of her hand. "What do you know of such matters? You're just a kitten. You need to grow up before you fall in love."

She propped her arm on the table and rested her chin on her hand. "You're an old cat, Mr. DeLange. Have you ever been in love?" She regretted the words the moment she said them.

For a moment his eyes clouded and grew blacker, and she could see his jaw clenching. Then he relaxed and leaned back in his chair. "The kitten has claws," he murmured, and gave her an indulgent smile. Jolene decided they'd better get off the subject of cats and love altogether.

An hour later she acknowledged she had enjoyed the steak dinner and the conversation. They had covered many topics, always coming back to his original proposal, but she was adamant that she wanted to be John Harris's wife. Period. Finally he suggested that she at least let him take pictures of her wedding to be used for advertising purposes.

"Advertising what?"

"Hair creations by DeLange Designs."

"But surely you have all the business you need without this?"

He sighed in exasperation. "A military funer—excuse me, a military wedding—is always exciting to the public. If my name were associated with that, it would be, shall we say, advantageous to DeLange Designs." He looked at her with grim humor in his eyes. "I would think, since you are turning down a modeling career that would make both of us rich, you could at least agree to free wedding pictures and free hairstyles."

She smiled at him contritely. "One would think that, I'm sure. It's just that … our wedding was going to be rather private and small, with just Rachel and my cousin's wife as my attendants, and one would think that it would not be worth your time or effort."

He studied her for a while before he spoke again. "Trust me, it's worth my time and effort."

Jolene drove to Denver the day before her wedding, so engrossed in her thoughts that she scarcely noticed the beauty of the countryside.

Dear Lord, I think I made a mistake when I agreed to let the hairstyles and pictures be handled by Mr. DeLange. It made John so upset. You know how we argued over it, practically the only thing we've ever argued about. Was it so wrong, Lord? When John realized my wedding dress was also going to be picked out by DeLange Designs, he was more than upset, he was angry. You know what he said, Lord. He practically insinuated that it was an insult to him to have another man pick out his wife's dress, and of all things, her wedding dress. Even when I told him Dexter was an old friend of my mother's, he wasn't completely reassured. Lord, if I've done wrong, please forgive me. When I apologized to John and said I'd cancel the whole thing with the salon, he softened, and finally agreed it would save us both time and money, but, Lord, I've been tied up in knots over all of this. I guess clearing out my Chadron apartment and getting everything ready to go to Germany has made things hectic, and I haven't even taken time to pray. Forgive me for trying to carry all this without coming to You.

Jolene took a deep breath and let it out in a sigh. She felt nervous about having her hair styled at the salon, having people fuss with her dress, working with a photographer, and, most of all, finalizing the details of the wedding. The day seemed to come upon them so fast, and she wasn't sure if she had done all the things she should have. But as John told her, the most important thing was that they were getting married. Amen to that!

The architecture of DeLange Designs impressed Jolene as she entered the spacious foyer. A woman with a trim, black suit greeted her from behind a desk. Upon learning Jolene's name and purpose, she smiled at her and came out from behind the desk.

"I'm Miss Grey, Jolene, and I'm to take you upstairs so you can try on your dress. But before we do that, let me introduce you to your photographer, Bob Lewis."

Bob was a friendly man, casually dressed, but she could see by the pictures in his studio that he was an expert in his field. He and his wife would travel to Colorado Springs the next day along with Miss Grey and Dexter, and they were excited, he claimed, to be able to have such a lovely backdrop as the military chapel there for the photo session. He had a release form for her to sign, and that meant they could use the pictures in several different ways. It also stated that the pictures would be used in an appropriate manner.

After she had signed it, she and Miss Grey ascended the curving oak staircase that led them upstairs to the second floor. Miss Grey walked with a brisk gait through another spacious foyer, and then they started up another stairway, equally grand, to the third-floor penthouse of Dexter DeLange. She explained that there were elevators, but she preferred to walk. She smiled and acknowledged that most of the staff used Mr. DeLange's gym on the second floor to keep as trim as their boss, but she found that running up and down the staircases worked for her.

Jolene caught a brief glimpse of the rich carpeting and soft colors of the penthouse before she was whisked to a bedroom where her dress was hanging.

"Oh." She paused and studied it again. "Oh."

"Are those ohs of delight, or ohs of woe?" Miss Grey looked at Jolene with her perfectly coiffed head tilted to one side and a knowing smile on her face.

"I'm just surprised. I wasn't expecting a dress like this, but it's … nice."

"Jolene, I've worked with Dexter DeLange for many years. He's never wrong on hair or dress styles, but it amazes me to this day what he comes up with. Let's try it on and see what you think."

Far from the long and flowing gown she was expecting, this dress almost had a western appeal. The top was an exquisite embroidered vest that fit over a tailored long skirt with insets of embroidered silk, and while she couldn't fault the richness of the material, it was so different from what her vision had been that she felt a stab of disappointment.

Miss Grey had just finished with the final buttons when her pager sounded. Promising to hurry back, she left at her usual brisk pace. Jolene stood before the mirror with a stunned look on her face. For several minutes she stood perfectly still, looking at the image reflected back at her, and even when she heard footsteps coming across the carpet, she didn't move.

"What's wrong with this vest? It isn't hanging right." Dexter's voice came from behind her. He frowned as he looked in the mirror at the imagined grievance, and then, walking in front of her, began to fuss and straighten, until at last he discovered a bit of tape that should have been removed. He ran his hand over her waist as he smoothed the material out, and then stepped back to appraise her.

He seemed satisfied, and then taking her hair in his hands and once again standing behind her so he could get the full benefit of the mirror, he took strands of blonde tresses and held them in different positions while he muttered about perms and damaged ends, and young women never listening to him, and about how this young woman in particular seemed hell-bent on destroying her natural curl.

Jolene wasn't listening to him very closely. She was thinking how she would have gotten the traditional wedding dress; yet this one reflected her personality completely. Not only that, she realized, it was a superb fit.

"Mr. DeLange." Jolene interrupted his mutterings. "This dress is absolutely perfect."

He looked shocked. "Did you think it wouldn't be?"

She was embarrassed to admit she had had her doubts, and for a moment their eyes locked in the mirror image, her green ones with a hint of apology, his dark ones with arrogance and a ghost of a smile. He let her hair slip out of his fingers. "I thought you would have remembered how you crabbed and fussed at your prom when I wanted you to wear a different dress. I'm usually right about these matters."

She defended herself hotly. "I did not crab and fuss. I just didn't know you had brought a dress for me, and I had to wear something, Mr. DeLange."

He turned her around to face him. "Miss O'Neil, you crabbed and fussed and didn't want me to, I believe the words you said were, 'waste my time' on your hair and clothes. Good grief, if it weren't for Betty's intervention, you would have worn that ugly red thing!"

"I sort of liked it." She grinned at him. "OK, I concede. You're the expert. Now what do we do?"

In short order she was back downstairs in the salon being introduced to Patrick and some of the other staff. As she was shampooed and clipped she felt a little like a poodle with a bad hair day. Dexter was completely absorbed in his work but occasionally murmured some comment to add to the conversation in the room. She was interested to know that Patrick had cut John's hair the day before, and that his two brothers had also come for haircuts.

"Three big guys," commented Patrick, who wasn't a small-framed man himself, "and all in the military. I think we are being well defended with them on our side!"

"They eat, breathe, and talk military." Jolene laughed. "I guess it's like any profession. I know my family does the same with ranching."

She quit talking when Dexter put the hat and veil on. It had the suggestion of a western hat, only much smaller, and he had arranged her hair so tendrils escaped from under it. It was a perfect match for the dress, and the dress was a perfect match for a young lady who loved the west. Miss Grey had boxed up the dress for her, and now she came in to do the same with the hat. She looked approvingly in the mirror and quickly left when Dexter took off the veil and hat and handed them to her.

"We'll do the finishing touches tomorrow when we get to the motel. It will be early in the morning, so be ready." He squeezed her shoulder in mock sternness. "I remember how you and Rachel can sit up all night and hen talk."

Patrick winked at her, and she shook her head. "We'll be ready," she declared.

Only they weren't. The rehearsal had gone well. The dinner and dancing afterward was fine, but she and John and Rachel had stayed up half the night talking. She was just waking up when the crew from DeLange Designs arrived, and she quickly realized that Dexter was in control, and his being in control meant that everyone had better march to a pretty fast step.

It seemed like time had wings and the hands of the clock were racing the hours past. Miss Grey was a strong second in command, and she had them all lined up and in their places at the chapel in no time. While the wedding party puffed to keep going, she looked like she exerted very little effort.

Finally the first round of pictures was taken, and then, just a little after lunch, Jolene was to get ready. She had thought some of the women would be with her as she pulled on her dress, but the others were busy making themselves gorgeous. It was a quiet time, and she reflected that the pace had been so hectic all morning that she hadn't had time to even meditate that this was the most important day of her life. She was dreamy eyed, thinking of her soon-to-be, handsome husband. They had had a hard time saying goodnight, knowing that the rule was not to see each other until the ceremony.

The light tap on the door proved to be Dexter, ready to arrange her hair and frowning when he saw she wasn't quite buttoned up yet. She was embarrassed when he finished the job himself and then plopped her down on the tall stool he had brought in.

He didn't seem to be in the mood for small talk, so she remained silent while he reworked her hair with the hat and veil on, and blushed when he snapped at her for daydreaming. Finally he stood back and observed his handiwork while lighting a cigarette. He scowled suddenly and said, "You could be a married model, Jolena, and we could all make lots of money."

She smiled at him and slid off the stool. "I don't think my husband would like that."

"He has no idea of how far you could go." He smoked for a while in silence, staring at her with a dark look that she found alarming.

"Do you always get so huffy at weddings?"

"No, I'm always incredibly charming, but you, woman, irritate me."

"How could I possibly irritate you? I've said a dozen times what a great job you did picking out a dress, and I stood still for hours at the chapel this morning during all those shots while you just kept getting grumpier and grumpier." Jolene's eyes felt as though they were beginning to shoot little flames. "This was all your idea, Dexter DeLange, so don't take out your little gripes at me!"

"I was not grumpy. I was irritated." Dexter's voice was getting louder. "I was irritated because I've made you absolutely beautiful, and you're walking up the aisle with this guy and throwing it all away!"

"Don't yell at me on my wedding day. How dare you yell at me!" Jolene's voice was louder than she intended, and for a moment she was afraid their argument could be heard all over the motel.

He must have had the same thought for he quickly put his cigarette out and started toward the door. "Let's get these pictures over with," he growled, and opened the door for her.

Pictures ... pictures. There seemed to be no end to them. In the chapel, outside the chapel, on the steps, with the bridesmaids, so many that Jolene felt her smile must be glued on her face. In between pictures she endured the touchups to her hair and makeup, and by the time the wedding started she wished she had opted for a homey, plain wedding without pictures.

At last she and Uncle Walt stood at the back of the chapel, waiting for the bridal march to begin. Uncle Walt had blown his nose quite a few times and told her this was the hardest thing he ever had to do. He softened that remark with a little hug and added that it also was the proudest moment of his life. He said he had never seen such a beautiful bride. Then he laughed a little shamefacedly and said, "Unless, of course, it was Aunt Arlene."

When the music cue began, they both took deep breaths and started down the aisle. She could see John and his brothers at the altar. They were standing with attentiveness, and when they saw her coming all three smiled in appreciation. She had eyes for only one. John was looking at her with love and awe written all over his face, and she couldn't wait to join him.

Arlene relived the entire weekend in her conversation with Walt as they drove back to the sand hills.

"Weren't they a handsome couple!" she enthused, going over all the details of John's uniform, Jolene's dress, the rose color of the bridesmaids' dresses, and the uniforms of John's brothers. "Think of it, Walt, three brothers and all three in the Air Force, and all three good-looking men. And our Sarah," she sighed contentedly, "our Sarah was so sweet the way she kept looking out for Jolene's dress and flowers, and Rachel with her black hair all done up with a rose ribbon. One thing I can say for that DeLange … the girls looked beautiful, didn't you think so, Walt?"

Walt muttered vaguely that they certainly did.

"But I don't know if I liked the way Dexter kept fussing over Jolene. Sometimes he was pretty sharp with her, and did you see the look Bob Lewis gave him at the reception when he danced with her? It was a pretty short dance, and then he stopped and said something to her and just walked off. I thought that was rude, but she just shook her head and said a few words to Bob. I guess they must have left then, because I don't remember seeing any of the crew around after that, did you, Walt?"

Walt muttered vaguely that he hadn't either.

"I was surprised to see Dale and his new wife there with Florence. I think that woman wears the pants in that family. She even rides roughshod over Florence. He danced with Jolene once, and she looked pained the whole while. Who could blame her with the way he has always treated her. I noticed Jolene sort of guided them back over to his wife. What is her name, Walt? I can't remember ever hearing it."

Walt muttered vaguely that he couldn't remember it either.

"Anyway, she sort of guided them back over there and said a few words to the Mrs., and waltzed away with Mr. Harris, her new father-in-law. Now he's a fine-looking man, and his wife seems like a nice woman. I got to visit quite a bit with them, and she told me that John has an apartment already picked out for him and Jolene over in Germany. Not a big one, but guess it's close to the base, and guess what, close to a riding stable! Now that was thoughtful of John, wasn't it, Walt?"

Walt answered vehemently that it was a pretty sad day when an O'Neil had to go to a riding stable.

CHAPTER 5

Family

$\mathcal{J}$OHN WATCHED HIS bride of almost one year walk toward him in the little park next to their apartment. She was holding the little hand of a toddler, the child of a friend of theirs, and they were deep in a conversation only the two of them could understand. He noted that the sun brought out the red tones in her blonde hair, and that a year of marriage had brought a new maturity to her face. She had lost some of the roundness of her youth, and her features were more pronounced. She hadn't changed out of her office clothes, and he admired her shapely ankles, accented by spike heels. When she glanced up and saw him, he reveled in the look of warmth that flooded her face.

"Lindsey was telling me that swinging is the most funnest thing anyones could does," she reported with laughter in her voice. John grinned at the two of them and took Lindsey's other small hand.

"Where did you meet up with Miss Lindsey?" he asked as they started back toward the apartment.

"Her mom called me at work and asked me to pick her up at the daycare center and walk her home." This was an oft-repeated procedure and one they both enjoyed. Lindsey's mother was a single mom, and when her work required late hours, she knew Jolene and John were delighted to watch her daughter until she came home.

The three of them entered the sunny apartment, and Jolene immediately kicked off her shoes and headed into the bedroom to find her jeans and T-shirt. Lindsey found her doll and other toys and soon was playing contentedly.

"Did I tell you David is coming over this evening?"

"Your brother David? I didn't even know he was in Germany."

"He just came over. He sure surprised me this afternoon. Said the folks were fine and Carl is back in the States and would probably stay there for a while."

"Is he coming for supper?" Jolene asked.

"No, he said he would be over after supper. I even told him you were a good cook, but he said he had other plans."

Jolene pulled her head out of the refrigerator and shook her head at him. Her cooking had been an adventure in the early months of their marriage as she tried to downsize the meals. She had been used to helping Arlene cook, and found that ten pounds of potatoes lasted a long time for two people who often ate out. More than one bag rotted, and finally she had learned to buy small quantities and less ranch-hearty foods. Since cooking was light and the apartment easy to keep clean, they were both glad when she found a job in an office where English was spoken and the bookkeeping was challenging. They took a lot of road trips when he had free time, and learned German history and tried to get a better grasp of the language. The airbase hosted several parties, and they had gotten acquainted with quite a few people. He knew it was a different life from what she was used to, but time had passed swiftly, and only on a few rare occasions did he notice she felt overwhelmed with homesickness for the sand hills.

When David walked into their apartment later that evening, Jolene hugged him and marveled at how closely he and John resembled each other. John was taller, and there was a kinder quality in his manner, but their blond hair and brown eyes made it obvious they were brothers. Carl also had blond hair and brown eyes, but his face was rounder, and in general, he had a jollier and less intense disposition.

Their men's talk was all Air Force and military, and Jolene tried in vain to gather information about their parents other than "they're fine." She was relieved when Shannon came to pick up Lindsey and provided talk of a different nature. She was also quick to note that David took much more interest in Lindsey after he had seen her mother.

The following week the five of them went to a zoo, and after that, they journeyed to a polka festival. Soon it was back to just John and Jolene, as David, Shannon, and Lindsey became an inseparable trio. They were married a month later and lived in Shannon's apartment next to John and Jolene. Before long, they were expecting a baby, and Shannon daily gave Jolene an update of her ups and downs of pregnancy, often ending with "someday you'll know what I mean." David was quite proud of the fact that he was soon to be a papa, and after their baby son was born, he needled Jolene and John incessantly to "get busy and get babies." It soon put a strain on their relationship, and Jolene was relieved when John received notice that he would be transferred back to the States. She hoped that being away from David would give John a chance to get his sense of humor back. He had seemed tense and edgy the last couple of months, and she thought maybe a change of scenery and company would help both of them.

Shannon knocked on their apartment door the day before they were scheduled to leave, and when Jolene opened the door to let her in she was shocked to see Shannon in a disheveled state, and close to tears.

"Are you sure you guys have to leave?" Shannon wailed, her eyes brimming over with tears. "I need you more than ever. You can't go now!"

"What's wrong?" Jolene asked more sharply than she intended, as all sorts of scenarios raced through her mind.

"I'm pregnant again!" Shannon blurted out, sobbing. Jolene stood gaping at her. Their baby was only three months old, and Shannon had seemed overwhelmed with a toddler and a baby. How would she ever cope with still another little one?

"David is as proud as a peacock that we're expecting again, but I told him I was quitting my job. Then he was sort of upset, but I just can't handle it all anymore. And if you're not here for me to unburden myself to, I don't know how I'll handle that either! You've been my sounding board, Jolene. All David knows is military, military, military. You were the one who really listens to me." She flung herself down on the chair and looked up at Jolene in a beseeching manner. "Can't you stay?"

More tears came as Jolene hopelessly shook her head.

"Then I'm going to hound David to get transferred too, at least back closer to my family or his. This is too much, Jolene. I can't take it!"

John had quietly walked in while Shannon was talking, and Jolene could tell by the white around his lips that he already knew what she was talking about.

"You don't have to hound, Shannon. David received his papers today, and you'll be leaving next month to go back to Colorado Springs."

Shannon bolted out of the chair and hugged John and then Jolene. She whooped that maybe they could both be in Colorado Springs, and then went tearing back to her own apartment. After she left, silence fell over the room.

"John, we won't be in Colorado Springs, will we?"

"I hope to God we won't."

It had been two years since Jolene had been back to the sand hills, and as she and John drove along the Nebraska roads in early July, she thought she would burst with happiness. The hay fields were filled with bales, the wheat fields were turning from green to a golden hue, and the big blue sky arched from horizon to horizon with huge white clouds floating serenely by.

"Careful, Jolene, you might eject yourself right out of the car if you don't settle down," John teased. She smiled at him and then ran her fingers through his blond hair.

"Have I ever told you how I like watching you wake up in the morning?"

He grinned back at her. "You might have mentioned it a time or two." In truth, she told him practically every morning. When she felt him stretching beside her, the daily ritual would begin. She would prop herself up on her arm and see his whiskered face turn toward her. A couple of sighs followed that, then a frown would furrow his brow, and finally his eyes would slowly open. He would look at her, close his eyes, and slowly open them again, only this time instead of a frown a little smile would quirk at the corner of his lips. "Good morning, angel," he would whisper softly, and she would answer back with all the love that was in her heart: "Good morning, my love." Neither of them ever tired of this exchange, and Jolene knew her heart would break if she had to start her day without his whispered words.

They had been delighted to be stationed in Texas. It was within reasonable driving distance to the sand hills and to Colorado Springs, but far enough to be away from David and Shannon. They were still settling in and had found a nice apartment close to the base. They found a church they liked, and as soon as it was possible, they took a road trip to the sand hills.

"The next turnoff will be Walt's," Jolene said. They had been glad to leave Germany and David. David talked about two subjects without end—the military and being a father. John could talk military with great enthusiasm, but to both his and Jolene's dismay, there were still no babies in their marriage. With David's competitive nature, the fact that he was a father and John was not added a certain amount of cockiness to his manner toward both Jolene and John that was almost unbearable at times. Perhaps without David's breathing down their necks they could relax. Certainly the tension had left both of them, and they were back to enjoying their marriage and each other.

"Wow! They put up a new sign!" Jolene almost shouted. "'O'Neil Cattle Co.' That has a fine ring to it, don't you think so, John?"

John agreed and then laughed as Jolene practically bounced out of her seatbelt in her enthusiasm to get to the ranch sooner. She seemed to note everything on the road to the ranch house and talked nonstop until he parked the car. When she opened the car door, she made a dead run into the waiting arms of Walt and Arlene.

"That was absolutely the best meal we have had in two years," Jolene said, pushing herself away from the table. "Aunt Arlene, no one can cook like you. Period."

Everyone laughed at that, and a contentedness hung over the table while Arlene and Walt's two sons, their wives and children, and now their claimed daughter and her husband were enjoying Sunday dinner. Jolene had been promised a ride later on in the afternoon, but right now was the time for coffee and visiting. Ben and Sarah's baby daughter cooed from her high chair, and John held out his finger to her. She latched on with one chubby fist, and slowly brought it up to her mouth. John glanced at Jolene with an amused look, and then back to his entrapped finger as the baby decided it was a fine chewable solution to her teething gums.

"Oh, John, if you don't want her to do that you can claim your finger back," Sarah said apologetically. But John didn't mind being drooled over, and in fact took the little one out of the high chair and set her on his lap. She leaned back to look at him, and then, satisfied that all was well in her infant world, continued gumming on her treasure.

Contrary to David and Shannon's endless ramblings about their children, the O'Neils were careful to discuss many other matters. And so it was that Jolene learned that Ben had repainted her parents' house on the inside, dug a new and better well, and was thinking of adding a pole barn. There was a slight pause, and then Ben leaned forward in his chair. His expression was both hopeful and wary. "Jolene, would you consider selling your folks' place to me?"

Actually, Jolene and John had talked about it on the drive up from Texas. It would mean some income for them, and when they had children, it might mean Jolene wouldn't have to work. There was no one better to take it over, and it should be an O'Neil ranch, because to Jolene's sorrow, it would never be in John's interest to have a ranch, or even as he said once, a country place. She looked down at her plate for a couple of seconds and knew everyone was watching her and holding their breath.

"Ben," she said, looking at him intently, "there is no one else I would rather see own that place than you, except of course, myself. I don't see John and me ever coming back, and I guess, if we can agree on a price, the answer is yes." There seemed to be a general expulsion of air, but when Ben wanted to talk details, Walt objected, and said they would work on that later on.

A couple of hours later, Jolene and Walt saddled up and walked their horses down a grassy path that led to her folks' place. Even in early July, there was still a trace of coolness in the early evening, and Jolene breathed in the prairie air and sighed in quiet rapture. Walt looked at her with a sudden frown, and said gruffly, "You've been gone too long, girl. You've got O'Neil blood; you're a prairie woman. You ride like an O'Neil, have the ranch instincts of an O'Neil, and I hate to think of you cooped up in some apartment and riding a stable horse."

Jolene looked at him and sudden tears came to her eyes. She quickly blinked them away and tried to make a humorous comeback. "I guess some people are blessed to have both a great love and a ranch. I seem destined to have only a great love." She paused briefly. "I really do love him, Uncle Walt."

He put a roughened hand on her arm. "I know. I know. Shouldn't have said anything. Didn't mean to upset you. Maybe I'm a little on edge because you're selling the place, even if it is to my own son. Jolene, I want you to have a fair price, even if it means that I help

Ben to buy it. I want you to be able to look back and know you got a fair deal. Ben and Sarah and even their little kids have done a lot of work there, and I think you'll be pleased about it."

As they rode into the yard, Jolene felt that indeed she had been gone too long. There were many changes, and far from looking forlorn, the house and outbuildings had a complacent look that spoke of good care. A quick walk through the house showed a neat but lived-in look, with toys and children's articles dominant. The room colors were more vibrant than what her mother had used, but all in good taste. Now it was Sarah's house, not Barbara's and not Jolene's. A walk through the yard revealed more flowers, a bigger garden, a new clothesline, the removal of some old buildings, and the addition of some new buildings. In the six years Ben and Sarah had been there, they had stamped their identity on the ranch, and Jolene made the inevitable observation that now it was more theirs than hers. She sighed and took Walt's arm.

"I had a happy childhood here. I learned about God, I learned how to pray and read the Bible, and I learned about love. When it comes right down to it, that is as important as it gets." She paused and looked at her childhood home. "I see Ben and Sarah and their three little ones, and they're teaching and learning the same values. What more could I ask from God than the chance to pass on this place to people I love and admire?"

Walt stopped, took out his big blue handkerchief, and blew his nose. "Jolene, you beat all." He paused and blinked a few times. "Let's talk business."

CHAPTER 6

After the Dance

"AW JOHN, DO we have to go with them?" Jolene wailed softly to her husband as they embraced in John's old room at his parents' house in late December.

They had endured an hour of David and Shannon while visiting the elder Harrises. When his mother had volunteered to watch Lindsey and the baby while John, Jolene, Shannon, and David had an evening out, the latter two jumped at the chance and left immediately to change their clothes and bring back the necessary articles for the children.

John kissed Jolene gently and answered grimly that he supposed they would have to. They, it seemed, were committed to an evening of complete boredom.

"Unless ... ," John said slowly, and Jolene noticed a calculating look in his eye. "Unless we decide to make it more fun. Did you bring along that new outfit I like so well?"

"You mean the purple sweater with the black sequins that matches a skirt?"

"Yeah, the one that makes your figure look like a million bucks, and your green eyes even greener, yeah, that one."

Jolene looked at him in astonishment. "John Harris, you've never noticed a thing I've ever worn before. What's the deal here?"

"The deal? The deal is that I'm sick and tired of Dave flaunting his kids with every conversation. All he talks about is kids and military. Good grief, I can talk military but . . Anyway, tonight I'll show off my beautiful wife. We'll dance up a storm!" He twirled her around and then brought her close to him again and whispered in her ear. "I'll be the envy of every man at the supper club."

"Hmmm, is that Christian, do you suppose?"

"Probably not, and I might regret it. But tonight I'm going to enjoy my wife, and, honey, we're going to dance and smooch and, hey, have one good time in spite of them!"

"You make me feel like a Sherman tank," Shannon groused across the table to Jolene. They were seated near the dance floor at the supper club, waiting for their order to arrive. "I am just huge. I don't remember being this big with the other kids. I even asked the doctor if he was sure I wasn't carrying twins. And you, you're just as slim and trim as you always were." She gave a huge sigh. "It almost makes me want to cry. I'm tired all the time carrying this load."

"And grumpy," David chimed in and received a withering look from both women.

"Are you too tired to dance with me across the floor the next time there's a slow tune?" John asked his sister-in-law kindly.

The delight in Shannon's eye was obvious to everyone. "Thank you, John, forever," she declared. "If you can handle a Sherman tank, I'd enjoy that!"

John seemed just as delighted as she was, and there were a few minutes of respite from David's monologue of government and military and, of course, kids.

When the band struck up a snappy swing tune, John pushed back his chair and held out his hand to Jolene. Together they moved onto the dance floor and began a fast jitterbug. They were masters of the six steps and could twirl around each other in perfect rhythm. Jolene felt herself beaming at her husband as he wrapped his arm around her waist so they could step the fancy footwork side by side. As the song ended John spun her around and they managed a perfect dip. To Jolene's great delight, he winked at her and kissed her lightly.

They were both out of breath as they came back to their table, and Jolene was grateful for the tall glass of lemon water. She had just set her glass down when Shannon leaned over and said in a low tone, "Who is that guy a couple of tables back? No! Don't look now; he's looking over here."

"What does he look like?"

"In one word, Jolene, handsome."

Jolene laughed at Shannon's rapt facial expression. "There's probably all sorts of handsome men in the world that I don't know, Shannon!"

"This one was staring holes through you and John while you were dancing. I think he knows you."

"Excuse me, ladies, your salads." As the waiter placed the salads in front of them and poured extra drinks, Jolene turned to furtively scan the tables behind them. It was only a quick glance, and she saw no one she knew.

They had scarcely finished their salads when the main course came, and even David was silent as they enjoyed their steaks. Jolene had just settled back into her chair, feeling comfortably well fed, when the waiter appeared again and handed her a note.

Puzzled, she opened it slowly. *Your hair is a disaster* it read simply.

"What?" she muttered to herself, and this time turned in a different direction to scan the tables behind her. "Oh, I should have known," she groused under her breath.

Sitting several tables beyond her was the unmistakable profile of Dexter DeLange. A lovely brunette woman was talking to him, but his eyes watched Jolene. Slowly he shook his head and gave her the briefest of scowls before turning to the woman across from him.

At least I don't have cap sleeves, she penciled below his note and gave the waiter both the note and the proper instructions when he returned. She pointedly refused to look behind her again. She only shook her head at her companions' inquiring looks, and as she heard the slow tune played by the band, asked John if this was Shannon's dance.

True to his word, John stood up and helped Shannon out of her chair. Shannon, flushed with pleasure, turned to her husband and said quite loudly, "Do Jolene a favor. Don't ask her to dance." She shook her head at Jolene. "He has two left feet."

Jolene thought her comments were hilarious, and she exchanged wide smiles with John as he escorted Shannon onto the floor. She realized instantly, however, that David found no humor in the situation.

He fidgeted in his chair momentarily, and then abruptly stood up, muttering something about the men's room. She watched his departing back with a sense of relief. Having danced with David before, she knew the truth of Shannon's words.

As she settled back into her chair to watch the dancers, the scent of wild musk slowly descended upon her. She knew without looking that Dexter was standing behind her.

"Shall we dance, Jolena?"

"The last time you danced with me you left me in the middle of the floor. I believe you called me a fool. No, we shall not dance, Dexter."

"Of course we shall dance, and this time I'll whisper sweet nothings in your ear and we will dance the whole dance."

He came around to the front of her chair and pulled her to her feet. Without saying any more, he guided her onto the dance floor. For a second he stood looking at her, and then he gently pulled her toward him until she felt he was holding her too close. Still he said nothing to her, and they moved slowly across the floor. She could see John and Shannon at the other end of the dance floor, but they were engrossed in conversation and didn't notice her.

"Are you mad at me for telling you that you were a fool?"

"I'm quite put out at you for telling me I was marrying the wrong man. A fool, maybe, but I definitely married the man I love."

"OK, maybe I was out of line to say that," he said, pulling her even closer, "but would you relax against me? You feel like a wooden doll."

"You're giving me claustrophobia!"

He released her slightly. Then he looked down at her with his haughty eyes, and they traveled up and down her whole being while a smiled played around his lips. "Do you want to know what I think of your outfit?"

"No."

"Then I'll enlighten you. It fits you perfectly. The color brings out the green in your eyes, especially with that little sparkly doodad of a necklace. It's devilishly low in front, which surprises me. If I were your husband, I would not allow you to wear it."

"That's because you're rather old and more Victorian."

He stopped abruptly, and she tripped a little because of the unexpectedness of it. When she looked up into his face, she saw a mixture of emotions, and she was very still, wondering which emotion would be victorious in his inner battle. She almost wondered if she should walk away. Then he drew her close once again, and they started moving with the music. She heard him sigh, and she stole another look at his face. He was looking at her with a bemused expression, and yet, like a cat, there was an undercurrent behind his eyes that boded caution in playing games with him.

For a while they danced in silence. Finally she looked up and gave him an uncertain smile. "Truce, Dexter?"

"Truce, Jolena." She relaxed against him slightly, and for a second his arms tightened around her. Neither could think of anything to say until she looked up at him again and said rather crossly, "My hair is not a disaster."

He smiled at her. "Kitten, unless I take care of it, it's always going to be a disaster."

After the music stopped, she was conscious of his hand on the small of her back, guiding her slowly back to her table. She thought

John looked surprised to see her with Dexter, but he instantly held out his hand to shake the older man's slender one.

"John, I didn't know the two of you were back in the states," Dexter said.

"Oh, yes, for several months now. Jolene likes Texas. A little closer to horses and home, you know."

"This is my sister-in-law, Shannon Harris, and of course you remember her husband, David." Jolene offered introductions, and then finished rather lamely. "This is Dexter DeLange from Denver."

Dexter nodded absently at David, and, taking Shannon's puffy hand in his, he softly said, "A lovely lady in waiting. So nice to meet you."

Jolene was amused at the look of awe that passed over Shannon's face, and her usually talkative friend bobbed her head several times and remained speechless.

Releasing Shannon's hand, Dexter gave Jolene a slight hug and thanked her for the dance before he walked away.

"I wouldn't let that guy hug my wife," Jolene heard David mutter.

Dexter sat on his cushioned couch with his feet propped up on the coffee table. With a cup of coffee in one hand and a cigarette in the other, he looked broodingly out at the snowy morning. His gas fireplace should have ensured a cozy Sunday morning reprieve from his usual busy schedule, but he was not enjoying the ambiance of the moment.

His thoughts took him back to Jolene's wedding. He well remembered dancing with her there, remembered how she looked when she thanked him for all he did to make that day memorable for her and John. He looked down at this creation of his and said nothing for a couple of seconds. Then he took a deep breath and told her she was welcome, that he had made her beautiful, but she was wasting all of it on a flyboy. She bristled at that, and her eyes flashed, but when she spoke again her voice was calm, and she told him of asking the Lord to guide her heart and mind when she was making the decision to marry John. She looked at him earnestly and said she believed in the power of answered prayer. He looked at her with a mixture of emotions, none of which were proper, and told her she was a fool. She should not be marrying this man. He walked off the dance floor, not caring that he left her in an embarrassing situation or what other people might think.

It was on the way back to Denver that Bob and Helen, and even Miss Grey, had chided him for his behavior. He had been ashamed of his actions then, and had taken special care to send her copies of all the pictures and several eight-by-tens, including the portrait of her and John, and a framed one of John looking at her as she walked up the aisle. He remembered so well standing by Bob as she entered the chapel. He was stunned at how radiant she looked, and then he had turned to watch John and had muttered to Bob to zoom in on the expression on the groom's face. He had sworn a little, and Bob had looked at him reprovingly. The picture had been one of the best. The others had decorated his salon and had been great advertisement for both him and Bob.

The snow fell more thickly, and he got up to pour himself another cup of coffee. Sitting back down, he thought of the people with whom he had gone to dinner the previous night. Yolanda Yates was a designer with a great line of clothes, but she wanted to branch out into something more western, and he had been intrigued with some of her drawings. They had decided to meet and discuss some business proposals with another couple. It was sheer luck, good or bad—and he wasn't sure which—that Jolena was dining at the same place. He hadn't recognized her as they walked in, but when John took off her coat and she turned toward her husband and flashed him a smile, Dexter knew immediately who she was. Dexter watched her with narrowed eyes, and from that point on had trouble concentrating on what was being said. He knew when they were dancing and when they came back. He watched as they were served and then, on impulse, scribbled the note and handed it to the waiter. As he sat and watched the wind start to pick up and fling the snow harder against his window, he realized he would not have sent that kind of note to any other woman. Other women would have been devastated to know Dexter DeLange thought their hair was anything but perfect. Maybe that was part of her attraction to him. She really didn't care what he thought. It was a new experience for him. No other person in his life had accused him of being Victorian. For that matter, no one had ever accused him of being old. He had prided himself on looking younger than most men of fifty-three. He had fought with disbelief on the dance floor, and then common sense prevailed. When she looked at him and asked for a truce, he was relieved. If she ever did come around to his way of thinking and became the model he thought she could be, they would spend a lot of time together. A congenial relationship would be a plus.

He thought of the way her dress looked and, in reality, couldn't fault it. Her hair had been cut far shorter than he would have ever considered, and yet framed around her face it gave her a perkiness that flattered her. When he sent the note, he hadn't seen her close up and had hated to think of her thick waves on a salon's floor.

He put his empty cup down and picked up the drawings Yolanda had given him. They were fine sketches of western wear and would need a model that could look like she had just stepped down from the saddle. His eyes narrowed as his thoughts began to form, and when the idea came to maturity, he mentally patted himself on the back. Dexter DeLange had done it again, he decided. Western wear, Texas, a fresh young model … Jolena. His face broke into a self-congratulatory smile. Yolanda Yates could be persuaded to develop her line of western wear, and what better place than Texas to portray it? A young model who could ride horses to show the clothes off would be invaluable, and Jolena was just the woman for the job.

He knew it would be hard to convince her and even harder to get a yes from John, but again he had confidence in his ability to charm. Timing would be crucial, he mused, and with those thoughts in mind, he headed for his office and started tweaking the sketches to flatter Jolena's frame. He was so absorbed in his task that the ringing phone almost startled him. Miss Grey called to remind him of his six o'clock dinner date, and for a moment his mind was blank as to who his date was.

He noticed it had quit snowing, and a weak December sun tried to shine through the last minutes of daylight. Walking into his room, he caught his reflection in a mirror. With his shirt half unbuttoned and his hair ruffled, he decided he looked anything but Victorian.

Walt O'Neil was awake before the alarm clock sounded. With a small groan he left his warm bed and sleeping wife in the predawn darkness and slipped into his clothes. He clicked the alarm button off on his way to the door and slowly walked downstairs.

By the time he stepped outside on this early April morning, his thoughts had already skimmed the list of heifers that might be close to calving. There was dampness in the air, and he slugged through not quite frozen mud from the rain the day before.

He grumbled to himself that cattlemen were slaves to their cow herd come spring. For that matter, the whole year through. Spend the whole summer putting up hay so they could spend the whole winter feeding it to the ungrateful critters.

Entering the heifer yard, he flashed his heavy lantern through the young cows. It was a ritual they were used to, and other than an occasional snort and lowing, they ignored him.

He snorted himself as he thought of Jolene's husband asking what the heck a heifer was. The young Harrises had been at the ranch for Easter, and John had asked numerous questions. Jolene had patted his arm and explained a heifer was a young cow that hadn't had a calf yet. John had looked puzzled and wondered why the constant check on the cattle night and day? Couldn't they have calves by themselves like the wildlife did? Once again she had explained that sometimes for various reasons the birth process was complicated. John had shook his head and said it sounded like a lot of work to him.

And it was work, Walt acknowledged. Especially during cold damp springs like this one. Even now, as he got on his horse to check the older cows in the bigger pen, a slow drizzle started.

His thoughts strayed back to Jolene as he circled the small pasture. She had practically drooled over Ben and Sarah's new baby daughter, but Walt noticed John had seemed strangely aloof. In fact, John had paid scant attention to any of the grandkids, come to think about it. Now that was odd; they both had seemed to want children when they were first married.

Walt stopped and shined the light on a newborn calf lying beside its mother. On closer examination he realized the mother had already licked her baby dry, and its little black face seemed to have a forlorn look at having left a warm womb for this chilly world.

Walt shivered, and, satisfied all was well for another couple of hours, he headed toward home. Dawn was still an hour away, and the warm house seemed like a bit of heaven when he entered.

Arlene always kept something baked up during that time of year, and Walt found cinnamon rolls in a covered cake pan. Taking two of them and a glass of milk, he sat on the hearth and contemplated the possible weather situation. He and his two sons would be busy if the weather took a turn for the worse. They would have to sort out all the cattle close to calving and get them near the barns.

"I must be getting old," he muttered softly. "It sounds like more work than I feel up to." Maybe, he mused, Jolene's fellow was smarter than he realized. John had a well-paying job with benefits, and no worries about a stupid cow. That should sure make him one easy fellow to get along with, Walt surmised. Arlene was always telling him and the boys they were nothing but grouchy in the spring.

The steadily falling drizzle turned to sleet by mid afternoon, and by early evening the wind was whipping in from the north and heavy snow was falling. After spending most of the day getting the cattle situated for the storm, Walt was tiredly eating the hot meal Arlene had fixed.

A couple hours later he once again put on his coat and pulled his Scotch cap down with his mittened hands. He trudged along the slippery path in his insulated pac boots. He had to take extra care not to slip, and by the time he reached the barn the wind had blown snow onto his weathered cheeks.

Danny was waiting for him, and after Walt pulled the barn door shut Danny pointed to a heifer that he already had put in a head catch.

"This little sister has been trying since supper to have her calf. Guess we'll have to pull it," he told Walt.

They quickly gathered all the paraphernalia needed and when Danny took off his coat Walt helped him pull a long plastic glove over his shirt sleeve. For almost an hour Danny wrestled with the unborn calf in the heifer's womb, trying to get it into position to be born. Finally, as Walt watch sweat pour off Danny's face, a contraction came and the baby's head emerged. With the young heifer mooing plaintively, another contraction came, and then suddenly, a live calf lay on the straw, and Walt stooped to clear its nostrils so it could breathe.

Walt dragged the slimy calf to a nearby pen that was bedded with fresh straw, and when Danny released the mother from the head catch he herded her also to the pen.

As many times as he had witnessed a young cow with her first calf, he was still impressed with the mothering instinct that happened when she nuzzled her calf and realized it was her responsibility to dry it off, nurse it, and protect it. *At least*, he thought wryly, *that's the way it's supposed to be, but some cows are like some human mothers: they couldn't care less.*

While Danny cleaned up and put his coat back on, Walt checked the other heifers they had put in the barn. In unspoken agreement, they also checked the cows in the outside pen.

"This darn snow makes it hard to see," Walt said, squinting at the beam of light Danny flashed around the cows.

"Oh, brother," he heard Danny mutter. "That old lop-eared bat looks like she has something brewing."

"Guess your eyes are better than mine," Walt observed, and waded through mud and soft snow to open the barn door.

After a few rounds of missing the paneled alley, the uncooperative cow charged into the barn with her head held high. They quickly shut the gate after she was in a pen and decided to let her settle down without any interference from them.

As they shut off the barn lights and closed the doors, the wind seemed to increase and the driven snow felt needle sharp in Walt's faces.

"Wished I would have built closer to the barns," Walt heard Danny say, and then they moved away from the protection of the barn, and neither had breath to say any more until they reached Walt's house.

Danny's house was around the bend, and Walt figured by the time he got his own outside gear off, Danny should be safely home. With Arlene's help, he peeled off the layers of warm clothing and gave her the details of the past couple of hours. He knew she would call Danny's house to make sure he arrived safely, and then—then, by golly—he was going to ask his wife to fix him some hot cocoa to go with those cookies she had baked that afternoon.

"Anybody call?" he asked.

"Oh, several neighbors, and Jolene."

"What did she know?"

"Just that she saw over the Internet that we were having some bad weather up here. Guess she wondered how everyone was getting along in the storm."

"Anything else?"

"Well, no, at least not anything she said." Arlene sighed. "We both know, Walt, there's something bothering the two of them."

CHAPTER 7

Jolene's Dilemma

"*M*RS. HARRIS, AS I told you before, you are an extremely healthy young woman," the middle-aged doctor said a little impatiently. "The only reason you are not conceiving is most likely your own anxiety. Now I can run all the tests, but I can tell you right now, you are fine."

Jolene looked at him. "Run the tests."

He looked at her sharply and ran his fingers through his thinning hair. "I would rather run tests on your husband."

She glanced down at her hands and realized she was twisting them in her lap. "It's not something he and I have discussed openly, and I wouldn't know exactly how to … well, how to …" She looked around the room searching for the right words and heard the doctor's exasperated sigh. "Well …" She glared at him. "He's so vulnerable right now, and if I asked him to be tested, it would, it would …" and to her embarrassment, tears came to her eyes.

The doctor seemed disconcerted by her emotions, and sat tapping his finger against his knee. Finally he said he could run the tests on her, and if everything was fine, which he was positive it would be, she would know for certain the problem was with her husband.

When Jolene left the clinic that afternoon, she felt mutilated and humiliated, but she comforted herself with the knowledge that when all the results were in she would have information about why there were no babies.

John had said very little when David had called to congratulate himself on their second son, and she noticed John had stopped paying attention to other little children. Their friends didn't mean to be cruel, but they seemed to bring up the subject of children constantly. Holding other people's babies was bittersweet to Jolene, but she was not going to bury her head in the sand and wait passively. If she couldn't have a child, then she wanted to adopt. John had no desire even to discuss such an option, and it seemed he had buried the whole issue deep within himself.

Two weeks later she knew for certain that she was indeed a healthy young woman. Everything checked out positive, and now she had to convince John to have his tests.

John refused and was upset she had even suggested it. In fact, he withdrew from her completely, and when she begged him to talk to her about their problems, he would only shake his head and tell her he couldn't believe she was so insensitive.

Grudgingly she decided to drop the whole matter for a while, and their lives seemed to slowly return to normal. She would have liked to talk to somebody about it but felt it would be disloyal to John. During her prayer time she poured out her heart to the Lord and gradually began to feel there would be an answer. Until Arlene asked her on the phone if she was really all right, she didn't realize her voice reflected her concern, but she knew the next time she called Arlene she had better pump herself up with good cheer, or she would be pouring out the intimacies of her marriage.

John had requested another transfer, and before she knew it they were heading to the East Coast. She was a little rebellious over the move. He had never consulted with her, and that was unusual in their marriage. John told her in an enthused voice that he had arranged it as a surprise for her, knowing she hadn't been happy in Texas. A change of scenery would do her good.

For several days she pondered the wisdom of telling him that Texas was not the reason for her sadness, but in the end she decided to simply resettle and let the chips fall where they may. She enjoyed the Atlantic coast, and once again they made friends, found a church, rented an apartment, and took in the sights, this time in New England.

It was June before she had an address to give Walt and Arlene, and quite frankly she had so little contact with Florence that she forgot even to tell her she had moved. She got an angry phone call from her grandmother in July and heard in no uncertain terms that Florence had had to call all over the country just to find out where her granddaughter was, and she didn't appreciate being the last to know.

Jolene apologized and listened to a lecture for several minutes. Then for several minutes more she endured all the news about Dale. Finally just before hanging up, Florence informed Jolene that Dexter had been trying to get hold of her. When Jolene wanted to know what for, Florence turned coy and said, "Now I know something you don't, and I'm not going to tell you."

Jolene said some pretty uncharitable things about Florence to the walls of her apartment after they hung up.

About six months later, John excitedly told Jolene he had been transferred to the West Coast. "All of this is a move up for me, Jolene—more money, more stripes. I know you would like to put down roots, but let's pack again!" He kissed her perturbed countenance until she laughed. Then he hurried out to gather some friends together for a farewell party.

"Goodbye, New England; hello, West Coast. At least I can say I've traveled," Jolene said to no one in particular. She held no regrets about leaving, yet she felt unsettled, and a yearning to be back on the prairie occasionally flooded her soul. The ranch life, horses, family, and, yes, babies—all those things had meant so much to her when she was growing up. In truth, Jolene was lonesome. John had a deep devotion to his military career. She knew that when she married him. She just didn't realize how devoted she was to her O'Neil heritage.

Perhaps it was homesickness that persuaded her to plan to leave New England before John and stay at the ranch for a while. He would live at the base on the West Coast until he found housing for them, and she would enjoy December on the prairie.

There was another reason. Rachel was getting married, and Jolene was to be one of the bridesmaids. Reverend Taylor would perform the ceremony at Sterling, and the wedding was to be the twentieth of December. The excitement of seeing her family and her friends made the final days in New England pass quickly, and before Jolene knew it she was back in Walt and Arlene's homey kitchen, drinking coffee, eating cinnamon rolls, and getting caught up on all the news of the ranch and community.

Florence had rather coolly invited Jolene to stay at her house in town, but Jolene declined, saying she would be too much bother for Florence. She thought her grandmother seemed relieved to have that question settled. Instead, the Taylors opened their doors and hearts to her, and she found herself once again in the same room she had been in when she was a junior at Sterling High School.

Jolene arrived at the Taylors the morning before the wedding rehearsal, and she and Rachel and Betty didn't stop talking from the time she got there. They introduced her to the rest of the wedding party, and Jolene and Rachel's sister-in-law-to-be tried on their gowns of red satin. The dresses were plainly made, but the necklines and hems were adorned with sequins that glittered and sparkled like new-fallen snow. The groom and his best men wore red ties and sashes, and the bride was to carry red silk roses in her bouquet. When Jolene met Rachel's fiancé she liked him immediately, and Rachel glowed whenever she talked about him.

The wedding rehearsal was fun, and everyone was in a lighthearted mood. Betty, however, looked worn out, and after the rehearsal supper, Jolene offered to take her back home. She accepted gratefully, and they pulled up to the Taylors' back door with the intention of finishing several details and heading to bed.

"It smells like cigarette smoke in here," Jolene observed as they walked in. Betty nodded, and they followed the scented trail into the living room. In the midst of the room overrun with wedding gifts and wedding preparations, Dexter sat idly on the sofa with his feet propped up on the coffee table, drinking coffee and, of course, smoking a cigarette.

"Hello, ladies," he purred, looking like a contented housecat. "I made myself at home."

Betty almost ran to give her brother a hug and kiss, and then plopped down beside him on the couch and wailed, "Dexter, I'm bushed!"

"Of course you are. Weddings are horrible things. All that hair, dresses, flowers. They give me the willies."

The thought of Dexter having the willies made Jolene break out into laughter, and she headed into the kitchen to get two more cups of coffee.

When she returned, Dexter was massaging the back of his sister's neck, and Betty's sigh was almost contagious.

"Sit down here, Jolene, and put your feet up. We can all enjoy a moment of sanity before the madness begins." Dexter indicated the space next to him.

The three of them sat with feet up and enjoyed very good cups of coffee. It was a comfortable moment, totally unexpected.

"The dresses are ready, the flower arrangements are done, the cake is made." Betty sighed and continued. "The caterers will do the reception, there's a photographer already here." She tried to think of what else there was to do.

"What color are the bridesmaids' dresses?" Dexter asked.

"Red, because of the Christmas season."

"Sleeveless," Jolene added because Dexter turned to look at her with a raised eyebrow.

"That's good. Did you say your neighbor down the street has a salon in her home that she's letting us use?" When Betty nodded,

Dexter continued. "I'll fix Rachel's hair first thing in the morning; then I'll do the other two young ladies." He stressed the word "young" and gave a tendril of Jolene's hair a slight tug.

She was beginning to think there must be something in the coffee. She had the ridiculous urge to curl up next to Dexter's warm frame and let him massage her neck as he was rubbing Betty's. It was almost hypnotic, she decided, the way he slowly rubbed his hand over his sister's taut muscles. No, it must be because the coffee was decaffeinated, she decided, because her eyes wanted to close. In fact, Betty's eyes were drooping and Dexter yawned. All three jumped when the back door slammed and Reverend Taylor came into the room. He took one look at their lackadaisical demeanor and gave a hearty laugh, then walked briskly over to Dexter and said with great sincerity how glad he was to see him.

The quiet spell was broken then, and Jolene gathered the cups and headed to the kitchen. Betty decided that whatever work needed to be done could wait until the next day. She headed to bed.

As Jolene finished tidying up the kitchen, Dexter came padding in. She thought again how much like a spoiled housecat he was, always sure of himself and completely self-satisfied. He leaned against the kitchen counter with his arms folded over his chest and watched her finish wiping the sink clean. She turned to face him and saw his eyes travel up her person and then stop at her hair. A frown came over his features as he studied her casual, mid-length hairstyle. He shook his head in dismay, and Jolene put both hands on her hips and glared at him.

"How would you like it if I looked you up and down and shook my head?" she demanded of him.

"I'm just trying to decide what I'll do with … this." He sauntered over to where she was standing and picked up a few strands of her hair.

"Uh, yes, uh, well actually you don't, ah, need to fix my hair tomorrow … because …" Jolene realized she was stuttering a little. "Because I can do it myself." She flinched at the deprecating look he gave her.

He turned her head this way and that way, and then cupped her face in both hands and kissed her lightly on the lips.

"Uncle Dexter!" she reprimanded him with astonishment.

"I'm not your uncle, or your father either." He still held her face in his hands and rubbed his thumbs lightly along her cheekbone. They both jumped when the back door slammed and Rachel came bounding in.

"Uncle Dexter! You made it!" Rachel fairly screamed her delight.

With two swift bounds he was over at his niece's side and giving her a very uncle-like hug. Jolene shook her head, put away another dish, and went to bed.

For a very long time she stared out the darkened window. What was it about the man that always unsettled her? If she was honest with herself, she would admit to the attraction he held for her. She scoffed at her silliness. He was a playboy, used to flirting with women, and she seriously doubted that he gave a passing thought to her other than for mild amusement. The rascal could get into trouble, though, if he kept kissing other men's wives.

"What do you think of this?" Rachel's delight in her uncle's hair creation was unmistakable as she turned around several times before Betty and Jolene.

Betty's eyes were soft and shining as she beheld her only child looking like the beautiful bride she would be that evening. "It is gorgeous, and you look beautiful!" she cried, hugging her daughter.

Dexter looked quite satisfied with his creation, and also with the other attendant's style. He had walked both of them back from the neighbor's salon, and was enjoying a cup of coffee and a piece of toast. Now he was studying Jolene like a biologist would examine bugs under a microscope, or at least that's the way it appeared to her. She looked at him quite exasperated and repeated her offer of doing her own hair.

For a moment he seemed to consider her suggestion, then to the relief of Betty and Rachel he put down his empty cup and held out his hand to Jolene.

"Let's get this over with," he groused, and, pulling her along to the door, he grabbed somebody's coat and threw it over her shoulders. She turned to say a hasty goodbye as he yanked her out the door. Dexter claimed her hand all the way to the shop and ushered her into the rather chilly salon. In no time at all he had her hair shampooed. She had kept her eyes tightly closed while he rinsed and added great-smelling conditioners. When he had her sitting upright again, he wrapped a towel around her head and turned the chair this way and that way while examining her with narrowed eyes. She felt nervous under his careful scrutiny and started to say something, only to have him put his finger across her lips and say, "Shh, I'm thinking."

"Oh, brother."

"I'm not your brother."

"Or my uncle or my father."

"That's true, Jolene," he said rather absentmindedly and finally removed the towel and started combing.

He seemed to have a plan in mind and started parting and snipping. Jolene tensed when he started on the area above her forehead and as she expected, he swore.

"Who did this? What imbecile cut this off? They must have used pinking shears!"

She looked at him in awe. "How did you know?"

"How did I know what?"

"How did you know that I used pinking shears?"

"Why would you use … ? No, I don't even want to know." He glared at her.

"I was packing, and that bunch of hair just kept hanging and getting into my eyes, so I grabbed the nearest thing handy that would cut, and … I …"—Jolene wondered if he might have a heart attack, and she finished very painfully—"just … cut it off." She made a dramatic whacking motion with her fingers.

"You butchered your own hair!" He looked at her incredulously.

"I had no idea you were going to be here, Dexter. No one said a word that you were going to work on hair. If I had known, I wouldn't have …"—she blinked a few times and continued—"butchered my own hair."

"What an incredibly"—he shook his head as if trying to find the word—"childish thing to do!"

She wanted to say that she probably did seem like a child to someone of his age, but wisely kept her own counsel.

He stood with his arms folded, looking at her hair, and then, lowering his eyes to her face, he said, "I know what you are thinking, Jolena."

"You do not!" she answered hotly.

"I most certainly do too."

"Do not!" she all but shouted, and it was that moment that the owner of the shop peered in and asked how things were going.

"Do too!" he whispered to Jolene and swung around with a smile and asked the sweet-faced lady when she needed her shop back. She waved her hand dismissively and said, "Not for another hour." When Dexter told her he would certainly have the young lady out of there by then, she smiled and waved a goodbye.

After she left, Dexter lit a cigarette as if to calms his nerves. "Do you think you should be smoking in her shop?" Jolene asked a little timidly.

"Yes!" To prove his exasperation he added, "And I should have a double martini to go with it!"

She thought he was very much overreacting and wanted to tell him so, but then he threw his cigarette into the toilet in the little bathroom and started cutting her hair with a speed that worried her.

"If you want a Mohawk, that's what you'll get," he muttered, all the while parting, cutting, and combing. She held her breath and closed her eyes, afraid of what she would look like when he was through.

The blow dryer felt wonderfully warm on her neck, and then the curling iron clacked away with amazing speed. She still held her eyes shut. He worked his hands through her hair, made a few more turns with the curling iron, added hairspray, and then whispered in her ear, "You can open your eyes now, Jolena."

After a heavy sigh, she slowly opened her eyes and stared into his intense, black gaze. He had a little, satisfied smile that worried her even more. When he twirled the chair around so she could see herself in the mirror, she gasped.

The pinking-shears disaster had been changed into a style that blended both long and short hair into a masterpiece. He had given her an entirely different look, sleeker, yet with a carefree air that would look right at home on a Pacific beach. She stepped out of the chair and pulled off the apron. She looked again, and then impulsively turned to him and hugged him around the waist. "It's wonderful!" she exclaimed, "absolutely wonderful!"

Slowly he wrapped his arms around her and sighed. "Kitten, you'll give me gray hairs."

Walt was enjoying the unexpectedly warm days between Christmas and New Year's. He had been glad for Jolene's sake that her long drive to the West Coast would be on good roads. He shook his head and marveled at her driving from one coast to the other all by herself. She had left early in the morning, and Arlene had been sniffing all day long, trying to avoid him. She never wanted Walt to know when she was crying. With the sun going down shortly after four at this time of year, the O'Neil men finished outside chores early. Walt figured he would have plenty of time before supper to coax Arlene into confiding in him.

"Well, girlie, let's sit here, and you better tell me all about it," he said, patting the seat on the couch beside him. Arlene sat beside him and gave a big sigh. Turning her reddened eyes toward him she said, "I'm worried sick about her, Walt."

"I know you gals had good talks. What all did she tell you?"

"Not a lot at first, but gradually as she let her guard down, more and more. But it wasn't until Florence called yesterday that I knew there was a lot more to it. Walt, that woman is nothing but trouble. I could hear Jolene's end of the conversation, and I have never seen Jolene act so defensive as when she was talking to her grandmother."

"What did she say?"

"She told Florence that she didn't know where they would be living, so she couldn't give a phone number or address. Then she said something like, 'He doesn't need to know either,' and then 'You two can just get off my case.' Then Florence talked for some time before Jolene said more. Then she sort of yelled into the phone and said, 'I'm not telling you anything anymore, and you can tell him that.' Then she slammed down the phone. Walt, for a while she just stood there, and her hands were shaking. She looked so vulnerable!"

"Must be something with that DeLange. He always could get Florence to tell him anything."

"Yes, she finally told me that both Dexter and Florence had cornered her at the wedding and were wanting her to do some modeling. Seems like Dexter had some scheme concocted last spring and wanted to find Jolene. When he couldn't get hold of her he lost some money on the deal."

"Too bad." Walt snorted.

"I guess Dexter had sent a letter to her and John in Texas, but Jolene never knew anything about it. Florence seemed to think John never showed it to her, and that the move to the East Coast was just to get her away, but Jolene would believe none of that."

Tears started trickling down her cheeks and she couldn't go on.

"What aren't you telling me, Arlene?"

It took awhile before Arlene continued. "Poor Jolene, it just seems like nothing ever goes right for her."

For a while they both sat in the darkening room and watched the fireplace crackle.

"Ours is the kind of life she wants, Walt, just a quiet place to call her own, with some children, a good husband. John is good, and she loves him, but she's afraid there won't be any children. It's such a heavy burden, and John won't talk about it, so she carries it all alone. My heart just breaks for her!"

Walt thought of his niece driving alone down the highway with too many hours to think, and he felt frustration in his inability to help her. No children. What a blow that must be to her. She had always had her dolls, then all her pets. She was a natural-born caregiver.

Walt sat up a little straighter. "Who has the problem, him or her?"

"He does."

"I wonder if Florence knows anything about this."

"Oh, I'm sure not, Walt. Jolene would never tell her anything of such a private nature."

"Sometimes that Florence is more clever than a witch. She may have figured it out on her own. If she knows it, she most likely said something to DeLange. I don't trust either one of them."

Arlene had a horrified look on her face and Walt thought she probably was contemplating a new round of worries. The phone started ringing but she didn't seem to notice.

"Are you going to get that phone?" he asked.

She immediately jumped up to answer it and Walt soon realized from the conversation on her end that it must be Jolene. When she came back there was a brighter look on her face than Walt had seen all day.

"Well?"

"Well! Well! Get this. Jolene said John had flown in to where she was staying tonight. Guess he was pretty lonesome for her and decided to drive the rest of the way to California with her."

"That's good. I hated to think of her driving all that way alone. How did she sound?"

"Better. Yes, I'd say she sounded a lot better."

They sat for a while in silence and enjoyed the last rays of the sun settling into the west. The winter evening shadows had darkened before Walt spoke again. "Since we've got some of her woes taken care of, why don't you get us some supper?"

After Arlene left, Walt continued gazing into the fire. He had suspected from the moment she got to the ranch that there was a problem in Jolene's life. He had watched her with Danny and Ben's children, and could almost feel the longing she had when she held or played with them. She had energy to burn and had gone with him every morning to feed cattle. She baked and helped Arlene decorate the house for Christmas. She helped the men cut wood. She was game to do anything, and Danny's older kids had delighted in her willingness to go sleigh riding or ice skating. In the evenings she played cards, and still at bedtime she seemed to be looking for something more to do. He remembered the morning they finished feeding the cattle and drove to the top of a big hill. The prairie glistened all around them with new-fallen snow. Diamonds twinkled in the grass as the winter sun touched the prairies with magic, and she had stood still looking at the panoramic scene and said in an awestruck voice that nowhere else in the world was there a more beautiful sight than the prairies. Walt wanted to tell her that few people had the gift to appreciate the hushed beauty of winter on the plains, but the longing he saw on her face matched the look she wore when she was with children.

Walt had grumbled to God a little about that. Here was a good young woman who only wanted the simple things in life. Why did it have to be denied to her? "But who can understand the ways of the Lord," whispered his heart, and he knew that in time answers would come.

He knew for certain that something had happened at Rachel's wedding. Jolene came home looking like the devil himself was chasing her. She had been preoccupied this past week, and said several times how she missed John even though she loved being back. On the day before she left she had taken a lone walk and he knew she had been crying. It was thinking of those lonely tears that almost brought tears to Walt's own eyes. Arlene had answered some of the questions, but he knew there was more to the story than what Jolene had shared with her.

CHAPTER 8

Roses and Baby's Breath

THE FLORIST HEADED up the steps to apartment 224 with a single red rose surrounded by baby's breath. It had been an unusual request, and the caller had been very specific on what the flowers should be and what the card should say. There was no name on it, only the words "Whenever you're ready," and he wondered if the recipient would understand or know who had sent it.

A blonde young woman in jeans and T-shirt answered the door. She thanked him as she took the vase with the rose, looking a little perplexed. He pointed out the flowers and the card and saw a horrified look come into her eyes. She regained her composure quickly, smiled, and set the vase down as if it were burning her hand. She hurriedly handed him a tip, and he thought her hand shook a little. Another smile and he was out the door, pondering the ways of people in general and this young lady in particular.

He wondered even more when he made the second trip to apartment 224 a couple hours later with a huge bouquet of roses, carnations, and greenery. It was one of the costliest arrangements they had, and the card read, "To my wonderful wife on Valentine's Day, All my love, John."

She looked at him warily when she answered the door again and saw all the flowers. He gave her the card and came into the apartment to set them down for her. He subtly looked for the single rose he had brought earlier. Not finding it, he turned and accepted the second tip and her gracious thanks and headed out the door. Now here was a story to tell the missus.

Jolene left the vase sitting where the florist had placed it, taking very little notice of all the bright flowers. She opened the patio doors and stepped outside onto the tiny deck. John had found an expensive, modest apartment with a great view of the Pacific Ocean. She had been thrilled with the view and had spent a great deal of time sitting and watching the sunsets. She had applied for several jobs, but so far only day work had been available. The apartment was easy to keep clean and since she found herself with time on her hands, she volunteered for almost anything their church needed help with. She was invited to a ladies' Bible study group, but when she found out there were many new young mothers there, she declined. She felt a growing restlessness within her that she wasn't comfortable with, and daily she took her study Bible and pored over the Scriptures, trying to find peace.

John wouldn't be home until the next day. His career was moving along with more responsibilities, and she was glad for him. She knew he loved her second best; the military came first. She knew it and accepted it, but she resented the fact that he refused to talk to her about a family. Several times she tried to open a conversation, a discussion on their options for parenthood, and he would close himself off from her in seconds. One night she asked him why he wouldn't talk to her about something that was so important to her happiness. He looked away for several seconds and then said flatly that maybe that was one area in which he could never make her happy, and he didn't want her to bring up the subject ever again. When she said she wanted to discuss adoption, he slammed out of the apartment. They never talked of the subject again.

A little breeze whispered over the deck and ruffled the lone rose surrounded by baby's breath. She knew exactly who sent it and what the card meant, and she cringed with the remembrance of what prompted it. She had tried so hard to forget what had happened at Rachel's wedding. Now the memories flooded over her, and she made herself re-examine them and herself.

Rachel's wedding and reception were over, and the happy bride and groom had left. There remained all the chores mothers and fathers and friends need to do after such an event. Jolene was helping when her grandmother tottered toward her on her high heels and said Betty was looking for her Bible and was wondering if she left it at the house. Florence asked if Jolene would be a dear and go see if it was really there so Betty wouldn't have to worry. Gathering up her coat and purse, Jolene headed down the block to check.

She found it at once, and decided since she was there she would change into some jeans and a sweater before returning to the church. Because she was alone in the house she hadn't even bothered to completely shut the bedroom door. It was after she had kicked off her heels and peeled off her nylons that she realized she was going to have trouble unhooking the miserable little hook and eye at the back of her dress. No matter how she tried, it seemed determined to be contrary. Finally she slipped her jeans on under her dress just to give her arms a rest, and then tackled it again.

She had no idea Dexter was watching her from the partially open door. She jumped when he said her name, and immediately wondered how much of her person he had seen.

"Trouble, Kitten?" he purred, and quietly walked over to her. He turned her around so her back was to him, and started working on the errant little hook. His hands were warm and he laughed a little at her predicament.

"How long have you been standing there?" she demanded of him.

"Long enough to see some very"—and he stressed the word *very*—"pretty legs."

"Oh, forevermore," she muttered. "A peeping Dexter."

"Hold still, Jolena, you're weaving back and forth." She gave a huge sigh and tried to stand perfectly still. She heard him swear softly, and then he unhooked her necklace and laid it on the dresser.

"It's the dress, not the necklace, I'm having trouble with." She turned and looked at him, puzzled. He looked at her with amusement and turned her back around. For a brief time he left his hands on her shoulders.

"Putting that necklace on your dresser reminds of the time I came into this very room to discuss a red dress with you and had to unwind a pencil from your hair. I really don't know how you manage at all without me." His voice held traces of laughter.

"I'll probably have to wear this red dress the rest of my life."

"Who put the miserable thing on you in the first place?"

"I don't remember who zipped it up and hooked it. Oh good! You must have gotten it. Dexter, you don't need to unzip me! I can do that myself!"

"Does it go down over your hips or over your head?"

She found it was very difficult to pull away while he was pulling at the dress, and even more difficult to get her arms loose while he was rapidly pulling it over her head.

"I can do this by myself, Dexter. For Pete's sake, quit pulling it off!" Her voice was muffled as the red dress slipped over her head as smoothly as a silken petal.

He was laughing at her as she sputtered and groped for a sweater to pull over her camisole, and then in one movement he turned off the light and pulled her close to him. His kiss was soft and it stirred a deep response in her. She hardly realized she was kissing him as fervently as he was her.

For a moment they clung together, and then he whispered her name. She looked up at him with eyes full of bewilderment. "I shouldn't be doing this, Dexter. I can't think what's come over me."

He kissed her again, and she sighed and leaned into him.

"This is nonsense. You know that, Dexter."

"Do you want me to stop?"

"No," she said honestly, and hated herself for being so weak. His hands were warm on her shoulders, and slowly he began to massage the back of her neck. She relaxed against him and for a moment neither said anything. When she broke the silence, the words came out dreamily. "I want a baby."

Dexter's massage stopped instantly. "What did you say?" he asked sharply, holding her away from him. Jolene looked as startled as he did.

"Who said that?" she demanded.

"There are only two of us in this room and I most certainly did not say that!"

"I can't think whatever made me say such a thing! Dexter, take your hands off me!" She jerked herself away from him and frantically hunted for her sweater. When she discovered it she hurriedly pulled it over her head, only to realize she had it on backward.

Dexter was sitting on the bed looking at her with a thoughtful expression that was making her even more nervous. She started out the door when he called out to her and asked her if she wanted everyone to see her with her sweater on backward. She stopped in her tracks, then turned around and walked back to where he was sitting.

"This is my room, Dexter, you leave."

He got up slowly and stood in front of her. With a gentle finger he caressed her cheek. "We'll discuss your baby and your modeling later. Right now I hear the Taylors coming back." He sauntered out of her room and softly closed the door.

Blast him! she thought shakily. *And blast me too!* After she rearranged her sweater and straightened her hair, she made her way downstairs. She and the Taylors compared wedding notes, and all the while they were talking she kept nervously glancing around. She told them she would be leaving quite early in the morning, and she would thank them right now for all their hospitality. She hugged them both, thanked them again, and headed back upstairs, relieved there had been no sign of Dexter.

She refused to think of what she had said and done and was glad to pack, as it gave her something to do. Finally, when everything was in its proper place, she considered leaving right then and there. It was eleven o'clock, and if she started out then she could be back at the ranch by early morning. But what would Walt and Arlene think if she came back that early? She couldn't decide what to do. Finally weariness won out, and after a long, hot shower, she settled back into her bed, willing herself to fall asleep.

By four the next morning, she was wide awake and tiptoeing through the silent house. She carried her suitcase and went quietly out the door. Her car started faithfully in the cold morning, and it wasn't until she was well down the road that she took a deep breath and stopped looking in the rearview mirror.

Now, sitting in the California sun, she shivered. She went back inside the apartment and made herself a full pot of coffee. While it was brewing, she touched the flowers in John's bouquet, read the card, and felt tears welling up. She didn't mean to be an unfaithful wife. She knew she loved John, and she didn't know what she felt for Dexter. He had a way with women, she decided. There was something about him that was magnetic. Her heart began to pound a little harder when she thought of being in his arms. He was wicked and so was she even to think the thoughts she had. She marched out to throw away his flowers and note, but found when she went out that she couldn't bear to, and that frustrated her all the more.

She paced back into the living room and stood before her Bible. *Dear Lord, why does everything have to be so hard? Why couldn't I have fallen in love with a rancher and had babies and served You on the prairie? Why is Dexter in my life, and what do You want me to do with him?*

Oh, Lord, he bothers me. I try not to think of him, and all he has to do is send me a stupid flower and I'm all upset. Why can't John talk to me about a family? Why, Lord, do I sometimes wonder if You made a mistake letting me marry him? Except I know You don't make mistakes, so did I make a mistake in thinking You wanted me to marry him?

You know, Lord, that my thoughts have gone around and around and I'm tired of thinking. My Father, I know You would forbid me to have Dexter's baby and be married to John. Why on earth did I ever say that to him? I still don't understand why I even let him kiss me. I don't understand why I enjoyed it so much. I feel so wicked, Lord. I ask forgiveness for not making him leave when I should have and for all the wrong things I have done, for all the wrong thoughts I have had. I am so sorry and I ask for guidance to do Your perfect will. Please fill my mind with Your perfect wisdom. Amen.

For a very long moment Jolene stood still. She didn't know the answers, but she did know her confession brought a certain amount of peace and a new resolve. Going back out to the patio, she quickly threw away Dexter's arrangement.

CHAPTER 9

Two Very Different Men

DEXTER'S STEPS OUT of his doctor's office were unhurried, and the nurses enjoyed exchanging pleasantries with him as he sauntered down the hall toward the reception desk. "See you next time, Mr. DeLange," the head receptionist cooed as he nodded to her and went out the door.

It wasn't until he got into his Corvette on this chilly raw February morning that he swore. For a man who liked to control destiny, the knowledge that his heart was ticking slowly to destruction irritated him beyond belief. Both of his parents had taken medications and been forced to live quiet lives because of weak hearts. Dexter had inherited problems from both of them. He chose the opposite way, and while he ate and exercised correctly, he lived life as he pleased, knowing that when his heart gave out he would have enjoyed his pleasures.

He started the car and took a moment to appreciate the sound of its motor. Heading skillfully into the Denver traffic, he weaved his way to his lawyer's office. He wanted to make some changes in his will, and from there he planned to meet Yolanda Yates and try again to set up a western-wear modeling session. This time he was determined that Jolene would be his girl.

He had been suspicious last spring when his letter to John and Jolene had been ignored, and then trying to find them had been more difficult than he would have imagined. He didn't take defeat lightly, and when Yolanda had gotten nervous about her whole western line and wanted to wait another year, he had wanted to stomp his foot. Yet he agreed gracefully with her, and set about replanning the whole affair. The only problem with waiting, he mused, was that time wasn't on his side. He realized there were plenty of other young women who could just as profitably model the clothes, but he had made up his mind it would be Jolena.

"Why did it have to be her?" Miss Grey had asked him. He answered rather brusquely that it just did. Her carriage, her long legs, and her expressive face were all perfect. It didn't make any difference when Miss Grey pointed out that she didn't have any experience. With Bob and him setting things up and taking the snaps, she wouldn't need experience. No, it had to be Jolena, and this time he was sure it would be.

He had taken several pictures of her at Rachel's wedding to show Yolanda. They were good clear pictures, and Jolene didn't have a clue he had taken them. Whenever he thought of the wedding, he had mixed emotions. Sometimes he raged at himself for missing an opportunity that he very seldom missed, but when she had looked at him with soft and dreamy eyes and said she wanted a baby, he was thrown completely off balance. He would be ready the next time she said it, but in the meantime he had to find her again. He also raged at Jolene for leaving the Taylors so early the following morning that he had no chance to talk to her again. He had no doubt before another year passed she would be his, and all his, but he wondered at himself for having such a deep need for her. She amused him, he decided. There was something so provocative and yet vulnerable about her that kept him thinking of her far more than he wanted to.

"Today," he said to himself as he zipped into a parking spot, "today things will start going into action." He permitted himself a small smile.

Indeed, that very evening he was handed Jolene's new address, and since it was very close to Valentine's Day, he decided to send her flowers. Only, and his devious mind chortled at this, they would be a certain kind of flower so his meaning would be totally understood. For a while he wondered if he was tormenting her too much, but then he recalled the days and nights that thoughts of her tormented him, and he made the call to the florist.

The doorbell rang wildly, and Jolene hurried to answer it, wondering who in the world would be setting up such a commotion. She unlocked and jerked open the door only to be met by the grinning face of her husband.

"Hey, beautiful lady!" he said and kissed her astonished face.

"Well, hey, handsome man, and when did you start ringing the doorbell?"

"When I realized I left my keys here." John walked in with his arm around her. "I see the flowers were delivered. Did they come yesterday like they were supposed to?"

At her nod he took her in his arms once again and thoroughly kissed her. Looking deeply into her eyes, he said, "I love you, Jolene."

John's declaration set the tone for the whole week they had together before his next flight. They went for drives and ate at supper clubs that had dancing. They lazed in the morning, walked along the beach in the afternoon, attended some concerts, and enjoyed each other more than they had for a very long time.

When he returned to the base, Jolene missed him and was thankful he would be back home the following day. She turned down a chance to work at a department store for a couple of days because she didn't want to miss any of this newfound closeness they were experiencing.

The following day when John came home, they packed a picnic lunch and headed up the coast to a little spot they had found. They walked and talked, and as the evening sun slipped into the ocean, John sighed with contentment.

"I never get tired of the ocean. I guess I enjoy it as much as you enjoy the prairie, Jolene." He hugged her. "Are you enjoying it a little, I hope?"

"Yes, it's beautiful, and the sunsets are pure works of God."

"Jolene." His voice sounded a little ragged and she turned quickly to him. He took a deep breath and looked away from her to the ocean. "In December I had those tests you wanted me to take." She watched in grave consternation as the emotions played over his face. "I … I can't have children."

"Darling." She wrapped her arms around him as tears streamed down both their cheeks. "Darling, it doesn't matter. It doesn't matter. We have each other, John. We have each other, and that's enough."

He buried his face in her hair, and a shudder went through him. For a while neither said anything, and then they looked up to watch the last glorious rays of the sun light the sky with a golden burst of color that reflected in the water for a few precious seconds. As the evening shadows slipped in, they talked. They talked of their disappointment, their love for each other, the options of adopting, the life they wanted to have, and John's military career. Jolene had never heard him speak so eloquently from the heart about their Lord, and she was silent for a moment.

"Have you ever thought of going into the ministry?"

"Would you want to be a minister's wife?"

"I want to be your wife, and whatever you choose, I'll be right there beside you."

"Actually, Jolene, these past couple of months I have thought about it. I've thought of a lot of things, and I have a confession I need to make to you." He took a deep breath. "You and I received a letter from that DeLange. I read it and burned it. He wanted to see if you could model a line of clothes for him last summer, and I … well, I … well, I'm ashamed to say that I just could not stand the thought of him having his hands on you. Jolene, I'm sorry. We should have made the decision together." He plunged on doggedly. "That's why I accepted that transfer so fast. I wanted us out of Texas." He looked at her pleadingly. "I'm sorry, Jolene."

She was silent for a moment. She felt humbled and guilty. "You probably were very wise to burn it, John." She made a self-deprecating laugh. "If some beautiful woman wanted you to be her model, and I knew she would be fussing and handling you, I would probably do the very same thing. In fact"—she looked at him—"I dang well know I would. Period."

In the following days she realized John felt like a huge weight had been lifted off his shoulders. They held hands and laughed, and when they were working, they could hardly wait to see each other.

In fact Jolene thought as she drove into the department store parking lot on a cool March morning that their marriage was back in the honeymoon mode, only better. She walked briskly into the store to start her workday.

What she didn't know that morning was that the tapestry of her life was again being woven in dark colors. Someday she would understand, the Master Weaver knew, but for now she would be walking in a lonesome valley. He would be with her, but He knew there would be many tears.

CHAPTER 10

Leaning

THE AIR FORCE plane carrying John's body back to Colorado Springs made its descent out of the cold March sky. John's brother Carl sat beside Jolene as they approached the runway, and with his brown eyes full of caring concern, he asked her if she was buckled up. She nodded, and they sat in silence as the plane hit the pavement and taxied in.

No brother-in-law could have been kinder than Carl, she reflected. He had flown to the coast as soon as he heard the news that John's plane had crashed, and he had guided her through the arrangements and steadfastly stood beside her throughout the week. He had been there when friends from the church came, had kept notes of who brought what, had made telephone calls, and had been the calming factor when her grief overflowed into raw sobs.

As they walked down the jetway they saw the Harris family huddled at the gate, and Carl took her arm and asked softly, "Are you ready for this?" Again she nodded, knowing how difficult these next moments were going to be.

They heard muffled sobs as they drew closer, and father Harris came toward them with tears flowing down his cheeks. Hugs and sobs permeated the scene, and then it was time to go to the same chapel where she and John had been married almost four years previously.

She fortified herself with constant prayer, and knew many others were praying for her also. She drew strength from the fact that John had loved the Lord and was even now in Paradise, but it was when she thought of her life without him that her courage left her.

The military service at the chapel gave her great comfort. The chaplain gave a powerful message and a personal account of John's faith. He spoke of John's love for his country, his family—especially his wife—and even mentioned that John had talked of going into the ministry.

She shivered at the cemetery, and suddenly Uncle Walt was beside her to put his arm around her. He said he could hardly bear the thought of her being a widow.

Afterward at the fellowship hall, he took her aside and said that he and Arlene wanted her to come back to the ranch. He told her that as long as she wanted to stay there, she was welcome. She wanted him to know how much she appreciated his offer, but somehow when she tried to say the words, only tears would come.

Spring danced into the sand hills with soft, gentle rains, balmy days, and great calving weather. Jolene took long rides through the pasture, checking cattle. She stayed in the saddle from morning till night. She knew she rode unnecessarily long, but there was something about riding on Tango with his rhythmic gait that mollified her soul.

She was rarely in the house, rarely still. She had vowed when she moved back that she would not make the rest of the family feel bad because of her grief. She kept her tears in check, laughed with the children, cried in private, and smiled in public. Many people would come up to her at church or other gatherings and tell her how sorry they were. She would hug them all, thank them, say, "Yes, it is hard," and change the subject. Rural communities, she realized, had a genuine understanding of grief. No one dwelled on her loss, but she knew they all cared.

At a branding in May she heard a neighbor mentioning a Bible camp in South Dakota that was desperate for help during the summer. The neighbor's mother had cooked there for years and had been concerned that volunteers were so few. After a few days of mulling it over, Jolene called the camp director and made arrangements to help out for the summer. She felt she needed to get out of her own thoughts, and how better to do that than to be with a camp full of children?

She thought Walt and Arlene had looked a little relieved when she told them, and she realized that her being home had placed a burden on them. Before leaving for the camp, she walked down to the little stone house that was close to the creek. It had always fascinated her, and since she had returned to the ranch, it had been in the back of her mind to see what kind of shape it was in.

Pushing open the door, she felt the coolness of the little house greet her welcomingly. It had two small bedrooms with a bathroom between them, and a larger living room and kitchen. It had been used years ago for hired men, but since Danny and his wife were living on the place now, there was no need for hired men anymore. She liked what she saw and decided that when she was back for the Fourth of July break she would see about fixing it up, if Walt and Arlene didn't care. Even though she didn't plan to stay there forever, it would be nice to have someplace to call home.

The weather the first two weeks of June was beautiful at the camp near Bad River, but then the temperatures started heating up. Days of hundred-degree heat baked the little camp huddled beneath the bluffs of Bad River. It was often like that, the camp director said cheerfully. They just worked around it with water games.

Jolene found herself withering. She groaned when she thought of the month of July and part of August she would spend there. She stayed right at camp in a small trailer and thanked the Lord every day it had air conditioning. When the weekends came, she visited in the home of Marie, another volunteer, and since Marie and her husband were remodeling an older home, she joined in that work on Saturday and part of Sunday.

The Friday before the Fourth of July dawned hot and dry. By noon the temperature was a scorching 110 degrees. Most of the kids were waiting impatiently for their rides home, and the camp help felt drained. The wind seemed to be blowing from a fiery furnace. Still—and Jolene marveled at this—the mission of the camp went on, and the staff showed and taught Jesus and His love up to the very last minute of camp.

A little girl held Jolene's hand as she waited for her mom to pick her up. She had touched Jolene's heart all week, soaking in the Word of God as each new lesson was presented. "You look really pretty," she said shyly, and Jolene hugged her and said, "So do you, and I love your yellow camp shirt."

When the mother came driving in, her little friend was wildly excited, and tore down the path to greet her. Jolene stood and watched the reunion of mother and daughter, both so delighted to see each other.

The smell of cigarette smoke wafted over her, and she wondered who on earth would want to smoke on a scorching day like this. She turned, and under the shade of one of the few trees of the camp stood Dexter with his casual air, leaning against the trunk. She wondered at her lack of surprise at seeing him. In fact, it almost seemed to her tired mind that she had been waiting for this moment.

He ground the half-smoked stub under his boot and called out to her, "Are you sure you aren't in hell?" Realizing he wasn't going to move from under the shade, she slowly walked up to him.

"No, but we both probably should be."

He seemed slightly startled by her comment, but bending down and retrieving the dead smoke seemed to give him time for a comeback. "We, Jolena? What wicked thing have you done that would merit such condemnation?"

She frowned and started to speak, but he carefully put one finger over her lips.

"No, let's not tease each other. I've come to take you to dinner in a cool, quiet place with real dishes. I have no delight right now in seeing you frown at me."

"How did you find me, and how did you get here? Or do I thank Grandma once again?"

He smiled at her and replied, "Why don't we tell whomever we need to tell that you are going with me, and then talk in the car where the air conditioner works so wonderfully well?"

It would have seemed rude and yes, even childish, to refuse to go with him, yet she knew instinctively what he would be asking of her if she went. After weeks of being in a godly atmosphere, should she go with the devil to his den?

Something of what she was thinking must have reflected in her face. He put his hand on her shoulder and said softly, "I won't mention babies. I'll be on my best behavior, Jolena."

The camp director stood nearby and watched Jolene standing underneath the shade tree with a dark-haired man dressed in black. His untucked shirt fit perfectly over his solid frame, and she decided he was the most handsome man she had ever seen. She noted his hand on Jolene's shoulder and the soft way he spoke to her. She observed something else that Jolene didn't seem to notice. The man looked at Jolene with a strange, intense look that could be construed as almost a pleading gaze. She swiftly walked over to them, greeted Jolene, and looked inquisitively at the man as she waited for an introduction.

When Jolene introduced Dexter, he shook the director's hand and asked permission to take Jolene away for a couple of hours. She looked at Jolene searchingly and said Jolene's duties were ended for the day. Tomorrow they would close the camp down for a week, but the rest of the afternoon was hers. Privately she thought if anyone asked her to a cool place for supper she would jump at the chance. Her many duties awaited her, and after a few more pleasantries, she said her goodbyes and walked over to the chapel.

"I'm hot and sticky and dirty," Jolene informed him. "Are you sure you want to be seen with me?"

He looked her over carefully. "You are all that," he agreed. "Grab some clean clothes and you can shower and change at my motel room."

"Forevermore, Dexter! I'm not going to a motel room with you. Good grief!" She looked at him with disbelief that he would suggest such a thing.

"Jolena, let's get something decided and get going. It's 110 in the shade."

"I'll get my stuff. It'll only take me a minute." She left him standing there and quickly went into the little trailer and grabbed her purse.

They started up the winding hill in Dexter's powerful Corvette, and he looked at her inquiringly. "No clean clothes?"

"I forgot I had a complete change at my friend Marie's. We can go there and you can wait for me while I shower and get ready. It's air conditioned for your comfort, Dexter."

"Why did you run away from me after Rachel's wedding?" he asked suddenly, taking his eyes off the road to look at her.

She looked out the window, seeing none of the scenery, and tried to think of how she should answer. "Because I was scared. Because when I was with you I had thoughts a married woman should never have about another man." She glanced over to him, not knowing how to say anything but the truth. "You almost bewitched me, Dexter. I had to run away to get my common sense back."

He pulled onto the highway and didn't say anything for several miles. Then he gave a little laugh. "And all this time I thought it was you who bewitched me."

After their stop at Marie's she at least felt clean. She had put on a pair of white capri pants and pulled a black top over her head, and quickly blow-dried and curled her hair. It was nice, she reflected, to be dressing up a bit again. It was especially nice to be cool!

Dexter seemed to know where he wanted to take her, and it was several miles from town. They followed the Missouri River for quite a while and then wound their way up to a bluff overlooking part of Lake Oahe that dammed up the river near Pierre. They stopped at a steakhouse situated where the view was breathtaking. Jolene stood and looked in appreciation. Entering the building, she was grateful all over again for the coolness.

Before their steaks came and while they were drinking some very cold iced tea, Dexter sat back in his chair and stretched out his legs. Lighting a cigarette, he blew the smoke out and looked at her with narrowed eyes. She mentally braced herself, knowing the look.

"So now you are a widow, Jolena." It was a statement, rather kindly spoken.

She closed her eyes and rubbed her forehead. Looking back up at him she sighed and said, "Yes."

He seemed to be waiting for her to say more, but when she didn't, he inhaled another puff of smoke. He slowly let it out, all the while scrutinizing her carefully.

"What are your plans?"

"I don't know, at least not long-range plans. For the next six weeks I'll be at this camp."

"Why camp, Jolena? What possessed you to come here?"

She took a drink of tea and waited for the swallow to ease her burning throat. It was harder to be with him than she thought it would be. Part of it was because she felt sitting here with Dexter was disloyal to John. Part of it was … no, she wasn't even going to think those thoughts.

"I came because I needed to get away from myself and all my thoughts. Kids have needs, and when I'm with them, I forget my own troubles. Some of these little people come from divorced homes, abusive situations. Dexter, they almost break my heart!"

"I thought your heart was already broken."

"My heart seems to be continually shattering into little pieces."

"Maybe it's time to start mending."

"Mending to shatter again?"

"If your heart wants to break all the time, I suppose it will, as you say, 'shatter again.'"

"What about your heart, Dexter? Has it ever been broken?"

"I think we'll leave my heart out of the conversation."

"I think your heart is out of most conversations."

"You would think wrong, Jolena."

Their steaks arrived before Jolene could get in the last word.

After they had eaten and were finishing up the wine Dexter had ordered, Jolene asked the question that had been on her mind.

"Why are you really here, Dexter?"

"I assumed it was to see you."

She digested that for a second and looked at him speculatively, waiting for him to say more. He smiled and reached in his pocket for another cigarette.

"It's a clever habit you have, Dexter, of giving yourself time to think while you light up another coffin nail."

He exhaled a cloud of smoke and said mildly, "With most people I don't need so much time to think." At her raised eyebrows he continued. "I actually did have several reasons for being here." He leaned closer and put his arms on the table. "I need your help, and I want you to listen to me closely, and"—he gestured with his hand that held the cigarette—"not interrupt."

He proceeded to tell her about Yolanda Yates and her western-wear designs. He needed a model who would look natural in a saddle, and Yolanda had a place in mind in western Colorado where they could do the shots. He wanted Jolene. The place was a guest ranch where he, Bob and Helen Lewis, Yolanda and her husband, and Jolene would have plenty of room and time to get Jolene used to the camera and whatever else she needed to know. It was reserved for the first week of September. He needed to know soon if she would come with them. After the week in September he had several other places tentatively lined up that would take them on into late December. His voice and actions were enthusiastic, but his watchful eyes never left her face.

She objected, and for every reason she gave for not going he had a counter answer. Finally she propped her elbows on the table and rested her chin on her hands. For a while she sat gazing at him.

"What if I get pregnant?"

"What?" he almost sputtered.

"What if I decided that, as you put it, I was 'ready' and I became pregnant?" She looked at him guilelessly.

An incredulous look crept over his face and he asked in a strangled voice, "Are you serious?"

"After you sent me the flowers and card I decided you were serious."

He looked at her with his eyes narrowed and said flatly, "I don't think you and I need any children, Jolene."

Her purposefully innocent look gave way to the laughter that was building up inside her, and she pounded the table with her hand and whooped in a most unladylike manner. Dexter sat back in his chair and glared at her hilarity for several seconds before a small smile hovered around his mouth.

"You'll be the death of me yet," he muttered as she continued to chortle with shaking shoulders, sometimes covering her mouth with her hands, other times holding her sides. Finally she sat up straighter, assumed a straight face, and in a voice that threatened to break into more guffaws said, "I think it's the wine."

He was puzzled. "The wine?"

"The wine. I always get the giggles when I drink wine."

"I'll remember not to give you wine if I want to talk business." He shook his head at her, but there was amusement in his eyes.

She sat back in her chair and wiped the tears of laughter from her eyes. "You made my day, Dexter. The look on your face was priceless. For once, I had you going!"

"How nice that I could contribute to the happiness of your day."

She smiled at him sweetly then turned to look out the west windows at the setting sun sending its glowing rays across the hot prairie land. Their colors reflected in the Missouri River water, and the earth seemed to be waiting patiently for the moment when the air would start to cool and night would bring its own whisper of freshness. Jolene felt a whisper of freshness in her own soul, just a quiet whisper. With a smile still on her face, she turned back to him and asked if she could have some time to think it over.

"I have to know in two weeks." He scrutinized her carefully. "Sooner would be better."

CHAPTER 11

The Harris Family

*J*OLENE HAD PLENTY of time to think during the long drive from camp back to the ranch. Now that she had spent a month working with the children, she had a better idea of what to expect the last six weeks. She knew it would be hot and the campers would take most of her energy. She looked forward to the challenge and the children, yet she would be relieved when it was over and her days would once again be her own.

For a while she mulled over how she would fix up the little stone house, but when she reached Nebraska she forced herself to think about John and this modeling business. If he were alive, of course, there would be no question of what to do. She would refuse, and that would be that. She turned off the road to a little rest area, grabbed her Thermos of coffee, and walked over to a rickety table with benches.

Oh, Lord, You know after the evening with Dexter I felt more alive than I have since John was killed. Why do You keep allowing him back into my life? I've wondered so many times, Lord, about those last days when John was here. They were so special to me, Lord, I can hardly think of them without crying because they were such beautiful memories, and I thank You for that. It was almost like You gave me a gift of perfect love before he had to leave.

But I don't know what You want me to do about Dexter. I know John's family wouldn't like it if I go with him on all these trips. I imagine that my own family would wonder if I'm doing the right thing. When it comes right down to it, the only person who would be happy is Florence, and that's a scary thought. But, Lord, it doesn't matter what the people here want me to do; it's what You want me to do that matters. Help me with the wisdom to do Your perfect will. Amen.

As Jolene sat drinking her coffee and looking at the hills, a small voice asked her, *What do you want to do?* It startled her, because she had never asked herself what she wanted. She poured herself a second cup of coffee and admired the miles and miles of prairie land. When her mind returned to the question of her future, she sorted out some truths that startled her. She wanted adventure, and the excitement of being with Dexter would definitely be an adventure. She wanted some time on the ranch with her family, but she needed something more than that right now. It wasn't her ranch or her cattle, and even though she loved it all, there was something a little unsettling about working there. She loved John and would always carry a place in her heart for him, but John was gone. She wasn't ready to head into another relationship, and in his own arrogant way, Dexter would keep away anyone who might be interested in her. Not that he wanted her for himself, she reasoned, but more because he didn't like to share anything or anyone.

As her thoughts became clearer, she sensed a growing peace. All the questions weren't answered, yet there was a plan taking shape, and the future didn't seem like the blank emptiness it had felt like before. She stayed there in the middle of the Nebraska prairie for several more minutes, letting the quietness of its rolling hills sink deep into her soul. She took a deep breath, and her thoughts once again turned heavenward. *Thank You, Lord. Take my hand and lead me on. Whatever would I do without You in my life?*

"And here's a picture of John when he was eighteen and had just entered the military." For the past hour Mrs. Harris had been sharing her scrapbook of memories with Jolene, fingering each photo with tenderness.

The Harris family had urged Jolene to join them in Colorado Springs and share the Fourth of July with all of them. David, Shannon, and their children were there, as well as Carl and his wife and children. Lindsey had hardly let Jolene out of her sight, and even now was on and off her lap, constantly talking to her and wanting Jolene's undivided attention.

David had seemed morose and had talked of John endlessly all day. He had been back to the coast and had seen the plane. He gave vivid details of the crash and seemed unsettled about how it had all occurred. He focused on two mechanics who had shown up to work on the plane, and yet no one seemed to know where they were now. He shared all his theories and suspicions until finally Carl stopped him and said maybe it was time to change the subject.

Jolene's head throbbed, and she could feel the muscles in her shoulders tighten. It was after lunch that the scrapbooks were brought out, and finally Jolene gently put Lindsey down and stood up. "Think I'll take a break and grab a cup of coffee," she said to no one in particular.

"Me too," Shannon said, and the two of them picked their way through the living room of adults and kids and headed into the less crowded kitchen.

"Maybe we need something stronger than coffee," Shannon muttered once they were safely out of hearing. Jolene agreed.

"So how are you really doing?" Shannon wanted to know. "My mind keeps seeing you and John dancing that evening, and it just doesn't seem right that he's gone. Oh, and did I tell you?" She continued on without waiting for Jolene's answer. "I went to that guy's salon, that DeLange Designs place, and your picture is plastered all over his walls. Wow, was David mad when I told him about it. Almost wished I wouldn't have said anything! You have on a red dress and your hair is so cute. Big pictures, more like posters. Lindsey! Quit hanging on Aunt Jo!"

Jolene was startled about the pictures. She smiled wanly at her little friend, and in an attempt to avoid more questions from Shannon asked Lindsey if she wanted to go with "Aunt Jo" to get her purse. They headed to the bedroom, where she retrieved her purse and the aspirin that was in it, and she mentally calculated when she could decently leave. She realized that while she had been moving on in her life with helping the children at camp, the Harrises had chosen to dwell on their loss. She felt it the moment she had arrived; the air seemed permeated with their grief. She dawdled in the peaceful bedroom for as long as she dared, and finally walked back to the kitchen with Lindsey hanging on her arm.

Everyone must have decided to take a break, because the kitchen seemed as crowded as the living room was. Someone handed Jolene a cold glass of punch, which she gratefully accepted and downed the two aspirin with it. For a while there was general chatter, and then during a lull Lindsey's little voice piped up.

"Aunt Jo's picture in a red dress is in a man's saloon!"

Complete silence greeted that announcement. Jolene giggled. "I think she means salon."

Carl laughed softly, but David's face was like a thundercloud. "That DeLange must have a case for you. If I had been John …"

"You are not John." Jolene broke in quietly, but her heart was pounding.

"Are you staying for the fireworks?" Mrs. Harris said, quickly changing the subject.

Carl laughed and hugged his mother. "Do you mean the fireworks this evening, or right now? Ah, now, Dad," he said at his father's protest. "I'm just kidding. David gets all wound up about things."

"I'm only being loyal to my brother," David said stiffly.

It produced a flat moment no one seemed to know how to end.

Before Jolene realized what she was going to say, her mouth opened and the words tumbled out. "Actually, since you were talking about Dexter DeLange, I should tell you that he asked me to model a line of western clothing this fall for a friend of his, and I have decided to accept." She was as surprised as the rest of them.

Shannon grinned and hollered, "Yes!" with wild gestures. Carl's wife nodded and smiled. Mr. and Mrs. Harris tried to act enthused, while Carl gave his sister-in-law a thumbs up. David stood without speaking and then walked out of the room.

Jolene didn't stay for the fireworks. In fact, within an hour she was heading back to the sand hills. David had stopped her before she left and said in a grim voice that she was making a big mistake working for that DeLange. He yelled at Lindsey to stop hanging on Jolene, and Lindsey ran off crying.

"David, worry about Lindsey, not me. I'm a big girl. That little girl wants attention. Her two brothers keep you occupied, but she needs you."

He smirked at her. "What would you know about kids, Jolene? You never had any."

He immediately looked ashamed, but the damage was done. Jolene glared at him with fire in her eyes. Without a word she turned around and left. If she never saw David Harris again it would be too soon.

CHAPTER 12

Modeling

THE LITTLE STONE house seemed peaceful after the past six weeks of camp. There had been days of rain, days of heat, and days of wind, but the camp stood like a beacon light of love all through the changing weather, and as the last little camper headed out, the staff congratulated itself on another summer of telling the beautiful story of the love of Jesus.

Jolene said a fond goodbye to all the volunteers who had worked without a murmur of complaint. They had all enjoyed their times of fellowship together, and she surmised she had learned as much as the children.

During the first several days back, Jolene relished the quietness. She would take her coffee, sit under the big cottonwood trees, and soak up the peacefulness. Sometimes Arlene would walk down the hill to visit, and they would sit outside together in quiet companionship and share summer stories. Eventually they would wander back into the house, and Arlene would note each new improvement Jolene had made. The little house was cozy, and Jolene had found several pieces of her parents' furniture in Arlene's basement that added special meaning for her.

She knew the weeks before she left again would go too fast, and said as much to Arlene.

"We always miss you when you're gone," Arlene said. "But then we have the fun of seeing you come back and catching up on all your news, so I guess there is a blessing in that."

"I was wondering what Uncle Walt thinks of me doing this modeling business," Jolene said. She hadn't had the courage to ask Walt himself.

Arlene patted her hand. "I'll tell you exactly what he told me. He said that DeLange was a taker, and most men hated to see those kinds of fellows around their womenfolk. And he kinda hinted that maybe I could tell you that for him."

Arlene chuckled a little, and Jolene had to smile. She sighed and looked out the deep-set, stone-framed window toward the fields beyond the fence. "Tell him I know that Dexter is a taker, a schemer, and a charmer. But for all that, he'll keep the wolves away from me. I appreciate that for now."

"But is he like the fox that guards the henhouse?" Arlene asked softly.

Jolene smiled ruefully. "Probably so."

"Well,"—Arlene's eyes snapped in good humor—"we will just keep praying that the little hen will know exactly how to outfox the fox!"

The fox in question was at that moment discussing his little hen with Bob Lewis.

"You're taking a chance, Dexter. It's really not like you to put an unknown into the equation."

"What do you think, Bob? You've taken pictures of hundreds of young women. What's your opinion of her ability to be photogenic?"

"Oh, man, you're asking me about someone I haven't taken pictures of in four years. Yes, her wedding pictures were great, but this is different. This is modeling."

The two men were lounging in Bob's studio, and both were poring over pictures of Jolene and two other young women. "I suggest you bring Tana in as backup if Jolene doesn't make the grade."

Dexter scowled at that. For a while he sat contemplating the three young women's pictures. Then he took a cigarette from his pocket and, while lighting it, told Bob he might consider Tana, but definitely not the other girl, Zodie.

"Remember how she tried to boss us around with this idea and that idea? She almost drove me crazy."

Bob laughed lightly. Then, growing serious, he studied the face of his longtime friend. "I believe Jolene drives you crazy, Dexter, in a totally different way." He didn't know what he expected the man across from him to say, but he was not prepared for Dexter's answer.

"She's never out of my mind. Sometimes I hate her for that." He inhaled and shook his head. "I want her, and she's thirty years younger than I am. It makes no sense to me." He looked across the smoke at his intent listener and added, "Now you know, Bob." He gave a short laugh. "You know I have a heart that isn't good and a mind that isn't working right. And I'd appreciate it if you kept that knowledge to yourself." Dexter walked out of the room.

Bob stared at the picture of the young woman in the red dress. He shook his head as he studied her. For all the world she looked like an innocent young lady enjoying her friend's wedding. How could a woman so unassuming catch and hold a spade like Dexter? It didn't make sense to him either.

The friendly September sun was going down on the western Colorado mountains, and Dexter stood back as Bob took the last few shots of Jolene. For four days she had changed from one outfit to another while her makeup was touched up and her hair sleeked down. She had proven to be capable of long sessions, and after coaching from both Bob and Dexter, she had quickly picked up the model's stance and look. She knew they were the experts, and her job was to do what they told her to. Dexter appreciated her willingness to be placed in various positions without complaint. He knew he had pushed her hard that day, but rain was forecast for the following day, and as always, time was limited. The weather was hot and muggy, and he could see she was visibly drooping.

"I'm finished," Bob called out. "Is there anything more you want, Dexter?"

"No, it's time to quit for the day," he replied and saw relief in Jolene's eyes. He watched her leave the stables where they were doing the day's photos and walk quickly to the lodge where they were all staying. He had discovered he had a sixth sense when it came to Jolene. He knew when she was tired and when she needed to be left alone, and he generally knew where she was most of the time. When he helped her with her clothes or touched up her hair he tried to be as aloof as possible, but always he could feel the tension between them, and he wondered if it also affected her.

He had been shocked at her appearance at the Bible camp. With her hair wind-tousled and the fine lines around her eyes, she had appeared older and sadder. She looked so tired when she walked up to him, and her words about deserving to be in hell shocked him. He had given himself time to recover by bending down and picking up the cigarette butt, and when he straightened up again he realized that the dancing light that had always been in her eyes was gone. It bothered him all evening. It wasn't until her little pitch about getting pregnant and his unbelieving reaction that her eyes once again looked like the Jolena he knew. When she called after the Fourth of July, her voice sounded troubled. She seemed unsure if he would still think she was the one for the job. He told her no one else would do, and in his mind, that was the truth. He was relieved and a little surprised that she accepted, and when she came to his salon he was also surprised at her calmness.

He grimaced as he remembered her hands. She had been helping her aunt with some canning, and her nails were chipped and her hands were rough. He was glad to see she at least looked rested, but he had yelled at Patrick to come and bring the manicurist and then spent a little time ranting to all who would listen that this woman was impossible. They looked at Jolene in awe because she seemed totally unperturbed by his ranting. It was out of character for Dexter to be rude to any of his customers, and Patrick tried to placate them until he saw that Jolene had an amused smile on her lips.

"Get over it, Dexter," she said, and Dexter noticed that Patrick didn't miss the look he and Jolene exchanged or the shocked expression on the manicurist's face.

Jolene and he had kept up a barrage of insults to each other during the days here at the guest ranch. It helped ease some of the tension between them, and yet if it had been possible he would have taken her in his arms and never let her go. And that, thought Dexter, was a miserable thing for a man his age to contemplate of someone her age.

"Hey, Dexter, give me a hand here," Bob called. They gathered equipment and slowly made their way back to the lodge.

Yolanda, her husband, and Helen were gathered on the porch enjoying a cool drink, and Jolene had changed clothes and was sitting on the ground looking sleepy. It was still hot, and Dexter noted how the clothes appeared to stick to everyone's skin.

Yolanda poured him a cold drink of water from a pitcher on a small table. "You've worked us hard today, Dexter," she scolded. "I think we're all bushed, and Jolene has been in and out of so many clothes that she is totally worn out."

Dexter looked over at Jolene and saw she had leaned back on her elbows and half closed her eyes. Without opening them, she nodded in affirmation of Yolanda's words.

"She's young." Dexter snorted. "She's got energy to burn."

"Good thing I'm not your age," Jolene muttered without opening her eyes. "I'd be half dead."

When Dexter chose to, he could move very fast. He swiftly grabbed the water pitcher and stood over Jolene. The rest of the group watched in silence, and then laughed nervously as she slowly opened her eyes.

When she realized her predicament, she didn't move, but her eyes flashed and danced as she looked up at Dexter and yelled, "Don't even think of doing that!"

He grinned like a Cheshire cat, still holding the pitcher at a pouring angle. It was double dog dare, and they both knew it, each coiled like a spring, wondering what the other would do.

In the next second he flung the whole contents of the pitcher on her, and as the cold water hit her she shrieked and grabbed him around the legs. He lost his balance and with a "Whoa!" rolled to the ground, half on top of her and laughing with abandon.

"You're soaking wet!" he said as he raised himself with his elbows to look at her. "Your hair looks like a sheepdog after a rain." He gave way to mirthful laughter.

She fished ice cubes out of the top of her blouse and threw them at him, her eyes flashing, and she alternated between muttering threats and laughing with him. For several moments they teased each other and listened to the catcalls of their friends. When they finally helped each other to a standing position, Jolene announced, "I'm going swimming," and strode toward the pool.

"You can't go swimming. You don't have a swimsuit," he yelled to her determined back.

"In Nebraska we don't even use 'em." She flung the words over her shoulder and whipped off her skirt.

"Jolene!" he shouted with a note of alarm as her blouse was next to go. She made a flying leap into the swimming pool wearing a white swimsuit.

Dexter stood in stunned disbelief then slowly turned around to look at the rest of the crew. He found himself staring into Helen's video camera and the amused faces of his friends. They grinned at him and at one another. Yolanda's husband declared they should all go swimming and left to get his trunks.

Yolanda, who had known Dexter for a very long time and had never seen him so disheveled, tucked her arm into his. "My friend," she said, chuckling, "this time I believe you have met your match."

Before long everyone joined Jolene in the pool. It was a great way to unwind from the long, hot day, and there was no lack of laughter and joking. It was after dark when they finally made their bedraggled way into the lodge.

After he had showered and changed, Dexter knocked on Jolene's door to take her downstairs for dinner. She answered with her hair partly blow-dried and her usual jeans and T-shirt. She looked like a tired kitten that had had a good time playing all day. Something tender touched his heart, and knowing it was a mistake, he stepped into her room, shut the door, and took her into his arms without saying a word. He had to hold her, he decided. If he didn't he knew he would yell at her, and he was tired of that. Better to just hold her and see what she would do.

She leaned against him and sighed a huge contented sigh. "Dexter?"

"Mm?" he smelled her freshly washed hair.

She tipped her head so she could see his face. "What are we going to do about each other?" For an answer he gave her a long slow kiss that took her breath away. When he drew away and looked down at her he noted she still had her eyes closed. Slowly she opened them and whispered, "I wonder if you would mind repeating that." He didn't mind at all. In fact he repeated himself several times, and then reluctantly pulled away.

"We'd better get your hair fixed or we'll be late for dinner." He was surprised his voice sounded a little ragged.

Dexter thought he would arrange her hair in curls, but when he saw the shadows under her eyes, he decided that for once he would just finish blow drying it and leave it alone. The back of his mind told him he should leave all of Jolene alone. The thought occurred to him that they were like two moths dancing toward a flame. They would probably destroy each other.

The rain the following morning made a good excuse to start the fireplace in the lodge. Yolanda modeled some of her own clothing with the snapping fire in the background, and then decided she wanted Dexter and Jolene together in some shots. She noticed both of them were professionally cool toward each other, and wondered at the relationship between the two of them.

Yolanda had often credited Dexter for being one of the best when it came to finding and working with models. He was usually the epitome of tactfulness with them, and it had been a shock when he sometimes barked at Jolene and she barked back. Yolanda remembered the many times Dexter would raise his voice slightly at some young woman and it would be enough to upset her for the rest of the day. Jolene was definitely different.

She remembered the second day at the ranch when he wanted Jolene to take a more seductive position. He had urged her several times to become more provocative, and finally in exasperation, yelled at her to unbutton the blasted blouse and get the shot over with. Jolene had fired back if he wanted to show his chest in public that was just fine, but hers was going to stay covered. Period.

For a minute Yolanda thought he was going to rip the buttons off the blouse. His eyes became even blacker, and he lit a cigarette. They were all relieved when he muttered to shoot it even if she wanted it buttoned up to her eyebrows. To everyone's amazement the picture of her in her buttoned blouse and blazing eyes was so arresting that they knew it would draw a lot of attention.

In the afternoon when the sun came out, the owners brought out a beautiful palomino mare named Pebbles. Yolanda thought if Jolene's beaming face was any indication, it was the highlight of the entire week for her. Jolene was to be pictured in several different poses both on and off the mare and in action with her. The camaraderie between Jolene and Pebbles was instant, and it was apparent this young lady loved to ride and could handle her horse. Yolanda saw Dexter smile smugly to himself several times during the shoot and knew he was giving himself a mental pat on the back. No doubt about it, she thought, the palomino horse and blonde girl in jeans, boots, and western shirt would make sales skyrocket.

When Sunday morning came, it was a tired bunch that gathered for breakfast. They were going to start packing up and heading home, but everyone was moving slowly. Dexter stood on the porch after breakfast, enjoying a cigarette and the morning beauty of the mountains. He was pleased with the week's work and with how well Jolene had adapted to the crew and to her work. Footsteps sounded on the porch, and she came bounding out of the door and almost collided with him.

"Where are you going, Jolena?" he asked mildly.

"Church. They say to take the path across the road and in fifteen minutes you can wind around and be at the little country church we saw when we were driving up."

"How do you know which path to take?"

"They say the one that has the little cross in rocks."

"Do 'they' say what I'm suppose to do if you get lost?"

"They say I can't get lost. Just follow the path. Dexter, I have to go if I'm going to get there in time." She skipped down the steps two at a time. When she got to the bottom, she hesitated, then turned around and looked at him. He drew on his cigarette and looked at her with narrowed eyes. Suddenly she ran lightly up the steps and took his hand. "Why don't you go with me?"

For a small space of time, he looked at her without speaking. Then throwing his cigarette down he replied, "I thought you'd never ask." He didn't release her hand as they walked down the steps, crossed the road, and found the path.

The narrow trail wound its way through the trees and around some big boulders. In places it was wide enough for them to walk together, in other parts they had to walk single file. The morning sun filtered its warmth around them, and the slow pace Dexter set made it an enjoyable stroll. When they reached the church, the congregation was singing the first hymn, so they quietly took a pew in the back. Dexter put his arm around her shoulder and gently tugged at a loose blonde tendril of hair.

The pastor had a calm demeanor, and his message was on knowing the only way to heaven was through Christ Jesus. He quoted Acts 4:12, which he read to his listeners, "Nor is there salvation in any other, for there is no other name under heaven given among men by which we must be saved." He made the point that even though we feel we have run a good race by doing good things and obeying all the rules, if we haven't made sure our name is recorded in the Book of Life by faith in Christ, we are not qualified to enter. He ended with another quote from Scripture, John 14:6. "I am the way, the truth, and the life. No one comes to the Father except through Me."

Jolene enjoyed the service and told the pastor as they were filing out how much she appreciated his message. He asked several questions about where they were staying and was pleased to hear the guest ranch had told them of the church.

As they were walking back Dexter groused that the minister should have been pleased. The only thing he had in his pocket to put in the collection plate was a hundred dollar bill, and he had parted with it quite reluctantly.

Jolene stopped abruptly in the path. "Dexter, the minister would much rather have your soul in heaven's gates than your money in his collection plate." Slowly he put both hands around her concerned face and kissed her.

He said rather carelessly as they continued walking, "Guess he'll have to be content with the money."

His remarked bothered Jolene, and she mulled it over for many days.

CHAPTER 13

Christmas with Dexter

SNOW WAS FALLING outside the little stone house on the grey December morning. Jolene had Christmas music on and had just finished baking the sugar cookies that had always been her dad's favorite. The past several days she had wrapped presents, hung her decorations up, and tried to stop a wave of nostalgia and sadness from sweeping over her. Her grief over John's death had seemed to deepen like the snow drifts outside, and she found that thinking of him and her parents threw her into a spiral of depression.

The Harris family had wanted her to come to Colorado Springs for the holidays, but she knew from the Fourth-of-July experience that she couldn't—or wouldn't—go there. She also had an invitation to be with Walt's family, and that was probably where she would go, but she remembered last year and how she felt a little like a fifth wheel during their family festivities.

Lord, I used to love this time of year, but now it just hurts.

She started washing the baking dishes and her thoughts drifted back to last year at this time. If only one could change the past. If John had come with her to Rachel's wedding. If Dexter hadn't come. If she had never left the church to find Betty's Bible. If she had confessed to John what had happened.

Oh, God, when I had the opportunity to tell John I let Dexter kiss me, I never said anything. I never said anything.

She felt overwhelmed by that burden. She rationalized to herself that had she known her time with John would be so short, she would have made a full confession.

But what good would that have done, Lord? Granted, I would have felt better, but how would such an admission have made John feel? He was already burdened by his inability to have children. Would knowing his wife asked another man for a baby make him happy?

Of course not, don't be ridiculous, her mind scolded her. She sniffed back tears of frustration and doggedly kept washing dishes.

Aw, God, we humans sin, and we fail, and what else can we do but start each new day asking Your Son to help us do Your will?

The clean dishes were stacking up in the little sink, and she reached for a towel to start drying them. "I hate bawling," she muttered as she sniffed again.

And sometimes I hate Dexter for muddling up my thinking. Lord, he's in my life again. Big time, now. What do You want me to do about this man? Sometimes it would help, Lord, if there was some great heavenly neon sign that said "Jolene, this is what I want you to do."

Her thoughts went over the past months and the places she had been with Dexter. They had had a turbulent time. There would be the moments when he would reach out and hold her, but more often they would bicker and insult one another. They were both worn out when December came, and they had parted hurriedly with hardly more than a simple goodbye.

The previews with Yolanda's designs turned out well, and some of the other pictures would be printed as full-page ads in magazines. When Jolene wasn't being self-critical, she admitted she had modeled the clothes and jewelry well.

But I don't think I'm cut out for this modeling business, Lord. Somehow, the O'Neil in me just can't get used to being fussed over. And You know how irritated Dexter becomes when anyone else tries to offer advice.

She shook her head and put some measuring cups away. Boy, did Dexter get irritated when other designers tried to help.

She remembered when Dexter had been at his wit's end with one of Yolanda's dresses. He and Bob had tried every angle, putting Jolene in several places, and nothing suited either one of them.

A young tousled haired designer from some unknown studio had been watching, and slowly walked over and winked at Jolene. He placed a filmy scarf across her shoulders and took time adjusting it. Then he quickly fluffed her hair and told Bob, "Now shoot it."

"I don't think so," Dexter had said coolly. He took the scarf off and handed it back to the young man. "We'll call it a day, Jolene. You can go now."

She gladly left. It wasn't the first time there had been unwanted interference from others, and Dexter was always testy about such matters.

Later as she sat in the lounge area of the resort, Dexter had quietly joined her. He put his feet comfortably on the coffee table, and without saying a word pulled her close to him. For several minutes they sat in silence while he absently rubbed her shoulders. Finally he muttered, "I could have shot him for messing with your hair."

"I could have shot all three of you and myself for ever getting into this situation," she replied.

"Aren't you enjoying yourself, Jolena?"

"My bank account enjoys the money and this is a wonderful opportunity, but my heart just isn't in it, Dexter." She added apologetically, "You and Bob couldn't be better. It's the O'Neil in me, I guess." She looked at him and sighed. "It's been interesting, I'll say that much. And I'm very grateful to you for all you've done." It was the first time she had ever admitted that it was anything less than great.

"I've put you through hard days. You're tired. When you see your pictures you'll feel differently."

She had turned slightly and noticed several people watching them.

"Dexter," she whispered, "people are staring at us."

"Good, pretend you're enjoying it."

She had whispered again, "I don't have to pretend."

That's the problem, Lord. I enjoy the man, and there is probably no two people on this earth less suited for each other.

She sniffed again, and became irritated that her eyes kept overflowing. "Pull it together, for heaven's sake, Jolene," she scolded herself.

With her tiny kitchen cleaned up, Jolene looked at the clock and groaned. It was only mid-morning, and she couldn't think of anything more to do. She wandered over to the window and noticed the snow still lightly falling. Finding a crumpled napkin on the counter, she used it to blow her nose, and then decided a cup of coffee would perk her up.

Leaning against the counter while the coffee maker gurgled it's brew, she thought again of Dexter.

I don't want to fall in love with him, God. No—no. It would be so disloyal to John. Besides, as Florence always says, Dexter loves 'em and leaves 'em and I don't need my heart broken by that rogue. And he's just too old for me, Lord. There is no good reason for me to love that rascal.

The pounding on her door startled her so much she gave out a little yelp. Grimly aware that she must have looked a sight with flour sprinkled on her shirt and those miserable tears staining her cheeks, she never the less hurried to see who her caller was.

Before she could open the door, however, it flew open, and an unsmiling Dexter strode in wearing a heavy black overcoat with a white scarf wrapped carelessly around his neck.

"Well, good morning, Mr. DeLange. Won't you come on in?"

"These are the most miserable foul roads I've ever driven on!"

"How inconsiderate of us to have only gravel roads. Are you staying awhile? Would you like to take off your coat?" Then looking at him incredulously she asked, "How did you ever find me?"

"Considering that you live at the end of the world, it's a small wonder!"

"Will homemade cookies make up for coming all this way?"

He let her help him off with his coat before he answered her. "It might help," he said, slightly mollified.

She laid his coat on a chair in her living room, and a wild musk scent surrounded her. "I can't believe you're here! You're absolutely the last person in the world that I would have expected to come here in this weather."

They stood looking at each other like two gunfighters waiting for the other to draw first. "Oh, forevermore, Jolene, come here," he said roughly, and she was in his arms in a flash.

"It would appear," she said rather shakily, "it would appear that we're glad to see each other."

"I missed you," he whispered. "I missed you, and after a week of biting everyone's head off and being told I was impossible—even by Miss Grey ..."

"If Miss Grey told you that, it must have been so."

"Exactly. They packed my bag and told me to go find you."

"I'm surprised you listened."

"I'm shocked, to tell you the truth."

"How odd for you to tell the truth."

He held her away from him and scowled. "I tell the truth more than you might think, and I'll tell you the truth right now. I want ... a cup of strong hot coffee. Your roads really are terrible."

"I know. No pavement, only gravel. And probably slippery and snowy on top of all that."

He looked at her and smiled. "I guess I'll just have to stay here until I can get out again. It might be months. Just you and me here alone." He raised an eyebrow and looked at her archly.

"Dexter, you rascal! I'm so glad you're here!"

Before lunch they drove up to Walt and Arlene's, and Dexter was at his charming best. He admired the ranch, said he knew very little about any of it, raved about Arlene's cooking, complimented

Walt on his sign by the road, and when Danny and his family came over to meet him, he talked to each child and learned their names. Ben and his family received the same treatment when they came over. By the time Dexter and Jolene went back to the little stone house, the O'Neils had been dazzled, and they knew it.

"Good grief, Arlene!" Walt groused. "You were supposed to be more objective than that."

"Than what, Walt? I tell you, that man is so good looking up close, and he smells so divine ..."

"What? What? Just what's so great about the way he smells? Good grief, Arlene!" Walt began muttering about pretty men wearing perfume and caught a look that passed between his daughters-in-law.

"It seems too soon for Jolene to have someone after John's death, though, doesn't it?" Danny seemed to feel he had to ask the question.

They all debated whether this was something serious or a passing fancy. They tried to decide if any couple could be serious with a thirty-year age difference between them. They wondered if a playboy could ever be considered "nice," if he could change, or if Jolene would become what she wasn't and change. They mulled it over rolls and coffee, and interruptions from the kids, and finally decided they just didn't know. One thing was for sure, and Dexter had made the point clear. Jolene would be spending Christmas with him.

While the family was discussing them, Jolene and Dexter were having a mild argument in the living room of the little stone house.

"I can't possible leave this afternoon, Dexter, I'm just not ready."

"What do you have to do?"

"Well," she fidgeted under his gaze, "you know, pack, and take care of the food in the fridge, and—" she stopped as he placed both warm hands around her face and looked at her intently.

"You were crying this morning, weren't you, Kitten." It was a statement softly said.

"Yes."

"You know I hate it when you cry."

"I hate it too. Makes my nose red."

"Red is not a good color for you."

She resisted the urge to giggle at that inane comment, but couldn't help flashing him a grin.

He smiled back at her lazily and kissed her.

"That is so unfair, Dexter," she muttered when she caught her breath.

"Life, my little kitten, is often unfair. Now. Pack. I told Miss Grey I would have you at her apartment this evening."

"Dexter, did anyone ever tell you that you are extremely bossy?"

"Actually, yes, and you can't teach an old cat new tricks."

On the drive back to Denver, she asked him what Christmas was like in Dexter DeLange's life. He told her that he had a supper for his family and close friends at about three p.m. on Christmas Eve. That left time for them to open gifts and go to church. Christmas Day was open for invitations to someone else's place, which, he informed her with a smile, was a selective choice.

She was puzzled about his reference to family, and wondered if he meant Betty's family. For a while he drove in silence, then glancing at her, he said he had a son. She raised her eyebrows in question, and he reached over and took her hand.

"OK, Jolena, bear with me, and I'll tell you about him." He sighed and seemed to try to gather his thoughts together before proceeding. "When I was young and dumb, I lived with a woman. She had my child, and we continued living together for the next several years. She married someone else, but I always kept in close contact with my son, and yes, Jolena, I see you trying to do the math in your head. He is older than you."

"Is he married?"

"Yes, he has a beautiful wife and two children."

"You're a grandfather," she breathed incredulously.

"It's a well-kept secret."

For a few miles Jolene turned all the information over in her mind. "Where does he live?"

"Denver."

"What does he do?"

"Hair stylist."

"What shop?"

"DeLange Designs." A small smile hovered around his lips. At her puzzled look, he said quite softly, "Patrick is my son, Marcella is his wife."

Jolene collapsed back into her seat and tried not to let her jaw go slack. Another few miles passed by before she could say more.

"But he doesn't look, or act, or even style hair like you. I never would have imagined he was your son."

Dexter released her hand and concentrated on his driving before answering.

"Patrick had no plans for being in my salon, or for that matter, being a stylist. He went into the army and was sent overseas, and because of necessity and boredom, he began cutting his friends' hair. He was good, and soon was in demand. When he returned home and was discharged, he decided to see if he liked it. I was skeptical, to tell you the truth, but when I saw how good he was, I offered him a chance to work with me. The rest, as they say, is history."

He turned to look at her and said lightly, "Any more questions Jolena? Ah, yes, I see it on your face."

He turned his attention back to the road before he answered her unasked question.

"Patrick looks like his mother, acts like her, and has her common sense. She was a good woman. I just couldn't ..." He let out a breath of air. "I just didn't love her or even want to spend my life with her. She married a good man. They have a good marriage and other children."

He faced Jolene again and raised an eyebrow at her with a slightly defensive gesture. "I never said I was a saint, Kitten, so quit looking at me like you've tasted something sour."

Jolene immediately tried to smooth out her features, but her mind was racing in several directions all at once. She folded her arms and brought one hand across her mouth as she pondered all his information. Finally she said, "You never cease to amaze me, Dexter. In one swoop I discover you are a father and a grandfather." She shook her head and looked at him in the fading daylight. His dark face with its strong profile and smoldering eyes gave her heart insidious little thumps as she studied him. This would be a most unusual Christmas, she decided.

Dexter kept busy in his salon with the holiday rush, and Jolene took the opportunity to go with Miss Grey on several shopping trips in Denver. She marveled at the efficiency of the older woman, and her no-nonsense approach to all of life's challenges was an education in itself.

One evening after such an excursion, Jolene questioned Dexter about his secretary. They were sitting together on the couch in front of the fireplace, and he had seemed especially interested in the hollow of Jolene's throat. She found herself trying to catch her breath and settle her heartbeat, and with some desperation, she blurted out, "What about Miss Grey?"

He slowly raised his head and looked at her blankly. "Do we need her for some reason?"

"Ah ... no, but," she continued hurriedly as he became interested in the softness of her shoulder, "but I was wondering how you and she came to work together." It was several minutes later before he remembered to answer her, and when he spoke, he sounded as breathless as Jolene had been.

"Let's see, I believe you asked me about Miss Grey."

"I believe I did," she answered vaguely.

For a short while he looked down at her, noting her luminous eyes and flushed cheeks, and with great effort turned away to regain his composure. Finally, clearing his throat, he began. A number of years ago Miss Grey had a friend who had called DeLange Designs for a hair appointment for her. There had been a mix-up, and she had been seated in the room where Dexter worked. When she realized she was in the room alone with him, she panicked, and with a shaking voice and trembling hands had told him to get out. He realized she was verging on hysteria, and without moving, and speaking softly, had called a woman hair stylist into the room. He left then, and it took a while before the reason for her behavior became apparent.

With many tears she told the beautician that she had been brutally assaulted and raped. She had spent the past year in virtual isolation, afraid of men, afraid to go out into society. She had no job, and it was with much persuasion that her friend had convinced her to get her hair styled. She was given special consideration and care that day at DeLange Designs and Dexter took over the appointments of the other beauticians while Miss Grey not only had her hair done, but was given a manicure and facial on the house. Finally he ventured back into his own space, and in the presence of his female staff, visited with the embarrassed Miss Grey.

He asked her what she did for a living before her attack, and she said she had been an accountant. She had left her job because she was too frightened to commute and too scared to be alone with any male. He asked her if he offered her a job as a receptionist in the salon, where she would be working mainly with women, would she consider it. She had been surprised but said she would think it over. He then suggested that she buy a pistol, learn to use it, and carry it at all times.

Miss Grey had been incredulous at such a suggestion, but a week later she began her duties as receptionist at DeLange Designs, and carried a small but deadly little pistol in her pocket at all times. She was very adept at her new job, and in short order, had taken over the bookwork. She worked tirelessly and was devoted to Dexter. Out of respect for her position, he had never touched her and always had called her Miss Grey.

Jolene's eyes rounded with wonder as Dexter finished. She silently mulled over all the details and sat grimly and silently looking into the fire. She was quiet for so long that Dexter spoke her name questioningly.

"Jolena?"

Turning to look at him she shook her head. "It's hard to imagine what victims of assault and rape go through all the rest of their life. It's hard to understand why it has to happen, and why it's allowed to happen. Yet," and she paused reflectively, "yet Miss Grey, with encouragement, took what was evil and turned it into something good. Or maybe I should say God took what was evil and turned it into something good."

She had pulled away from him and was sitting on the edge of the couch. "It's amazing, isn't it, what happens when a helping hand reaches out. In this case, your offer of a job must have been quite an incentive for her."

"She's been my right hand for many years." He smiled at Jolene's seriousness and tried to add a lighter note. "At any rate, she's well paid and I'm well served." He reached out to pull her back to him. When she was well settled in his arms again, she was still quiet, gazing at the flames. Finally she looked at him and said, "I almost like you for being so kind to Miss Grey." She smiled impishly.

He leaned over to kiss her and said wryly, "I feel so blessed, Jolena."

Dexter's penthouse was decorated with a profusion of poinsettias and scented candles. On Christmas Eve, the fireplace provided an inviting gathering spot, and with the softly falling snow, a joyous Christmas celebration was underway. Patrick and Marcella and their two children, along with Miss Grey and Bob and Helen Lewis, were greeted at a cedar-decorated door. Mr. and Mrs. Runski, Dexter's employees, became cook and butler for the evening, and the aroma of delicious food wafted over the visitors.

Soon they all gathered around the table, and after Patrick said a short grace, enjoyed Mrs. Runski's own version of roast goose. She had added all the trimmings, and was beaming in the kitchen over the compliments.

Later they gathered around the tree and slowly opened presents. Patrick's children were first to unwrap their gifts from their grandfather, and Jolene wondered if he had actually picked them out, or had let Miss Grey decide what to get. They were perfect gifts for an eight-year-old boy and six-year-old girl. She looked with wonder as they both sat on Dexter's lap with total ease and thanked him with hugs. She loved the gentle look he gave both of them and thought if she hadn't seen it she would not have believed he could be so … so grandfatherly.

After all the gifts were opened, they sat around the fireplace with small glasses of wine for the adults. They included Jolene in the conversation and seemed genuinely pleased she was there. She marveled at that too. She knew Helen and Bob had become aware of the feelings between Dexter and her at the modeling locations. In fact, more than once when Dexter was abrupt with her and her response was equally brusque, Bob had eased the tension with some timely remark.

Soon it was time for the church service, and all of them donned coats and headed out the door. Dexter took Jolene's hand as they walked out to his car, and before he opened the car door for her, he put his hand on her shoulder and asked if she had enjoyed herself. She nodded. "I had a good time, Dexter. Thank you for asking me here."

Sitting beside him at the service, hearing the familiar carols and the timeless story of Baby Jesus, brought unexpected peace into her very being. She had been dreading the holidays, but spending them with Dexter and family and friends had been uplifting. At that moment he turned to look at her. Giving her hand a gentle squeeze he winked at her, throwing her new found peace into turmoil.

Dexter and Jolene had decided to open their gifts to each other after the church service, when they were alone. Dexter wanted his gift first, and he thought she looked anxious as she watched him unwrap it. She had bought him a leather-bound study Bible with his name in gold letters on the front. He couldn't hide his astonishment.

She looked a little flustered, and said, "I … I wanted to give you something that means a lot to me." She looked down before continuing. "Dexter, I … I don't know what you really feel, but it is so important to me to have my loved ones know Jesus and have eternal life." She looked at him imploringly.

Never in Dexter's life had he been given a Bible by anyone other than his mother or sister and he thanked her with sincerity. He gently reached over and ran the back of his hand across her cheek. "I know Jesus, Kitten. I may not act like it most of the time, but I was raised in a Christian home." He decided against kissing her then, but it was a serious act of self denial.

He knew when he put his package on her lap that she would suspect jewelry. The diamond and emerald necklace and earrings he gave her matched her eyes perfectly, and she looked both aghast and delighted when he helped her put them on.

A slow smile crept onto his face and reached his eyes. "You are so beautiful, Jolena." He ran his hands down her arms and thought again of kissing her.

She fingered the necklace. "What does it look like on?"

"Check it out in the hallway mirror, Miss O'Neil."

When she returned she settled herself primly across from him. With her hands folded in her lap, she stated softly, "I never ever, no never, have had such a beautiful and expensive gift." She was silent for several seconds. "Where are we going with this relationship, Dexter?"

"Where do you want to go with it?"

"I don't know." She looked at the fireplace, then back at him. "Where do you want to go with it?"

"To the altar, Kitten."

Her eyes widened and her hands flew to her necklace. "To the altar? What are you saying, Dexter?" She almost shouted his name.

He sat back on the couch and put his feet on the coffee table. "I'm saying—forevermore, Jolene, come over here so I don't have to talk across the room."

When she was snuggly at his side and his arm was once again around her shoulders, he looked at her with his usual raised eyebrow. "Now then, Kitten. We need to be married. I can't have you staying at Miss Grey's indefinitely while we fool away time."

She frowned at him and said slowly, "People usually get married because they love one another."

"Of course." He paused for a moment and then said mildly, "I thought you did love me."

She bolted upright and glared at him with glowering green eyes. "You have to be the most infuriating man I ever met! I'm talking about you loving me! Good grief, Dexter, you can't ask a woman to marry you without ever telling her you love her. What kind of a playboy are you, anyway?"

"Obviously a very ignorant one," he said, bursting into laughter and pulling her indignant frame against him. Finally he kissed her the way he wanted to all evening long, and when she was slightly mollified, he kissed her again.

"We're not right for each other, you know that," she groused.

"I'm way too mature for you, Kitten."

"You're way too old for me."

"That's what I said."

She was silent for a while. "Dexter, we need to be serious."

He reached into his pocket and pulled out an emerald and diamond ring. "Jolene," and suddenly he was very serious. "I don't go chasing after women in a blizzard unless I have plans for them.

I want you to be my wife. And yes, Kitten," he said, seeing the question that was forming in her eyes, "I love you. I wouldn't ask you to marry me unless I loved you."

He saw a glowing look come into her eyes, and then she quickly looked down at her left hand and then just as quickly glance back at him.

"You'll have to take John's ring off if you're going to wear mine," he informed her softly.

Early the day after Christmas, Dexter walked into the salon and asked to speak to Patrick privately. He leaned against the doorway to their office, and looked at his son with affection.

"I guess I have four things I need to tell you, Patrick. The first and probably most important to me is that I'm marrying Jolene."

Patrick nodded. He hadn't missed the signs. If it bothered him that his new stepmother would be younger than he, he gave no indication.

"Second, I'm retiring from the salon."

Patrick looked dumbfounded. It was obvious he had not expected anything like that. Before he could reply, his dad continued.

"Third, my will says you are to inherit all this building, including the penthouse on the top floor, and of course, this business."

Patrick held up his hand to stop but Dexter continued on.

"Fourth, I don't have a lot of time, Patrick. You know I have this heart condition. The doctors tell me probably a year at the most. And no, Jolene doesn't know."

Dexter looked at the astonished face of his son. "I'm too proud to tell her, and I'm too selfish to get out of her life. I … I know that it's a low thing to do to her, but I want her for as long a time as I have." He gave Patrick a searching gaze. "Can you understand it, Patrick?"

Patrick slumped into the nearest chair and ran shaking fingers over his face. "You have …" He swallowed painfully several times.

"No!" He looked at Dexter with troubled eyes, and repeated it again, only more agonizingly. "No! I knew you had heart trouble, but not this bad. Are you sure the doctors … have you gone somewhere else for another opinion?"

Dexter went on into the office and closed the door. He stopped by the chair his son was sitting in and squeezed his shoulder lightly. Then he walked over to the office chair and sat down. For a while he didn't trust himself to say anything.

"I have gone to the Mayo Clinic. They ran every conceivable test. I have what my dad had. I lived a different lifestyle than he did, and it had certain advantages, but in the end, the heart gives out. Thank God, Patrick, you have your mother's health."

Dexter stopped speaking and looked down. "I guess I could handle this better if it weren't for Jolene. For the first time in my life, I can't have my way." He smiled ruefully before continuing. "I would so like to have a lifetime with her, but I can't, so I'm grabbing minutes." Again he stopped and then composed himself again. "I've convinced her to get married quickly." He smiled. "Like today quickly. This evening. We would like you and Marcella to stand up with us."

Patrick blew his nose, and leaned his head back against the wall. For several seconds he was unable to speak. Then in a choked voice he said, "Sure, sure. We'll be glad to. Is there anything else we can do?"

Dexter let out a long sigh. "For right now, I'd appreciate it if you could keep the heart matter to yourself. I don't want pity. I've actually had a good life. You are certainly the best part of what I've done with it." He looked at Patrick intently for several seconds and then continued briskly with the details of his plans for his marriage and for the business.

When Dexter left a half hour later, Patrick allowed himself fifteen minutes to crumble. Then he took several deep breaths, asked for Divine Help, and strode out of the office into the magic of DeLange Designs.

CHAPTER 14

Hawaiian Honeymoon

THE WAVES OF the Pacific Ocean could be heard through the open bedroom windows of Dexter's Hawaiian rented house. He had been awake for several minutes and occasionally looked down and caressed the sleeping form of his bride curled up next to him. After a couple of weeks of marriage, he found himself unable to imagine life without her.

He had regretted his plan for a reception on New Year's Eve. His original plan had been to show her off with fine jewels and clothes, but after their first night together, he only wanted Jolene to be with him. It was too late to cancel the party, and she had endured it graciously. The men had hugged her, the women had hugged him, the laughter flowed, the congratulations rolled in, and all the time his eyes were on her, wishing it would all end so he could have her to himself.

He also regretted that he had lined up some modeling for her. Bob and Helen would be flying in next week for those pictures. He knew by now that Jolene would work hard to make it a success. He had already decided how he would fix her hair to complement the styles. The clothes she would be showing were the creation of a friend in Honolulu, and this too he regretted, because Sy Baxter would want to have his hand in on the photo shoots. Dexter knew he would be jealous if Sy even touched her.

He thought of her sitting on the porch of their bungalow, drinking coffee, reading her devotions out loud to him, and then looking at him with pleading green eyes. God and Dexter were not as far apart as she feared, however he admitted to her that he just couldn't give up control of his life to the whims of God. She had questioned his use of the word "whims." He acknowledged that maybe that wasn't quite fair to God, but he wanted his life to be his own to manage.

"I want to do it my way, like the song says," he had told her.

She had looked at him with concern and slowly said, "There's a better song, Dexter. It says, 'I surrender all. All to Thee, my blessed Savior, I surrender all.'"

He had sat there with the wind tousling his hair, gazing at her with amusement, and reached over and closed the Bible resting on her lap.

He ran his hand over her bare shoulder and thought how enthused she had been to discover they would be living in a bungalow by the sea. Her eyes had flashed and danced and she hugged him around the waist.

"Ours? This is ours, Dexter? Wow! We can sit here and see the sunrise and the sunset over the water! We can walk in the water whenever we want to! We can watch it rain over the water!"

"You can watch me walk on the water," he had interjected mildly, and was rewarded with a light smack delivered with a delighted grin.

Even the remembrance brought a slow smile to Dexter, and when he looked down at her she was watching him with kitten-sleepy eyes that blinked lazily up at him.

"Good morning, Mrs. DeLange," he murmured softly, and rubbed his whiskered chin gently across her cheeks. "How is my favorite wife this morning?"

She assured him that Mrs. DeLange was very well indeed. Raising herself on her elbow, she studied him with great seriousness.

"I just thought of something profound."

"This early in the morning?"

"Yes, sir, this early in the morning." She reached over and traced his lips with her finger. "There has never been another Mrs. Dexter DeLange, has there?"

He pulled her close to him and said softly, "You are the only one, Jolene, the first and the last. How does that make you feel?"

"Surprised."

He shot an eyebrow up and looked at her inquiringly. "Surprised?"

She ran her hands over his face. "I can't think what you ever saw in me."

"I believe you scared me into marriage by wanting a baby."

She laughed softly into his cheek. "I can't imagine you being scared. You always seem so self-confident."

His eyes searched her face for several moments. "I have my fears, Jolene, but we won't talk about them now." He rolled over on his back and again pulled her close to him. "Do you know that Bob and Helen will be here next week for the modeling pictures?"

She groaned. "Yes, I know. It will be fun to see them, but this is so nice. This, Dexter," and she looked up at him. "This being with you, just with you, and enjoying a very special time in our lives. Sometimes these moments are so fleeting."

He wrapped his arms around her and held her tightly. In a voice not quite steady he said, "I plan to enjoy every moment that God allows us to be together, Jolene. Every moment."

Arlene looked out at the snow piled up over a foot deep on the sand hills prairie. Whenever the O'Neil men left the house they would bundle up in layers and lace heavy snow boots. Wading through snow banks wore them all out, and as soon as fresh snow would fall, they would take the tractor and scoop and level out a path between the houses and barns.

Temperatures hovered around zero, and more than once Walt had mentioned to her how grateful he was that Dexter had hired someone to drain the pipes in the little stone house. The man had come from town and said he had been contacted to completely winterize it, and though Walt had complained about it in the beginning, he was grateful the job was done.

Now as the snow swirled around the buildings, she and Walt were immersed in a folder that bore a Hawaiian address. With fresh coffee and cinnamon rolls, they were comfortably settled for a winter afternoon.

Arlene had her reading glasses perched on the end of her nose and admired several huge photos of Jolene and Dexter.

"They look happy, Walt. We've been so worried that he wouldn't make her happy, but she looks better than I've seen her for a long time."

"Umm," Walt took the pictures to peer at with his own reading glasses. "Didn't she say that the modeling business was gonna go by the wayside?"

"Well, I guess they did the two weeks they planned, and then Dexter said 'no more.' Don't you think he's a little controlling, Walt? Seems like he pretty much calls all the shots." Arlene thought privately that if Walt looked anything like Dexter she probably would let him rule the roost too.

"Well, he's so dang much older than she is, I suppose he does have the upper hand a little, but knowing Jolene I would bet she doesn't let him talk her into anything she doesn't want to do." Walt started looking at another batch of pictures. "Where were these taken at?"

"Those are from a magazine. An interviewer came to their house. Isn't that quite a place? So close to the ocean, and she said they walked the beach almost every day. She said the magazine puts out a special Valentine's issue, and I guess somebody, a Sy somebody, had Bob take the pictures. See that necklace she's wearing? Rubies! Another gift from Dexter."

"Good grief, he looks like he isn't going to let her out of his sight." Walt frowned a little.

"Oh, phooey," Arlene scoffed. "How can you tell that from a picture?" Taking it away from him, she studied it with a furrowed brow. Jolene was sitting on a chair with a white sweater and skirt outfit. It had little swirls of red throughout that made it a very striking set. She wore a red ruby necklace and earrings that matched, and Arlene thought she looked extremely beautiful.

Sitting on the arm of the chair with his usual black shirt and slacks and gazing down at his wife with glittering eyes, was a man of unusual handsomeness. His features were strong and arrogant, and his slender hands were possessively on her shoulders. He wore an amused smile, and her upturned face had a look of quiet contentment.

The caption beside the picture read, "Rubies instead of roses" and told how newly-married Dexter DeLange had surprised his bride with an untraditional Valentine's Day present. It was a short article, but there were several very good pictures of Jolene and Dexter in and around their home and beachfront.

Arlene set the picture and article down. "Did you read Florence's letter? It almost made me sick."

"Nope, I wasn't going to waste my time reading that gibberish."

"Well, she goes on and on about how famous Dexter is, and how Jolene is such a lucky girl, and her Babs should have been as smart as Jo to snag him. Then she babbled on about Dexter marrying Jolene because Babs jilted him. The clincher, though, was her stupid remark that she guessed Dexter just had to have one of her girls. 'Her girls!' Walt, as if she ever lifted a finger with Jolene." Arlene burned with resentment against the infamous thought.

"Well," Walt said placidly, "what else does Florence have in her life? Dale and his wife don't have very much to do with her, and she manages to make everybody irritated at her so she doesn't have many friends. Dexter is thoughtful with her. Didn't Jolene say he had her send Florence a box of candy for Valentine's Day?

He said she was a lonely old lady, and it wouldn't hurt to pay her a little attention."

"Huh!" snorted Arlene. "She's lonely because she's a royal pain in the neck."

"Period!" Walt laughed.

Jolene had sent them quite an assortment of pictures from Hawaii. She had written on the backs of them, and then had included the magazine article and pictures plus some wedding pictures and modeling shots. She missed them, she wrote, but was happier than she had thought she would ever be again. She said there were cattle ranches there, and she and Dexter had been invited to one. She had been able to ride and had an enjoyable afternoon in the saddle. Dexter had visited with Bob and Helen and their hosts, so they both had a good day. She didn't know when they would be home, but would keep her family updated. She asked a lot of questions about everyone and the ranch and gave them her phone number and address again.

Walt and Arlene spread all the pictures out on the dining room table, knowing that their family would enjoy seeing them. Their talk drifted off into neighborhood news, and weather related topics, but Arlene had one more thought about Jolene.

"I wonder how the first anniversary of John's death will affect her."

In her dream she was walking along the beach. In the mist ahead of her she saw John staring at her, and she called his name. He kept moving away and no matter how hard she tried to catch up, he would always keep the same distance away from her. Finally she had shouted and asked him why he didn't wait for her. His words came back thinly through a thickening fog. "Dexter is coming." She kept shouting, "No! No!" She woke up shouting it, and found herself sitting up in bed with her heart pounding.

Dexter had spoken her name softly, and gently pulled her back against him. She had lain there trembling, and when he asked her what was wrong, she couldn't answer. "Was it a dream," he asked, and she finally said it must have been. When he asked her if she could remember it, she stiffened and said she didn't want to remember anymore. It was a long time before she relaxed against him and even longer before she fell asleep again.

In the morning while she was making coffee for them, he started to ask again what was wrong, but when she looked at him, he stopped abruptly. For a while he searched her face with narrowed eyes. Then with a sigh he wrapped his arms around her and said softly, "Don't shut me out, Jolena. I know what this week is." He ran his hands up to her shoulders, and then cupped her face in his hands and kissed her.

Tears sprang into her eyes, and she said in a husky voice, "Can you be patient with me, Dexter? I ... I need some time to think."

"You dreamed about him last night." It was more of a statement than question.

"Yes, but I don't want to talk about it."

Once again he searched her face. His hands went back to her shoulders and then to her waist. "I can be patient." He smiled ruefully and added, "For a very little while." He looked away for a few brief seconds, and then back to her as tears dripped down her face. Abruptly he pulled her closer to him. "I can't compete with a dead man, Jolene, and it makes me jealous." His lips brushed hers, and then he quickly released her and walked into the living room.

Finishing with the coffee maker, Jolene started after him then changed her mind and went out to the porch. The ocean stretched ahead of her with its waves lapping mindlessly onto the shore. It was a moving force—always coming in, always going out—and she had respect for the power that lay beneath its deceptive, blue serenity. It wasn't like the prairie, she reasoned. She understood the prairie and its many moods. The ocean was more willful, more treacherous. A great longing for the sand hills came over her, and she wrapped her arms around herself to ward off the chill of the morning air.

Dexter came out with two coffee mugs and silently handed one to her. For a while they both gazed at the water and watched the waves rolling in.

"I'm going to drive down to the grocery store this morning. Is there anything you need?" He was still looking out to sea.

She shook her head and didn't volunteer to go with him.

He took another swallow of coffee and looked at her. "Are you going to be OK by yourself, Kitten?"

It was the way he said "kitten" in his caressing tone of voice that brought more tears to her eyes. She leaned against him, coffee mug and all, and nodded. "I'll go for a walk," she murmured.

Not only did she need a walk, she told herself as she started out along the beach, but she needed a talk with God.

Where have You been lately, God? I guess You are where You always are. Everywhere. It's me that's been wandering away. Lord, it's already been a year since You took John. A year. I feel so disloyal to him that I remarried so quickly. I wonder what our lives would have been like if he were alive now. I wonder where we would be, and if he would have decided to quit the military and become a minister.

She sat down on a rocky point that jutted out into the sea. Overhead the sun had begun to warm the air with its rays. Jolene thought how good it felt to have sunshine on her back, almost like the warmth of Dexter's hands when he massaged her.

Dexter. Oh, Lord, Dexter! What is there about that rascal that makes me almost giddy with love? I love being with him. I love sleeping with him. I love loving him. I feel guilty, Lord, because I love loving Dexter more than I loved loving John. There. I've finally confessed it. You knew the truth all the time, but I've fought it tooth and nail because I was ashamed to admit it.

She stopped for a moment to take in the picturesque sailboat that was skimming along the waves.

I'm also ashamed that I've not been thinking about John. Until that dream last night, I've not had him on my mind the last couple of weeks. I must be exceedingly selfish, Lord. These days with Dexter

*have been so full of excitement that the first love of my life seems like
a dim memory.*

She sighed and grabbed a little rock to throw into the water. It
skipped along several times, and she watched the widening rings
form after it sank.

*I often think, Lord, that our lives are like these rippling rings.
Everything we do or say has an effect, and it branches out wider and
wider. I think back to how Dexter and I first met. It was Florence's
idea to have me stay at the Taylors; what if I would have stayed with
Walt and Arlene that winter?*

She paused, listening to the sound of the waves.

*You are so powerful, Lord. Like these ocean waves. Yet You let us
come to You with all our doubts and fears and little woes. I want to
lift up Dexter to You, Lord—I want him to love You and serve You as
You would have him to. I pray that he and I can do Your perfect will.
This is my prayer, Lord, that this man You have sent to me, and who
I love so much, that Dexter and I can do Your perfect will.*

She blinked away the tears that had been brought on by the
intensity of her prayers, and was startled to hear Dexter's voice.

"I don't know how long I'm going to be able to watch you cry
for another man."

"Sit down here beside me," she said smiling as she patted the
ground.

He looked a little miffed as he lowered himself beside her. She
brushed at her damp cheeks, and then hugged his arm. "Dexter,
do you know why I was crying?"

"I don't know if I want to know."

"I'll tell you why. I just realized how very much I love you. It's
… it's like God's gift to me. I'm not going to feel guilty about it
anymore. I'm going to enjoy it, shout it to the world, and … why
are you looking at me like that?"

He was staring at her incredulously. He stayed that way for so
long she finally reached over and took off his sunglasses to see if
he was really looking at her.

"Dexter? Are you OK?"

"What happened here? I've been worried sick all morning that you're sitting out here all alone, grieving, crying for him. What are you saying, Jolene?" Dexter's normally controlled voice almost shouted.

"I'm saying again that I love you, Dexter DeLange! What do you think about that?"

She had never seen him laugh with such carefree abandonment.

CHAPTER 15

Only Today

BOB AND HELEN knew when they left Hawaii that Jolene's career as a model was probably over. They discussed it on the flight back to the states, and Bob wasn't surprised when Helen laid the blame on Dexter.

"He is the most controlling man I've ever seen," she groused. "Poor old Sy knew he didn't dare touch her or Dexter would have his head. Why is he that way with Jolene, Bob? We've known him for a long time and he's never been so tense on a photo session."

"He's never been in love before, and he knows he's too possessive, but when it comes to her, he's a little out of control." Bob mused over his words several minutes before continuing. "Don't feel too sorry for Sy. The interview and pictures for his magazine will make a great Valentine's Day feature, even though it was a quick, last-minute change for the publisher."

"The necklace and earrings Dexter gave her were expensive! And beautiful. He made a remark when I complimented him about it, something like, 'I had to make amends for last Valentine's flowers.' I guess I didn't quite understand what he meant."

"He's a complex man," Bob muttered as the plane droned its way homeward. "But, and I guess this is the most important thing, both he and Jolene are very happy."

The stewardess came with drinks, and after their selections they made themselves comfortable. They had both enjoyed the DeLanges' little Hawaiian paradise, and they couldn't fault Dexter's congeniality as host. It was only when they started taking the pictures that they realized there might be trouble. Jolene had learned her lessons well, and appeared graceful and photogenic, but when pudgy little Sy had bounced over to adjust the fold of her dress, Bob could feel the coldness radiating from Dexter. Apparently Sy had felt it too, because he never adjusted any more dresses on Jolene.

"I was surprised he let her out of his sight to go riding the day we visited the cattle ranch together," Bob commented while trying to find a more comfortable position for his long legs.

"Huh! She was only gone a little more than half an hour, and he smoked three cigarettes while we were visiting."

"Yeah, but it was cute when she came up behind him and wrapped her arms around his neck. She looked like a kitten getting ready to pounce on an unsuspecting old cat." Bob chuckled at the memory.

"I wish you could have gotten a picture of that."

"I did. My little sneaky camera caught it all. Even the expression on his face when he realized she was back. He always could move fast, but I don't believe she realized how fast until he spun around and pulled her onto his lap. I have it all on film," Bob said in a self-satisfied manner.

Dexter and Jolene pictures were popular. Bob always displayed them in a prominent place at the salon and found they made good advertisements for his photography business. He was always amazed at the interest they generated and the source of chatter they provided for the customers. Even the stylists enjoyed the saga of Dexter and Jolene and always pointed out the new pictures. He thought Jolene would be embarrassed if she knew.

"Bob," Helen's voice was serious. "Did you think Dexter feels good?"

"Why do you ask?" He didn't mean for his voice to sound so abrupt.

"Just little things. He has always walked slowly, only with him it becomes sort of a conceited stroll. But I noticed he stops more than usual, like he's trying to catch his breath."

When Bob finally answered, he lied. "Guess I didn't notice anything."

Jolene and Dexter strolled hand in hand along the beach the last of March and enjoyed the final breathtaking minutes of another sunset. The air was balmy, and a breeze was blowing Jolene's hair into little disarrayed strands. Dexter stopped, but instead of reaching for a cigarette, he attempted to straighten her hair. Finally giving up, he kissed her on the forehead.

"I want my own bed, Jolene."

She looked at him with such a shocked expression that he broke out into laughter. "Listen, Kitten." He stroked her cheek. "I mean I want us to go back home to Denver and share *our* bed. Can you pack in a couple of days?"

Part of Jolene knew she was ready to leave. She missed her family and friends and the prairie. But part of her loved having Dexter all to herself, and they had spent three months being together every waking moment. They had driven all over the islands, taken boat rides, looked at the attractions, and always returned to their bungalow knowing they would spend their evenings on the couch in complete privacy. They had many serious discussions and just as many lighthearted bantering sessions, and the joy of snuggling next to his warm body and having his arms around her was a source of constant happiness.

However, in a week's time they were winging their way across the Pacific and back to Denver. The weather was cold and blustery as they headed out of the airport into the waiting car driven by the ever efficient houseman, Mr. Runski. After the quietness of their days alone together, the bustle and busyness of DeLange Designs took them both by surprise, and yet it was good to be back.

To help Patrick and Marcella with their hectic schedule, Jolene and Dexter started picking up the children after school and bringing them back to the penthouse. It was good for all concerned, and Mrs. Runski, cook and housekeeper, delighted in having hot cocoa and cookies waiting for the children. Dexter enjoyed his grandchildren, and the four of them played countless games of Go Fish and Kings on the Corner. To the children's great enjoyment, Jolene and Dexter would get into loud arguments over which one was cheating the most, and would settle their differences while moving cards when the other's back was turned. The grandkids felt it was their duty to inform each of them of the other's unacceptable behavior, and Patrick and Marcella would walk in the door to merry bedlam. It was decided the children won the game because Dexter and Jolene had disqualified themselves, and while Mrs. Runski brought out more goodies and coffee, the children would pick up their games and let Patrick and Marcella share their day's news with Dexter and Jolene.

It was a routine they all came to look forward to. Patrick was amazed his father showed no interest in styling hair at the salon. For as long as he could remember it had been his father's consuming interest, but soon he came to realize that Jolene had taken that spot in Dexter's life. He watched his father's happiness with his bride and appreciated the fact that she was equally happy.

During the spring, Jolene and Dexter took several drives out to the O'Neil ranch, bringing boxes of doughnuts that brought gratification from the whole family. Dexter was always politely interested in the ranch but made no move to view cattle herds or look at horses. They would leave after a couple of hours, which Jolene could tell made Arlene slightly upset. She wanted more time with them, but everyone enjoyed the time they were there, and as Dexter said, better to leave while the family still liked him.

Jolene did put her foot down and flatly refused to visit Florence. Dexter said he thought she was acting childish, and she glared at him and said she didn't care. If Dexter wanted to see Florence, he could go by himself. Dexter said mildly that he would rather be with Jolene by himself, and that seemed to end that. However, when they went to Sterling to visit Betty and Reverend Taylor, it was the only logical thing to do to stop at Florence's house also. After forty-five minutes, Dexter politely stood up and said he and Jolene had appointments back in Denver and would be on their way.

"What appointments?" Jolene asked him as they were driving down the highway.

"You have a hair appointment. Surely you didn't forget?" He looked at her self-righteously.

"Pish-posh, Dexter DeLange, I have no such thing as a hair appointment and you know it. You were as tired of hearing about her 'girls' and her 'Babs' as I was. And I didn't know my mother jilted you."

"For that matter, neither did I."

"I didn't know you were madly in love with her."

"Neither did I."

"I didn't know that I married you for your money and you married me because you thought you were spiting my mother." Jolene's voice was rising.

"Neither did I." Dexter had an amused little smile on his face.

"I didn't know ..."

Dexter interrupted her. "Jolene, you're shouting."

They drove down the highway several minutes in silence, and then Dexter burst out in unsuppressed mirth. "When did you start saying pish-posh?"

Jolene glared at him. "When you started making me go visit my grandmother!"

He turned to grin at her, but when she refused to smile back, he pulled off the road and stopped. Getting out of the car, he watched for traffic and then came over, opened her door, and helped her out of the car. For a short time he held her gently, and then in a quiet voice said, "Now, Jolene, let us get this understood. Florence is an old lady who babbles on without thinking. Lonely people do that. Your mother and I had no secret love. She was an attractive young lady I thought would look good at the salon. She was going to marry your dad, and when she told me that, I was relieved. I know you didn't marry me for my money, and you know I didn't marry you to spite your mother. That's ridiculous ... even though she did name you Jolene when she knew I was going to name my supermodel Jolena."

"Huh?" Jolene blinked at him in bafflement.

Dexter touched the tip of her nose. "I had rambled on to her that someday I was going to discover a beautiful woman and make her into a supermodel who would be world famous. I would name her Jolena." He laughed softly. "When I found out that she had named her baby Jolene, I was irritated. When I finally met you, I was, shall we say, rather intrigued."

Jolene leaned into him and sighed. She could hear the traffic going by the road, and an occasional honk. "So 'this is the rest of the story,' as Paul Harvey would say. I always wondered why you called me Jolena." She looked up at him and added, "You don't call me Jolena much anymore."

"No, Jolena was my creation. You are your own person." He kissed her and she wrapped her arms around his waist. She gave a contented sigh and rested her head against his chest.

"Let's get back on the road, Kitten. We're going to cause a wreck if we stand here much longer."

"Is Jolene back yet?" Dexter asked Miss Grey when she clipped into the salon on her high-heeled shoes.

"Actually, she just called and said to tell you she would be about an hour late," Miss Grey informed him, noting the frown that immediately appeared.

"Did she say why?" he asked mildly. Miss Grey was not deceived by his quiet manner.

"No, she was in a bit of a hurry and just wanted to let you know. If she calls again I'll tell you." Miss Grey and Patrick exchanged glances, and then she clicked back to her office.

One of Denver's debutants had planned for over a year to have DeLange Designs style her bridal party's hair, and she herself wanted Dexter. She had been very upset when the polite receptionist told her Dexter had retired the first of the year and wasn't taking any more appointments. It was a June wedding, and mother and daughter were frazzled with all the details. Their one consolation had been that the hairstyles would be perfect, but only if Dexter was the stylist. The mother called Dexter personally, and even though he hinted that Patrick was in every way capable, the mother was insistent that it be Dexter himself who styled her daughter's hair. They had brought in the dress so he could see it, and immediately he had pictured a hairstyle that would complement the beautiful wedding gown.

While Dexter was busy in the salon, Jolene had decided to volunteer at a stable where handicapped children were brought in to ride the gentle horses. She had gone several afternoons, and that morning she was helping one last time. Dexter had reminded her when she left that it was the last time. He wasn't altogether pleased with her plan. In fact, when he first knew he would be working, he had suggested she come down and wait in the salon. She raised her eyebrows at that, and when she heard about the handicapped program, had decided it would be a worthy cause.

When he started with the bride to be, he realized she was about Jolene's age, but her maturity level seemed to be much younger than his wife's, and her hovering mama quickly became an irritant to him. It had taken much longer than what he had planned, the problem being the indecision of the bride after he explained what he was going to do.

Dexter soon realized that he was more impatient than he used to be, and he stepped back and reached for a cigarette, only to be chided by the mother. She didn't want the bride's hair to smell of smoke. Patrick caught his father's eye with a slight shake of his head, and while acknowledging Patrick's unspoken thought, Dexter held up his hand to the mother and slowly walked outside. When he returned, the decision had been made, and he started once again, only to be interrupted every few minutes by the mother's questions. Marcella noticed the problem and tried several tactics to divert the over-anxious woman. Finally, after Patrick had finished the maid of honor, he guided the mother to his chair. There was the usual idle chatter among customers and staff, and Dexter was chagrinned to discover that he was bored with the talk.

During a lull when the only sound was the soft music being piped in, Miss Grey came clicking in again, and informed Dexter that Jolene was home and would be down in a little while. Dexter narrowed his eyes at that remark, and with a gesture from Miss Grey, stepped away from the chair and exchanged a few private words. Most of the wedding party had seen the Jolene and Dexter photos, and there was an air of curiosity among them to see the young woman who had apparently captured the heart of the playboy Dexter DeLange.

He heard her footsteps before the others did, and his eyes narrowed once again. When she came into the room, she slipped over to Dexter. Still holding his comb, he brushed his lips against her forehead and asked how her ride had been.

She looked around the room before answering that all had gone well, and then she moved a little stiffly around the chair and leaned against the counter. Dexter looked her up and down, then still combing and coaxing, he told her to look at the dress the bride was going to wear that evening. She didn't move away from the counter but admired it from a distance, and then also admired the creation her husband was working on.

Dexter's work was finally finished except for some beadwork he was having woven into the hairstyle. He looked at his work, satisfied that it was good, and then sauntered over to where Jolene was. Everyone from the manicurist to the bride paid close attention.

Standing directly in front of her and putting his hands on the counter on each side of her, he looked carefully at her.

"So what happened?" he asked softly. Everyone strained to hear.

"Happened?" Jolene echoed.

"Why were you so late?"

"Oh, one of the little girls had a convulsion, and we had to wait for it to pass so she could ride again." Jolene looked uncomfortable.

"You were riding with her when it happened." It was a statement and Jolene looked startled.

"Let me guess. You were holding her and she was about to fall so you took the fall with her and landed on the ground." It was flatly said, and once again the bride sitting in the salon chair was beginning to act nervous. Even the mother was quiet, wondering what might happen next. "Am I right, Jolene?" He stared intensely into her green eyes.

She grinned up at him, twined both arms around his neck and kissed those accusing lips in front of their audience. After a few "ahs," everyone erupted in a gale of laughter. His arms went around her and for several seconds he held her close with his face brushing her hair. Suddenly he released her and looked only slightly apologetically at the bride and said to no one in particular, "She makes me forget what I'm doing."

Once again he looked at the bride. "Marcella will wind the beads in for you." Indeed, Marcella was already standing there with them, and she began at once to work the glittering pieces into a design.

While Dexter watched Marcella, he pulled Jolene away from the counter. She winced slightly.

"Didn't I tell you to be careful?"

"You might have mentioned it," she said, remembering how he had continually repeated it while she was getting ready to go that morning.

He stood behind her and gently massaged her shoulders, all the while keeping an eye on Marcella's work. Jolene mentioned how nice everyone looked, and she asked the bride several questions about the wedding. She was introduced to the mother and asked Patrick how he planned to style her hair. The hum of voices soon picked up, and all the while Dexter stood there smiling with amusement, gently rubbing her tensed muscles. He knew he should stay and help the staff with the last finishing touches on the bridal party. It was expected of him, he supposed. Yet the only thing he wanted to do was take his aching wife and his own tired body upstairs to their bed. He looked at the bride and the bride's mother and both seemed to be satisfied with their hairstyles and Delange Designs. He caught Patrick's eye and raised an inquiring eyebrow. Patrick said rather loudly, "Better get Jolene upstairs, Dad. We'll finish here."

Jolene started to protest, but Patrick shook his head, almost unnoticeably. Jolene got the message. She congratulated the bride and then said she was going to steal Dexter so he could finish giving her a massage. When she started walking toward the door she barely limped, but it was noticeable.

Dexter said some parting words to both mother and bride, and then laying his hand possessively on Jolene's aching behind, he gave it a gentle pat as they walked out the door.

"Patrick," Marcella's voice was troubled. They were the last ones at the salon after the wedding party had left in a great fervor of wedding gaiety. The staff had also gone, and DeLange Designs was closing down for the weekend.

Patrick was cleaning both his combs and his father's. As long as he had worked with his dad, he never remembered Dexter leaving his combs on the counter and walking out. It bothered him as much as seeing his dad acting irritable with a client. He gave a troubled sigh and asked Marcella what she wanted.

"I thought Dexter looked a little tired when he left. Do you think he's feeling OK?"

For several seconds Patrick thought about rebuking his wife. Instead, he laid the cleaned combs down and took her by the shoulders, guiding her into the office. Once inside he closed the door, and for the first time since Dexter had confided in him, he repeated to his wife all the words that had troubled him for so long. It was emotional for him, and by the time he was finished they were both in tears.

"Now it's a waiting game, Marcella, and we don't know when or how it will end. I don't know how I can bear to see him getting weaker." Patrick's voice trembled.

"And Jolene doesn't know?"

"I doubt he's told her anything, but I think she knows a lot more than she's saying. Today it didn't take her long to catch on that he needed to go upstairs."

"Oh, I wondered why you thought he should take her up there! That was clever of you, Pat, to play on his concern for her." Tears welled up in Marcella's eyes again. "I wonder why this has to happen now when he has finally found what he's always looked for."

The thunderstorm that had growled over Denver all afternoon finally broke into a wild pandemonium in the early evening. Wind and rain swept into town, and lightning crackled in the air. Once the fury was spent, a slow, steady rain beat against the windows, and Jolene thought as she brought two mugs of coffee into the living room that nothing was cozier than an evening of rain. She said as much to Dexter, who was absorbed in his reading, and he looked up at her with his glasses on to smile his acknowledgement.

It was a week after her fall from the horse, and she was grateful the aches had disappeared. Dexter had laughed at her groans when she got up or sat down, and had reminded her she was too young to make those sounds. She knew she was healing. It was Dexter's health that was a concern to her. She often noticed he looked tired, and lately he seemed to stop more, as if trying to catch his breath. She blamed the cigarettes, and wondered if she could convince him to quit smoking.

Setting the cups on the coffee table, she picked up the book she had been reading and was getting ready to settle under a blanket on the opposite end of the couch from where he was sitting.

"I don't think so, Jolene," he said softly, and patted a spot next to him.

In seconds she was snuggled beside him, and all thoughts of reading had vanished. He laid aside his glasses and the Bible she had given him for Christmas and reached forward to hand her a steaming mug of coffee. Taking the other for himself, he planted his feet on the coffee table and looked the picture of a contented cat.

"I wonder if it's raining in the sand hills like this," she murmured. "Walt and Arlene said it was dry there. It would mean a lot to all the ranchers and farmers to get moisture."

"You should call them tomorrow and see." He kicked off his shoes and moved into a more comfortable position.

"Did you realize it was almost a year ago that you took me out for supper in South Dakota?"

"Mm, already a year."

"Next week will be the Fourth. Where were you last year for the Fourth?"

He knew very well where he had been. The road back from the Mayo Clinic in Minnesota loomed in his mind's eye, and he remembered all the emotions he had dealt with along the way.

"Probably all alone somewhere and missing you."

She reached over him and set her half empty cup on the stand beside the couch. "Dexter, I hate it when you say you were alone. In my mind you were always with some gorgeous woman, doing something exciting."

"In my mind I'm with a gorgeous woman right now doing something," he set his cup beside hers, "exciting." He caught her close to him and nuzzled her cheeks before finding her lips. The rain continued against the windows, making the moment a satisfying memory.

He drew the blanket over them and they snuggled even deeper into the cushions.

Absently rubbing a spot on her shoulder with his finger, Dexter closed his eyes and took in the fragrance of her hair. "You called me after the Fourth to say you'd come with me to western Colorado," he reminded her.

"I did, and I was nervous about it too."

"Of modeling or being with me?"

"Both, Dexter." She ran her fingers over his face and then with her forefinger traced the straight line of his jaw.

He turned slightly to see her better. "Do you miss the fun of seeing your picture in the magazines?"

"No, darling, I love the fun of being with you," she murmured, curling into the warmth of him. Then without explanation she added, "I haven't talked to the Harrises for quite a while."

"What does it have to do with them?" he asked flatly.

"It was after I spent the Fourth with them that I knew I was going to go with you." She paused for a while. "David made me mad, and before I even knew what I was saying I told them all that was planned. I made David mad, and we really haven't spoken since."

He whispered her name. "Jolene, were you terribly disappointed we didn't drive down to Colorado Springs for Memorial Day?"

She was silent for a while. She had planned they would go, but Dexter had refused even to consider it. When she said she would go by herself, he wouldn't hear of it and had become quite upset with her. She had accused him of being spoiled, and he replied that he certainly was and wasn't going to change now. He seemed to know he had acted like a three year old. Then he had left the room. They never discussed it again.

She ran her fingers through his hair and kissed him. "I was upset for a while, but it would have been awkward to see the Harrises at the cemetery. I called a florist and had flowers taken to John's grave.

He tightened his hold on her and then gently released her. "I'm selfish, Jolene. I don't want to share you with anyone. I want you all to myself, to have moments like these." He gave her an apologetic smile, longing to hold her forever. The rain continued its patter on the windows, but Jolene and Dexter were oblivious to it.

A couple of days later Dexter had their Fourth of July plans made and was taking Jolene shopping. She knew from experience that walking into a high-end ladies apparel shop with him was an unmatched event. He loved parading her on his arm, looking at the one or two dresses that met his criteria and having her try them on. The sales ladies would fawn over him and ignore Jolene, until of course he would point out his bride. He took great delight in patting her here and there to make the dress fit better and looking at her with smoldering eyes. Dexter practically had the staff swooning by the time he and Jolene left, even if he didn't buy anything. She knew her part by now, and it was her lively bantering with him that amused him the most. It shocked the ladies to hear her talk to him in such a manner, especially since his every whim was their command. By the end of the excursion he would have bought her at least one outfit, complete with matching heels and even occasionally some jewelry.

This particular day he was after an appropriate patriotic outfit to wear to a benefit dinner theater. He found what he was looking for after a couple of stops and decided the ruby necklace and earring set he had given her for Valentine's Day would be perfect with it. While they were still in the boutique, he worked her hair this way and that way until he found the style he wanted to complement the dress.

"Isn't it nice you have a real live Barbie doll to play with, Dexter?" she groused.

"Sort of a mouthy one at that," he flashed back at her with humor in his voice.

They walked out of the shop holding hands and decided to end their excursion with lunch in downtown Denver.

While they were getting ready for the benefit he began to work on the hair creation he wanted for her. He took great delight in pulling her long hair into a ponytail, and then making it a cascade of curls. He added a rhinestone comb around it, and when he was done he looked in the mirror at her. Their eyes met, and for a while neither said anything. He bent over and kissed the back of her bare neck, and Jolene had to choke back her tears, because for a moment he had looked vulnerable, as if he was yearning to say something to her but didn't know how.

That night he escorted Jolene in all her finery into the lobby of the theater. He had on a black suit with starched white shirt and a patriotic tie, and he took great pride in his wife and the way she looked. They were the object of a lot of attention. People came up to speak to him, and he introduced them to "Jolene, my wife."

For Jolene it was a night of enchantment. The food was delicious, the program was filled with good music and patriotic speeches, and the ladies and gentlemen present were well attired and well heeled. The benefit made money, and so it could be said, "A good time was had by all." Jolene didn't have to act the part of the adoring, young wife, because everyone who spoke to them realized that Dexter's bride was very much in love with her husband, and he equally so with her.

She remembered her situation last summer—the Bible camp, the little campers who stole her heart, the dedicated camp staff, and the desire to serve the Lord. Being in high society was not comfortable for her, but she could see Dexter was as much at ease as if he were in his own living room. Sometimes she wondered how two such different people could be happy together.

It was while they were strolling back to his car that he stopped her. For a while he didn't say anything, just looked at her and smiled. She thought he looked pale, but the street lights could be deceiving, she rationalized. Finally he murmured that he had been proud to have such a lovely wife with him that night, and he continued his slow pace.

"Mr. DeLange," Miss Grey spoke to him as he stood on the balcony of the penthouse and watched Jolene swimming in the pool below, "the clinic called to remind you of your appointment tomorrow."

"Cancel it," he said without turning around.

She stood silently behind him, trying to decide whether to make an issue of the matter or not. "Your doctor feels you should come in," she said crisply.

"Cancel it, Miss Grey."

"You really shouldn't ..." She was brusquely interrupted.

"I said, and this is the third time, cancel it."

"All right," she snapped, turning toward the door, "but it's against my better judgment"

He waited until he heard the door shut behind her before he muttered, "I really don't care about your better judgment, Miss Grey."

Dexter knew he was losing ground, and it infuriated him. He found himself irritable with everyone, including Jolene, and yet he refused to talk about his health to her. She watched him with a worried look, and this morning he had told her in the harshest tone he had ever used with her to stop looking at him like that. Her eyes had flashed and she snapped back that if he would just tell her what was wrong maybe she could help him. He had looked at her coldly and walked out of the room.

That was why, he supposed, she had flung on her swimming suit and was getting rid of some pent-up frustrations in the pool. He had grappled with an idea for several days and knew that if he presented it to her, or Patrick and Miss Grey, they would instantly reject it. Yet it was taking hold in his mind, and the more he mulled it over, the better he liked it. Taking a deep breath he made his decision, and went to the phone to put his plan into action.

Feeling better for having decided something, he mellowed toward everyone. The lot of them were flabbergasted when he brought his Harley bike out of storage in the garage and took it to be tuned up.

When he told Jolene he had a little modeling for her to do in the Black Hills, she looked surprised and rather reluctantly agreed. His mood had improved so much over the last couple of days he knew she hated to refuse him anything.

It was the day before they left when he informed everyone that she would be modeling leather outfits at the Motorcycle Rally in Sturgis and that he and she would be traveling on his Harley bike.

Bob was hurt that he hadn't been included as a photographer, Patrick was upset thinking of the long bike ride in the heat, Miss Grey shook her head and worried that he could kill both of them, and Jolene said she didn't even know Dexter could handle a motorcycle. For every objection they voiced, he had a solution—even, he informed them, to the extent of having two men ride with them for an extra precaution.

He wooed Jolene with extreme tenderness and charm, but she was adamant that it was a bad plan. He would have liked to lash out at her with his temper, but he knew it would have the opposite effect of his desired results, so he remained calm and placating, and as he expected, she finally agreed, very reluctantly.

The phone call came just before they left for the Black Hills. Jolene was still in their bedroom and took the call from there.

"This is David Harris," the voice was curt. "I just wanted you to know that I've done a lot of investigating about John's death. There's something you should know."

Jolene remained silent. After a short pause, David continued, "Those two mechanics that I told you about were hired by someone from Denver. Some of the crew is suspicious that they tampered with John's plane."

Jolene turned around and saw Dexter waiting for her by the door. "Yes, well, thanks for the information. I'll, ah, keep it mind." She hung up quickly and grabbed her purse. Before he could ask who called, she hastened out the door and down the stairs.

Jolene could see the concern on Patrick's face when she got on the Harley. It matched her own dismay. Clear to the pit of her stomach, she knew this was going to be a disaster.

CHAPTER 16

Bedlam

in the Black Hills

$\mathcal{B}$IKERS AND BIKES of every size and description lined the streets of Sturgis. Thousands of them descended every summer from every state in the union, roaring down the highways that led to the cities and towns in the Black Hills. The South Dakota August sun glared down at them with a vengeance, and rightly so, thought Jolene, as she looked at the mass of bared bodies and tattoos.

All around her the din of bikes and voices of the thousands rose and fell in discord, and when they reached the motel she was irritated that she had been coerced into a situation she found so unappealing.

She showered for a great length of time, hoping to restore a little of her good humor. Dexter was asleep when she finally stepped out of the bathroom, and she noted the fine lines of fatigue on his face.

He had reserved a small suite on the top floor and the room next door was for the two men who had accompanied them. They were men of average height, yet they gave her the impression of hardness. They said very little to her, yet they seemed to know Dexter quite well, with a familiarity she found puzzling, because to her knowledge he never consorted with the cruder elements of society. The men fit in well with the rest of the bikers, she decided, and it gave her no comfort.

She lay down beside him and wondered again why he had insisted on coming. She had thought Patrick wanted to tell her something and tried unsuccessfully to get a minute alone with him, but Dexter seemed to have eyes in the back of his head, and allowed her no chance to slip away. She was convinced now that he was having heart problems, yet she couldn't get him to say what was wrong, and she wondered how serious his medical condition was. Sleep didn't come to her that late afternoon. She was out of her element, and it worried her.

In the evening the two men who seemed to be nameless drove them to Deadwood in a rented convertible. The gambling houses were full of bikers and gawking tourists, and Jolene felt immoral in the low-cut leather top and black leather shorts that Dexter had insisted she wear. They had argued about it loudly until in exasperation she had looked at him and said, "This isn't fun, Dexter. What's wrong with us?"

He had pulled her close to him and kissed her, and in a quiet voice asked her to humor him. She had wanted to shout that his behavior wasn't like him, and to wear this type of outfit wasn't like her, but he looked grimly determined, so she gave in and dressed to suit him.

From one place to the next they wandered, dodging people, listening to the hubbub of voices cresting with profanity, seeing the machines that people were feeding religiously; and all the while the din of revved-up bike motors pervaded the air. Deadwood glittered and preened, and enjoyed its status as a gambling town.

Dexter urged Jolene to try some of the machines, and she looked at him in open rebellion and said she would rather have supper. Finally they found a somewhat quiet spot that served reasonably good meals at a fair price. They ate in silence.

The ride back to Sturgis was the best part of the day. In the open convertible with a full moon shining down on the hills, she began to relax and reached for his hand. For a few seconds he was unresponsive. Then he gave a gentle squeeze and withdrew it to put his arm around her bare shoulders. She snuggled into his warmth but her heart was pounding, and she wondered what she would ever do if he decided he didn't want her anymore.

She slept badly that night. The air conditioner droned on. Often there were shouts and then bursts of laughter from outside their window, and in the background was the constant rumble of bikes. There was no comforting conversation with Dexter. He had lapsed into a cool, distant state, and even in bed had remained aloof. She was too proud to make the first move again, and had lain in a forlorn lump on her side of the bed.

She woke up with a headache and realized that he was already up. He had showered and shaved and was dressed to go biking. She wondered if he intended to go without her, or if it would be more togetherness without contact. He gave her the choice and said her modeling wouldn't be until evening. He was going out to breakfast and when he came back she could decide. She wondered if he knew he was breaking her heart.

While she showered she prayed, but there seemed to be no answer. Her oft-repeated, *What's wrong, God? What happened?* was met with complete silence. She applied her makeup, found shorts and a tee that were comfortable, and still didn't know what to do. She drank the coffee provided by the motel, and then the door opened and one of the men brought her a couple of doughnuts from the continental breakfast downstairs. Finally she decided the thought of staying in the motel room was less appealing than riding a bike all day, so she gathered her purse and filled it with what she would need. Taking her key, she walked out the door. It was midmorning by that time, and the sun was blazing down with fiery heat. Dexter was sitting on his bike visiting with two young women and good humor was radiating from every charming pore.

Her jealousy was almost out of control, and she stopped to take several deep breaths and pray a quick *Help me, help me*, before she continued down the steps.

"Well, Mr. DeLange," she drawled out slowly as she walked over to him. "Fancy meeting an old cat like you here in a place like this."

His eyes snapped at her, but his voice was deceptively mild as he started up the bike. "Get on, woman. I almost left you."

She smiled amiably at the two young women and straddled the seat behind him. She hardly had time to buckle on her helmet before he roared off, followed by the nameless men.

They spent the day touring the Hills, weaving in and out of traffic, and stopping occasionally for something cool to drink, with only a few remarks made by either one of them. By mid afternoon they were back at the motel, and once again she was under the shower. She asked him what she was supposed to wear for this session, and he said it was already at the photographer's. She reapplied her makeup and looked questioningly at him about her hair. He wasn't gentle. He wanted a straight look, and quickly had her blow dry it, and then with a few tweaks here and there found the style he wanted.

Her head was pounding and she almost felt sick to her stomach. She decided that evening they would have to have a full-blown discussion. She had to know where this behavior of his was leading them. All the while, she was remembering David's phone call, and his insinuation that Dexter might have had John's plane tampered with. An insidious fear was beginning to creep over her.

He stopped to refuel and she bought several granola bars and threw then into her purse. He hadn't seemed inclined to take her to supper before this modeling session, so she reasoned they would go afterwards. She wondered if he was as upset as she was and couldn't tell by the look on his face.

The studio was on the far end of town, and as usual, the two men followed them. Dexter seemed to have new energy as he got off the bike, and bursting into the shop in front of her he gave a cheerful yell for Shirley. Shirley came running into his arms. With purple tights and clinging sweater, she laughed and called him "Dexter darling" and rewarded him with all sorts of passionate kisses. Her hair was brilliantly red, and with big, dark eyes she gazed at him with adoration. Neither paid the slightest attention to Jolene, so she wandered around the studio until they suddenly broke apart and called her over to them.

"So you're the one who's gonna model these clothes," Shirley's husky voice rasped out.

"Yes," answered Jolene. "I'm Mrs. Dexter DeLange." She didn't smile and she didn't offer to shake hands.

"Whoa, Dexter Darling, you didn't mention she was your wife."

"He is temporarily insane," Jolene added, and then asked where the clothes were that she was to wear.

Shirley's throaty laugh echoed throughout the room. Jolene didn't even glance at Dexter as she went into the dressing area. The clothes were laid out on a table, and even a novice could tell they were cheaply made. She tried on the one that seemed to be better than the rest. It was skintight and the waist gapped on her. The leather tops were flimsy, and cut low. Finally she pulled one over her tee and walked back out to where the camera was set up. Dexter and Shirley were talking in low voices when she came out and stopped abruptly when they saw her.

"These clothes don't fit me," she said quietly.

Dexter sauntered over to where she was standing and looked her insolently up and down. With an exasperated sigh he pulled the pants down low over her waist and shook his head at her. "Why are you wearing that ridiculous tee?"

"Because as a married woman it would be indecent not to."

For a brief moment an emotion flickered over his face. Then Shirley called out in her hoarse voice, "Let's shoot it that way, Dex. It looks kinda cute." She laughed her throaty laugh again.

It took Shirley forever to get anything done. She tried the camera at all different angles, adjusted the lights, had Jolene sit in dozens of different poses, couldn't seem to decide on the background, and all the while she and Dexter carried on a conversation and completely ignored Jolene. It took several hours, and Jolene wondered how much longer she could endure it. Finally Dexter looked at her and in a cold voice told her to get out of the tee. She looked at him for quite a while, fighting between rage and tears, and got up without a word to go back into the dressing area. She slipped off the cheap pants, put her jeans back on, slipped off the leather scrap of material, and gathering her purse, she quietly slipped out of the room and out the door.

The two nameless men were waiting in the streetlights, and Jolene went up to the one that had brought her the doughnuts and said she was feeling sick and needed to go back to the motel.

A surprised look came over his face, but he motioned for her to get on the back of his bike, and soon they were scooting out into the street. He drove maddeningly slow, and to her chagrin, by the time they arrived at the motel, Dexter and the other man pulled up right behind them. She was conscious of a nameless fear growing inside her.

She could hardly trust herself to speak to him, and he looked the same way at her. Inside the motel room she turned to him and with her eyes flashing demanded an explanation for the way he was behaving.

"When did I have to start answering to you?" he snorted.

"What are you, a Dr. Jekyll and Mr. Hyde?" she burst out. "Why are you doing this to us, Dexter? Do you want a divorce already? Are you tired of me? You could have said so in Denver and spared us these two days of hell!"

"You don't know what hell is, Jolene," he spat out.

"I know I came here with a man I thought I knew, and you've turned into somebody I don't know at all!" A horrible suspicion was looming in her mind.

"Well, poor little you," he sneered at her.

"What is wrong with you, Dexter? Are you cracking up? Did you hire those creeps to kill me like you did John?" Her eyes blazed with uncontrolled fury.

His face paled and then he raised his hand and slapped her. It took her by surprise, but she reacted instinctively and backhanded him with her left hand across his cheekbone. The impact of her ring on his face immediately broke the skin, and it started bleeding. He cussed her and slapped her again, and she reeled back against their bedroom door. For a second they locked eyes. She cried out hoarsely, "I'll never forgive you, Dexter, never!"

She slammed the bedroom door shut and locked it. She was shaking so badly she thought she would collapse. "God, help me!" she moaned softly. She could hear the outside door slam shut and his footsteps descending down the stairs. Soon she heard the roar of his bike, and went to the window in time to see his taillights disappearing. She also noticed the two men pulling chairs up to her door. She supposed they were to guard her so she couldn't leave. Or, her frightened mind thought, to get rid of her.

"God, help me!" she pleaded again and took off her ring and laid it on the dresser. She realized she still had her purse over her shoulder and that she hadn't turned on the bedroom light. She quickly exchanged her sandals for socks and tennis shoes, and was grateful she had on jeans and a T-shirt. A plan was pumping into her brain, and with a last look around the bedroom, she slipped into the bathroom and locked the door. Standing on the stool, she took the screen off the skinny window above it, and cranked it out. Then she turned on the bathroom fan to deflect any noise she might make, and remembering her skill as a youngster, she shimmied out the window and crawled up on the roof. Had she even taken a minute to think about it, she would have realized it was impossible, but she had asked for help, and she was getting it. She carefully made her way along the roof until she came to the rain gutter, and then just as carefully worked her way over the edge of the roof and slid bumpily along the drain till she reached the ground.

It was close to midnight, and the town was still buzzing, but nearby was a creek, and she slipped along the back alley until she could hear the water gurgle. Then she lowered herself over the bank and discovered in the moonlight that she could walk along the edge of the water for quite a way without being seen.

She followed the creek's winding course toward the north and walked under two bridges. When she came to the third bridge the road was quiet, and she quickly slipped out of the creek and scrambled onto the road. She jogged until she felt she was a good distance from the town and then settled into a brisk walk under the stars. She knew by the dippers she was heading east on the gravel road.

On and on she walked, not crying, not thinking. Only her repeated prayer for help went through her mind. She had walked for over an hour when she heard a motorcycle traveling on the road. The moon broke out from behind a cloud at that second, and she noticed a barbed wire gate going into a pasture to the north of the road. She ran over to it, dropped down on all fours, crawled underneath, and then started trotting down the faint trail that led to a draw with trees. When she reached it she stopped and could hear the motorcycle going on past the gate, following the gravel road.

For a few minutes she rested and let her pounding heart settle down. Then she started down the pasture trail and was grateful the moon was full and she could get her bearings again. It wound along the draw for several miles and then gradually started up toward the ridge. When she reached the top, she stopped again and looked toward the west. Sturgis was just a dim glow behind her, and she couldn't see the interstate at all. She was out in the country where she felt safe.

She felt in her purse for one of the granola bars and realized she hadn't eaten for most of the day. It tasted so good she ate the second one and then wondered if she should have rationed them out to herself. The air was warm, yet the pureness of it buoyed her, and she realized that somewhere along her walk, she had lost her headache.

Once again she followed the trail, and another hour later she came to a second gate. The trail forked, with the easterly way going through the gate, and the other heading back to the west. She crawled under the gate, and started heading east. The trail ambled along, sometimes heading north, sometimes east. She kept walking until she heard the sound of rushing water and realized she was getting close to a river. Her watch said it was four in the morning, and she decided rather than crossing the river in the predawn darkness, she would wait until it was lighter. Finding a tree close to the running water, she slowly eased herself to the ground and leaned against the trunk. For several seconds she sat there, still unthinking, not even praying. For the first time she realized her cheeks ached from Dexter's slaps, and then the jolt of the whole scenario hit her. She laid her head on her arms and sobbed.

CHAPTER 17

Chauncey Sullivan

CHAUNCEY SULLIVAN FINISHED cinching his horse and pulled the stirrup down. In the early dawn he could only faintly make out the Black Hills to the west, and when he looked east he could see the beginnings of a magnificent sunrise. Chauncey enjoyed watching the sun come up when the world seemed new and fresh; he could almost hear the orchestra of nature tune up to present another glorious day.

"Ready, Buzz?" he asked his border collie. Buzz had been waiting patiently beside his horse, and now that it looked like their ride would begin, he began to wag his tail excitedly.

Chauncey stepped into the saddle with the ease of someone long accustomed to riding. With his long legs and powerful build he sat tall and lean, his black hat pulled down low and his blue shirt unbuttoned around his neck.

When people talked of Chauncey their faces brightened and they would recall how his blue eyes twinkled constantly and his talk was fun and usually kind. There was a time when his Irish eyes were not smiling, and no one wanted that to happen again. He had decided that after two losing affairs with women, he would wait and see what the Lord provided. He mused that his choices must have been pretty bad, as neither one worked out worth a darn.

Chauncey loved the Lord and didn't care who knew it. He neither preached nor criticized but lived his life in day-to-day worship. It was his habit to point out special things of beauty to the Lord whenever he was riding, and Tango, his horse, was used to an occasional burst of praise coming from the man in the saddle.

On this particular morning he was riding to the far west pasture where his cow and calf herd were grazing. He knew he needed to throw the whole bunch into a fresh pasture and had decided he would start this morning by opening gates and seeing how many of his black cows could find the way out themselves.

The day was going to be hot, so the early start was imperative. Soon they were miles from home and Tango was pressing on with the mile-eating trot that he could keep up for a long time. After making a swift ride around the pasture to check water and any other problems that might have cropped up, he opened the gate and hoped his cows could figure out what he wanted them to do. He started down the trail to the Belle Fourche River with an uneasy eye on the storm coming in from the west. It had begun to look darker with every mile he rode.

Suddenly Buzz growled and dashed down to some trees by the river, and Tango snorted and danced. Chauncey's first thought was mountain lions, and he wished he had more than his little pistol on his saddle. He could see something against a tree and whatever it was, Buzz did not like it one bit. He was growling and barking and looking at Chauncey for some help.

As he rode up, he heard a woman's voice saying distinctly, "Oh, shut up, you stupid dog!"

It raised his hackles a bit to hear Buzz talked to in that manner, and he was about to say something sharp, but then he saw the sorriest face he had ever seen in his life turn to look at him, and he could only stare before saying, "I hope the other guy looks worse." Both of the young woman's cheeks were red and turning black and blue. Her eyes were also red and swollen, and her mascara was smudged and running black sooty streaks down her face.

She made no effort to either get up or to talk to him, and she glared at Buzz, who continued barking at her. Chauncey took a quick look around to see if she had friends waiting to waylay him, and satisfied that she was alone, dismounted and came a little closer to her.

She transferred her glare from Buzz to him in short order and asked him, "Can't you make your dog be quiet?"

"Well, now." Chauncey regarded her for several seconds before yelling, "Buzz off, Buzz!" at the barking dog, and was amused to see the disgusted look on his dog's face as he went to lie down by Tango.

He turned to her with a grin on his face and admitted a little sheepishly, "I always wanted to say that to him." Then he became serious and asked her if she was hurt.

She shook her head and gave a huge, shaking sigh. It brought a frown to Chauncey's face. "Look, my lady, I don't usually have visitors here by the river. I don't know where you came from or where you're going, but obviously you've had some trouble. Right?"

"Right, and I'm not your lady."

"Right, and I'm not your rescuer." Her sharp retort had nettled his good humor. Chauncey remounted his horse and looked down at her. "So I'll ride along. You'd better get some shelter from the storm." Buzz whined a little as some thunder rumbled in the distance.

The look she flashed him was somewhere between panic and anger. Chauncey rode over to a small boulder and asked her over his shoulder, "Can you ride?" When she nodded, he told her to get on the rock and swing up behind him.

He was surprised how tall she was when she stood, and he watched her stride over to the rock with long shapely legs clad in tight fitting jeans. In no time she was behind him, gripping on to the cantle and not saying a word.

Tango danced a little at the extra weight, but soon Chauncey headed him into the Belle, and they splashed through to the other side. For a while they rode in silence, then she cleared her throat and muttered, "I'm sorry. I was extremely rude."

"Yes, you were," Chauncey amiably agreed.

They rode in silence for quite a while then she said, "This is your ranch?"

"Yes, ma'am, mine and the banker's."

He wondered if she was smiling, and turned to look at her over his shoulder. She gave him a small smile, and he was satisfied with it.

The thunder was rumbling louder, and a wind began to pick up over the prairie. The dark blue in the west was getting closer and he could see streaks of rain showers in the distance. He wondered if she would bounce off if he pressed Tango into a trot.

"Hang on," he ordered and gave his horse some rein. She seemed to know instinctively how to get a better grip, and they began to cover the miles home at a faster pace. The thunder, lightning, and wind chased them all the way back, and horse, riders, and dog were grateful when they reached the shelter of the barn.

The woman slid off the back of his saddle with one easy motion, he noted with admiration before he dismounted and led his horse into its stall. He noticed she seemed to be comfortable around his horse, and when Buzz came up to her she spoke softly to him. As Buzz's tail wagged pleasantly and he let her pet him, Chauncey decided his dog was a pushover. He gave Tango some oats and then asked her if she wanted to make a run through the rain to the house. She seemed game, and they charged up to the house in the increasing downpour.

They were both puffing as they stood in the mudroom off the kitchen, and when he caught his breath he said, "I don't mean to be disrespectful, ma'am, but you look cold, wet, tired," he stopped and studied her a little more closely, "and hungry."

She had quit breathing so hard, and nodded a little to each description.

"If you take a left through that door," he pointed to a door that led into a hallway, "you'll come to my bathroom, and you're welcome to shower or whatever. I think I have a pair of my sister's jeans I'll lend you. I'll leave 'em by the door."

She nodded again and without saying a word followed his directions. He heard her give a little gasp as she caught her reflection in the mirror, and then the door closed and the shower started.

He looked a little embarrassedly around his house; it was definitely a comfortable bachelor home. He thought ruefully that he should tidy up some but then decided that people who don't telephone before they drop in should expect the worst. Quickly he found his sister's jeans, and also a warm T-shirt. After leaving them by the bathroom door, he went into the kitchen and started the coffee.

She took quite a while, he thought, but by the time he had made scrambled eggs, toast, and coffee, she had reappeared with a clean and made up face, damp blonde hair, and dry clothes. She went over to Buzz and patted him again, and Buzz—very undignified—rolled over on his back so she could scratch his belly.

"You're a shameless beggar," Chauncey told him disapprovingly, and Buzz gave him a canine grin from his upside down position.

She obligingly scratched, and then stood up and looked at the rain pelting the window. He saw a shadow of sadness pass over her face. Then with apparently forced good manners, she turned and complimented him on how good everything smelled.

When they sat down, he bowed his head. "Lord, thank You for this food. Thank You for this young lady. Thank You that we are here where it is warm and dry. Amen."

"Amen," she murmured.

After a few minutes he began to wonder if he was ever going to fill her up. She was hungry, and she complimented him several times on how good everything tasted. Finally she sat back with her refilled coffee cup and sighed.

He sat back also, and stretched his legs out in front of him. "Now then, I think we have established that this is my ranch, and my dog's name is Buzz," he was interrupted by a tail thumping heartily near by, "and we have had breakfast together. Other than that, it's a pretty blank slate. My name is Mr. Sullivan." He reached over to shake her hand.

Her eyes smiled. "I'm Mrs. DeLange." She shook the proffered hand.

"Mrs. DeLange, who hit you?"

Immediately the smile left her eyes.

"Sorry, I shouldn't have asked that question yet. Let me try another one."

She spoke tiredly. "Let me tell you what happened. I ran away from my husband. We were at the Sturgis bike rallies, he was acting like a jerk, we got into an argument, we both lost our tempers, and he hit me, then I hit him, and he hit me again. Please understand, Mr. Sullivan, he has never done this before. I crawled out a window, found a gravel road, and ended up under the tree where you found me."

He looked at her incredulously. "You were in Sturgis last night, and ended up here? You walked a lot of miles! Tell me how you came."

She struggled to remember but finally he was satisfied that it was possible by going through the pastures she talked about.

"By the road I'm at least forty miles away from Sturgis, but I suppose by going through the pasture like that it would be more like sixteen miles or so. At any rate, you must be exhausted." He looked at her tired and bruised face and decided any more talk could wait. "Why don't you grab a blanket and lie down somewhere. There's a spare bedroom in back, or the couch over there." He gestured toward the living room.

Once again she nodded, and slowly got up. "Thank you, Mr. Sullivan. You've been very kind to me. I appreciate it." She saw the couch with pillows and blankets thrown in disarray, and walked over to burrow down into the cushions. Covering herself, she closed her eyes and was asleep in seconds.

Chauncey sat and listened to the rain and drank another cup of coffee. He didn't think much of men who hit women. He thought of her walking all night in the dark and wondered if she had been afraid. Even if she was, he decided, she must have been more afraid her husband would find her. He hated to think of anyone crying alone. It bothered him whenever he saw a child crying without someone there to lend a supportive shoulder. He had lent his broad shoulder to a number of heartbroken toddlers.

He glanced into the living room at her quiet form, and hoped he wouldn't wake her when he started cleaning his kitchen. He need not have worried; she didn't stir. He went outside after the rain stopped, and the morning freshness greeted him. He took care of his girls in the hen house, and they listened to his cheerful voice with cocked heads and matronly clucking. By the time he finished with chores, it was almost noon, and as he ambled toward the house he could see her sitting on his old bench underneath the branches of the cottonwood tree.

She held a coffee mug in her hand. He nodded to her, went into the house to pour himself some coffee, and then rejoined her by the cottonwood. He eased his big frame down beside her, hoping she wouldn't think he was sitting too close.

"You have a beautiful spot here, Mr. Sullivan. Do you sit here often and enjoy it?"

"Yes, ma'am, I do. In fact Buzz and I have been known to have deep and profound conversations sitting here admiring the view."

She gave him a shy smile. "I hope you don't mind that I made us some coffee."

He turned sideways on the bench and took a good look at her. The bruises on her face would be there for a while, but her eyes looked more rested and she had pulled her blonde hair in a neat braid down her back. "Feeling better?" he asked her mildly.

"My body is grateful for the food and rest," she smiled briefly at him, "but my mind is in turmoil. I ... I really don't know what to do, Mr. Sullivan, and that's a fact."

Chauncey took some time before he replied, "Let's eat dinner and go fencing. Sometimes it's easier to figure things out when your hands are busy."

Her eyes brightened at the suggestion, and she nodded her head in agreement. "And how better to keep your hands busy than pounding staples?" she almost laughed.

He looked at her quizzically. "Said like a country girl, Mrs. DeLange. Do you have some background in fencing?"

"My maiden name is O'Neil, and we have wind and prairie and cattle running through our blood." He thought her eyes almost held a sparkle, and it transformed her whole face.

"O'Neil, you say, well begosh and begorrah, lassie, we must both be Irish!"

This time she laughed outright and stuck out her hand saying, "My name is Jolene."

"And my name is Chauncey." They shook hands again.

It was late afternoon by the time they started back to the ranch after taking his four-wheeler fencing. There were several places where the bulls had been fighting, and they fixed the resulting broken wires. They also traveled to the fresh pasture and checked the fences there.

Chauncey had complimented Jolene on her fencing savvy, and she in turn admired his ranch. They had stopped on a high ridge where the breaks fell into folds of cedar trees that tumbled down to the river.

"What a fantastic place for cattle," she said quietly.

Chauncey swung his leg over to the side of the Honda and gazed at the grass blowing in the breeze. The rain had freshened the air, but already the winds had dried most of the ground. For miles the rougher breaks met with softer rolling hills, and just below them wildflowers dotted the prairie with hues of yellow and purple. The river wove a pattern of green, and the summer clouds under a canopy of blue made a breathtaking scene.

"I usually remember to stop here and count my blessings," he answered.

"Was this place in your family?"

"No, it belonged to an older couple who wanted to sell, and they were kind enough to work with a green kid out of the army."

Jolene had remained seated on the back of the four-wheeler. She looked all around her slowly, and then sighed. "It refreshes my soul to see sights like these."

Chauncey heard a longing in her voice and recognized it as a counterpart to his thoughts. Without turning to look at her he asked, "And you, Miss O'Neil, with prairie and wind and cattle in your blood, married a hairdresser from Denver?"

She said very quietly, "I believe, Mr. Sullivan, that when you asked me where my husband worked, I said he owned DeLange Design in Denver."

"Sure, and when I said, 'What does he design?' you said he was a hair … I believe you used the word 'stylist.'"

She didn't answer him for a while. Then in a low voice she said, "I love him, Chauncey, and when he asked me to marry him I put every reason why I shouldn't out of my mind."

"Ah well," Chauncey swung his leg back over to straddle the four-wheeler, "love makes us all blind and a little crazy."

He asked that night at supper if she would like to stay another day and help him move his cattle out of the pasture. She nodded yes rather slowly, admitting that she still didn't know what to do or where to go, and if he could put up with her tomorrow she would get something figured out for the next day. Since the August weather promised to be hot, they decided to get started at daybreak.

He hoped she didn't mind the old bed and mattress set in the guest room, but one look at her drooping eyes made him realize it probably didn't matter where she slept. By nine o'clock she was headed toward her quarters, and by nine-thirty the lights were out at Chauncey's house.

Jolene woke to a gentle tapping on her door and a voice telling her it was time to ride. She had been in a deep sleep, and it took a few seconds to wake up in the early morning darkness. She was a little confused as to where she was and muttered and mumbled to herself. Quiet chuckling sounded through the door. She finally gathered her wits enough to call out that she was awake, and then as she heard booted feet walking down the hall, she slipped out of the uncomfortable bed and hurriedly dressed.

Lord, what am I doing here? Help me today to make a decision that would honor You. I'm too confused to think straight, and I need Your help ... again.

She had been uttering similar prayers the previous day. Chauncey's decision to go fencing had been a balm to her troubled mind, and she was looking forward to riding that morning. She could always think better in a saddle, and she was interested in seeing more of the countryside. Yet always in the back of her mind was the hovering image of Dexter. She had to go back to him; she knew that. But her emotions played havoc with her common sense, and she was grateful for some time to settle her nerves.

She walked out to the barn as the sun was just peeking over the eastern rim, and at once disapproved of the horse Chauncey picked out for her. It was a quiet, gentle mare that looked sleepily at the oats in the manger before her. Her wide girth proved she hadn't been ridden much, and Jolene immediately unsaddled her, and went searching for a horse that would have more to offer. There was one other choice in the corral, and she hoped he wouldn't disgrace her by being too rambunctious. Leading him into the barn she met Chauncey's irritated look with one of her own.

"Mr. Sullivan," she countered before he could say anything, "is this horse broke to ride?"

"Yes, ma'am, he is."

"Any bad habits?"

"Yes, ma'am."

She looked at him suspiciously. She found she had a hard time knowing when he was teasing her. He began saddling his own horse and didn't say any more.

She tied the horse to another manger and put the saddle blanket on. Chauncey was right behind her with the saddle and quickly threw it on and cinched it. He also had the bridle ready, and taking both horses, led them out.

"Now, Mrs. DeLange. I don't have a clue how well you can ride." He paused reflectively. "However, if you ride as well as you fence, you can probably handle him. He gets a little spooked, so sit tight in the saddle." He handed her the reins. "Oh, one more thing. If you get hurt, don't think you can sue me for the ranch. I am on record as trying to get you to ride a more gentle horse."

He was standing by her horse's head waiting for her to mount. Taking the reins, she put her foot in the stirrup and quickly mounted. Chauncey hastily mounted his own horse, and they trotted out of the corrals in the early morning light with Buzz following close behind.

There was a slight haze in the air, making the brown prairie hills appear softer. Meadowlarks were visiting with one another and mourning doves were making their melancholy coos. All the while the sun gently sent its beams into the low-lying clouds, turning them to a rose colored hue. Jolene was always affected by the beauty of nature, yet she was surprised to hear Chauncey telling his horse to smell and enjoy the freshness of the air.

"Does he listen to you?" she asked.

"Only when it pleases him," he answered ruefully.

They started walking their horses several minutes later, and Chauncey began explaining to her how the pasture lay, how he generally gathered the cattle, and where they would be crossing the Belle to get to the other pasture. She appreciated his information ahead of time. She remembered the times Uncle Walt forgot to tell her what was happening and then tried to shout it to her while they were in the midst of a mooing and moving herd of cattle.

A couple of hours later they were pushing the herd through the river and up the long hill to the gate. The cattle had been anxious to head to the fresh pasture, but now were tired and mulish, and it took a lot of convincing on the riders' part to keep them moving. Buzz was great help as he barked and nipped at a laggard's heels, but even so it took a lot of yelling to reach the top. A black white-faced cow realized she was heading into better grass and started taking off at a run. That enthused the rest of the herd, and soon the usual cluster of calves at the gate was all that remained to be herded in.

After he closed the barbed-wire gate, Chauncey walked over to Jolene. She was looking at his cattle with obvious interest, and he wasn't sure if he was amused or irritated.

"You have good cattle. Looks like they've summered well."

"Well," he stated, swinging himself back into the saddle, "no sense in having poor cattle."

She flashed him a quizzical look, then glanced down at the puffing Buzz. "He's quite a cow dog."

"And you, ma'am, are quite a hand." It was quietly said and greatly appreciated.

"Normally," Chauncey said, eyeing his herd, "I come back later and take out the bulls, but I see five of them pretty close. Are you up to helping me get 'em out?"

Jolene hated to admit that she despised chasing bulls. They bellowed and fought, and it generally meant a lot of hard riding, but her pride was at stake, so she merely nodded.

Once again Chauncey told her the direction they would be taking them, how they would use the fence line to make chasing them easier, and where the gate was.

"There's eight of 'em in here, but if we could get these five, that would be a great help."

The bulls were as difficult as Jolene imagined they would be, but eventually they were convinced to head down the fence line, and with Buzz doing his job effectively, they were soon through the other gate. Once the bulls decided they were being escorted away from the cows, they settled down, as if relieved that once more their duties were over and they could just graze and rest.

Chauncey had a smaller fenced pasture in mind for them, and when he opened the last gate and Jolene chased them in, they both gave a sigh of relief.

Even though it was only ten o'clock, the air was hot and sultry, and all the prettiness of the early morning had disappeared. Their horses were tired and walked wearily toward home. When they crossed a little creek that made its way to the Belle, they let their horses drink, and Buzz threw himself into the water and alternated between swimming and drinking. With a few loud coughs from ingested water, he made his way to the bank, shook himself with vigor, and then plopped down to get a few seconds rest.

"I don't know about you, but my breakfast is wearing out," Chauncey said idly, watching his horse nuzzle the water. "Oh, say, Jolene! Watch out for Fox Trot, he likes to lay down when he's drinking." Chauncey turned at the loud splashing behind him, and saw Jolene in a frenzy trying to jerk Fox Trot out of the water. She succeeded, but not before her pant legs and T-shirt were splattered with water.

Her laughter rang out as Fox Trot lunged across the creek and gave a huge shake as he reached the dry bank. "This must be one of his bad habits you forgot to tell me about!"

"Stupid horse," Chauncey muttered as he crossed over and looked at her anxiously. Other than being a little drenched, Jolene looked fine and seemed to be revived during the rest of the ride home.

Dinner was steaks on the grill, and since they were in no hurry now that the work was done, they added baked potatoes. Jolene fixed a salad from the offerings in Chauncey's fridge. The temperature shot up to one hundred degrees, and the central air in the house was a welcome respite.

They chatted lightly about the weather and cattle but avoided anything personal. Finally after they had finished eating and were enjoying another glass of iced tea, Chauncey stretched out his long legs and looked at her with blue knowing eyes.

"I think I can make this easier, Jolene."

She looked out the window at the sun-baked grass, and then sighed. "What do you have in mind?"

"You need to go back to him. Fly back to Denver." He studied her reaction before he continued. "I can take you to the airport tomorrow morning."

"You don't think I should go back to Sturgis?"

"No, during the rallies Sturgis is no place for a woman alone. The law has all it can do, and they couldn't help you if you needed them."

She looked at Chauncey for a while before she sighed again and nodded her head. "You're right, of course." She hesitated before saying more. "I need to tell you some things and I don't know how to start." She looked down at her ringless left hand. "Chauncey, it might be better if you didn't tell anyone that I was here." At his surprised look, she plunged on. "There were two men with us that I didn't care for, and ..." She wondered how much more she should say. "Dexter seemed to know them well. It would just be better for you if ... if you didn't know me at all."

His eyes seemed to be bluer and colder when she looked up at him. "Maybe you should tell me the whole story," he said softly.

Once again she looked out the window. Then she took a deep breath. "I don't know if I even know the whole story. Dexter has always been able to find me. I don't know how these men fit into the picture, but they didn't seem like nice guys. I'll tell you one other thing. The reason Dexter slapped me was because I accused him of some pretty harsh things—like trying to kill me." She noted his startled expression and hurried on. "My first husband was killed, and now some think that it wasn't accidental. I don't know," she gave a shaky little sigh, "I just don't know, but when I was yelling at him I blurted that out, and ... well, you know the rest."

He was looking at her incredulously. "You married someone you think murdered your spouse?"

She covered her face with her hands and said in an anguished voice, "Oh, what you must think of me." It startled her to realize that she wanted him to understand. She looked at him pleadingly. "It was something that I was told about just before we came here—it may not be true—-I can't think he would—-but yet—-" She pressed her hand against her mouth and lowered her eyes. Then taking another deep breath she looked at him again. "I just love him, Chauncey," she said softly. "I just love him." Her eyes threatened to spill over.

Chauncey slowly stood and started picking up dinner plates. "You'd better make the plane reservation," he said flatly.

Later that evening Jolene finished her shower and headed into the bedroom. She was sorry that the afternoon had fizzled into dismal small talk and that Chauncey had gone out in the heat and spent most of his time avoiding her. She had found one of his old T-shirt, and some basketball trunks that fit her decently, and they served her well as pajamas. She thought of how she liked this house and ranch on the prairie, how much she had enjoyed the ride in the morning, but most of all she thought of Dexter and how he had hurt her with his actions. She relived all over again his coldness and his flirtation with Shirley, even to the point of kissing her in an embrace that tore Jolene's heart in two. The tears started again, and she decided to go outside and not keep Chauncey awake with her bawling.

Softly she headed out the door and went to the east side of the house where the steps were shallow and headed upwards toward an open porch. She sat down and put her head on her hands and let the memories and the tears and muffled sobs continue. For some time she sat there in total misery. Then in embarrassment she heard Chauncey's steps coming around the corner of the house. He sat down beside her, handed her a roll of toilet paper, opened a bottle of flavored water, and handed it to her.

"I absolutely can't stand hearing you cry by yourself," he informed her, taking another bottle for himself.

"I'm sorry," she sniffed, sounding nasal from all her tears, "I thought you couldn't hear me out here." She made good use of the paper, wiping her eyes, blowing her nose, and trying to compose herself. The water tasted good and she guzzled quite a bit of it.

"Well," he sighed, "I have to admit I've spent a little time crying out here myself."

She drank more water. "You've heard my woes. Maybe you should tell me your sad story."

Chauncey tried to be brief. "Boy meets girl, boy thinks he loves girl, girl dumps boy. Boy meets another girl, girl lives with him, girl wants to get married, boy wishes she'd move out. Instead, boy marries girl." He looked at Jolene and sighed again. Her bottle was empty and she was looking intently at him. He continued on, "Girl doesn't like Buzz or ranch. Girl's daddy thinks they should move to town. Girl's daddy buys house in town." He heard her gasp of dismay. "Boy says good." She gave a grunt of disproval. "Moves girl out. Divorces girl. Boy stays mad for over a year. Not good."

"The dumb broad!" Jolene exclaimed. "She had it made, great ranch, great guy. What was her problem?" She reached for another bottle of flavored water but had trouble opening it.

Chauncey looked at her a little surprised and then quickly twisted the top off and handed it to her. She took several large swallows.

"Who knows, Jolene? She thought she wanted to be a cowgirl. Got her boots and hat, and rode like a sack of potatoes." For some reason the sack of potatoes part was funny to Jolene, and she sputtered a little as she drank some more water.

"Terrible of her not to like Bizz," she muttered.

"You mean Buzz," Chauncey corrected her with raised eyebrow.

"Yeah, I mean Buzz," she echoed. "Did she visit the girls?"

"What girls?" He was puzzled.

"Your girls in the ... in the—what you call that place?—the rooster house!" she finished triumphantly.

He looked at her with a little frown. "Not to my knowledge."

She stared at him and in the moonlight could see his black hair blowing softly across his forehead. For quite awhile neither said anything and then she leaned back against the step and finished up the second bottle.

Chauncey was about to suggest they go in when she announced, "Our little children will have mottled hair." She fumbled for her third bottle. He took it from her and opened it, then handed it back.

He leaned back so they were side by side, and looking up at the moon asked her how many children she thought they should have. The conversation wasn't going anything like he thought it would.

She took a long time to answer. "Fourish. The first two would have that mottled hair 'cause of the back and the bond."

"You mean the black and the blonde," he corrected her again and had trouble keeping a straight face.

"Yeah." She looked at the moon and said rather testily, "That's what I said, Chaun." She gathered her thoughts together again. "The third would be ... am I already on the third one?" She gave a huge sigh. "Time flies. Where was I?"

He reminded her that she was telling him what color hair their third child would have.

"Oh, yeah, black, of course, like their daddy. How many do I have left?"

"You're on the last one," he said rather regretfully.

"I mus be a buzzy woman," she lamented and took another drink. "That fourish one would be bronze." She frowned. "Do I mean bronze or do I mean blonze? Sorta confusing. It's a good thing we're on the last one." She sighed again. "Chaun, this is the best flavored water I've ever had."

"Jolene," he said, horrified. "Those are wine coolers, not flavored water."

She looked at him, startled, then at the half empty third bottle. For a while her eyes were wide and uncomprehending. Finally she said with a loud wail, "Chaun O'Sullivan, you got me drunk, and now we have all these poor lil kids." Her voice rose to a squeak, "You mushn't ever, ever, let me drink so many wines."

Chauncey's shoulders shook with suppressed laughter. "What ever made you think flavored water tasted like that?" he finally choked out.

"Well, now," she started to put her hand on her chin, "Well, now, Chaun boy, things are jus better here in ... here in ... where ever the heck we are," she muttered.

Chauncey couldn't help himself, and gave in to howls of laughter. She looked so befuddled and cute, and he thought it was the funniest thing that ever had happened to him.

"I'll have a stopover when I go 'ome to what's his face!" she grumbled.

"Hangover, Jolene, not stopover!" Chauncey whooped. When she didn't answer, he turned and saw her eyes were closed. "Hey, let's get you to bed before you pass out on me!" It was too late. A most unladylike snore whistled into the night.

CHAPTER 18

Dexter's Secret

OLENE'S FLIGHT TOUCHED down in Denver shortly before noon. She debated about calling Miss Grey to pick her up but decided to grab a taxi instead. When she arrived at DeLange Designs, she had the driver take her to the back, and she quickly entered the coded key door and slipped upstairs to the penthouse. Once again she opened another coded door, and without calling out to anyone, she hurried to the bedroom. She had no idea what would take place, but she wanted to be dressed in something better than jeans and a tee, and to have her hair fixed.

The bedroom looked exactly as they had left it on Monday, only to Jolene's surprise, her ring that she had removed at Sturgis was sitting on the dresser. She hurriedly changed her clothes into white Capri pants and a v-necked green top. Adding sandals and some earrings made her feel more assured, and then with a curling iron, she quickly arranged her hair into a more sophisticated style than her braid. She looked at her ring for quite a while, trying to decide if she should wear it or not. Finally, she slid it onto her finger and walked out of the room.

The apartment seemed strangely silent, and she wondered if Mrs. Runski was in the kitchen. There was no one there, so she headed downstairs to find Patrick. When she walked into the back of the salon she could hear the usual murmur of staff and clients and with her heart pounding, she walked quietly to where Patrick was fixing a smiling woman's hair.

He saw her reflection in the mirror and turned quickly to look at her. He visibly flinched when he saw her face. Without letting her say anything and with a hurried apology to his customer, he hustled her into his office and shut the door.

They both started talking at once, and he stopped her with a raised hand. "Let me go first, Jolene. Did you know Dad had a heart attack?"

She stood frozen and could only shake her head.

"He's been asking over and over for you. Listen, stay here while I get someone to take my place, and I'll drive you to the hospital."

She felt shaken from head to toe but managed to tell him she would go upstairs and grab her purse. In seconds she was back downstairs and they were in Patrick's car heading toward the hospital.

"He did hit you. He kept saying that. None of us could believe it." Patrick's voice was agonized.

"How bad is this, Patrick?" From the grim look on his face she realized it was serious.

"If he can come home he'll be lucky. He was hoping to get a chance to talk to you before ..." Patrick swallowed a couple of times and couldn't go on.

Once again Jolene was praying for strength, for wisdom, for help. Over and over she repeated that prayer. Her thoughts were scrambling to put together the puzzle pieces to Dexter's health and their marriage, and then Patrick's voice broke through to her.

"He knew when he married you, Jolene, that his time was short. He has a bad heart. He went to the Mayo clinic last year, and the news wasn't good. Now he thinks he should have told you about it. Whatever happened in South Dakota has hit him hard. He can hardly bear to think about it, and yet it's all he can talk about."

"It wasn't good, Patrick. I ... ran away after we fought. And I mean we fought. He changed right before my eyes and became a monster. Was he on medication?"

"Yes. I don't know what it was. Some kind of quack pills to give him energy. I guess they were over-the-counter pep pills or some such thing. His doctor was definitely unhappy about it." They were pulling up to the hospital, but before they got out of the car Patrick had one more thing to tell her. "I think he knew he was declining. I think he just wanted to get it over with."

She was grateful Patrick was with her to guide her through the hospital maze. In the elevator he touched her arm. "Jolene, he loves you, and he's pretty emotional right now." He looked at her pleadingly.

"Pray for me, Patrick. I need all the help I can get," she whispered.

They stepped out of the elevator and soon were by a door leading to a private room. She took a deep breath and walked slowly into the room and toward the bed. She realized there were other people in the room, but her eyes were riveted on the man who was watching her with agony written all over his features. Even in a hospital gown he was a commanding figure, yet there was pain in his eyes, and she wasn't sure if it was physical or emotional.

When she reached the bed she smiled at him and said softly, "Dexter, let's not play with motorcycles again."

He sobbed her name as she bent to kiss him, and the arm that was free from the IV held her tightly.

His voice was agonized as he whispered, "Jolene, I'm so sorry. I'm so sorry." He couldn't seem to say any more but looked at her with eyes that were tired and hopeless. She kissed his cheek where the ring had dug in, and he raised his hand with the IV tube and traced the bruises on her cheek.

"No." It was a moan, and he repeated it with a heavy "Oh, no." His voice was so low she could hardly hear him. "I never meant to hurt you like that." He trailed off to a whisper, "I never wanted to hurt you."

She smiled at him a little shakily and said, "We had our moments, didn't we. I came back to you, Dexter." She put both hands around his face. "I came back because we love each other and we belong together."

185

Dexter was profoundly shaken and it was evident to everyone in the room. For the first time Jolene noticed those around her. Reverend Taylor cleared his throat and stepped forward. "I think," he said softly, "that a word of prayer is needed, and then we'll leave the two of you alone." He took both Jolene's hand and Dexter's and bowed his head.

"Dearest Lord Jesus, we thank You that Jolene and Dexter are reunited, and that their love for each other is true and strong. Give them both the strength and peace that only You can give. In Your precious name we pray, Amen."

Several tearfully echoed "Amen."

He quickly ushered Betty and Miss Grey out of the room. Patrick followed them and quietly shut the door.

When he heard the door shut, Dexter's shoulders shook and he let out a muffled sob. For several minutes Jolene held him until she felt him slowly regain his composure, and all the while she was murmuring to him that she loved him, that it would be all right.

He let out a deep breath. "Jolene ..." He was more in control. "Jolene, it won't be all right. I'm ... I'm dying." He took another deep breath and let it out. "I just thought that I might as well get it over with rather than go by inches." He ran a gentle finger over her cheek. "I even had the crazy idea that if you hated me it would be easier for you." He was begging her with his eyes to understand.

"When I came back and found you were gone, I was so shook up I hardly knew what to do." He stopped to catch his breath. "I saw your ring on the dresser, and then I knew I was having a heart attack." Once again he breathed deeply. "Jolene, my only thought was to live long enough to tell you ... all the things ... and to ask you to forgive me ..." He couldn't go on. Finally he patted the bed next to him and whispered to her. "Lie beside me, Jolene. I want you next to me."

"The nurses will be scandalized," she muttered, kicking off her sandals. Gently she slipped beside him and laid her head on his shoulder.

He slipped his arm around her. "You always just fit against me," he said softly. She looked up at him, and for the first time there was a little smile on his lips. The look that passed between them would linger long in her memory. They were together again, but the knowledge their togetherness was limited was heartbreaking.

When he spoke again his voice was stronger. "The ribbon in the Bible you gave me was placed at the story of David and Bathsheba." He looked down at her lying so still beside him. "Was that for a reason, Jolene?"

She absently rubbed his chest with her hand and didn't answer for a while. Once again she looked up at him, and her answer was a faint whispered yes.

He closed his eyes and she could feel his heart pounding.

"Dexter, the reason I put the ribbon there was because I was guilty of wanting you when I was married to John. He and I were having trouble right then. It would have been the easiest thing in the world for me to have slept with you. I have been so sorry that I was unfaithful in my heart to John. I—I've prayed for forgiveness."

"Was there any other reason?"

She took a deep breath. "When I gave you the Bible, there was no other reason."

"But now?"

Her voice trembled. "Dexter, what do you want me to say? I had a call before we left for Sturgis that a man from Denver hired two thugs to tamper with John's plane. You were acting so weird—I just didn't know what to think." She broke into a sob and felt the trembling in his hand as he silently rubbed her shoulder.

"Do you think I had John killed so I could have you?"

She buried her face into his chest. She loved this man. How could she possibly believe he would do such a thing? She slowly raised her head and looked at him. "In my heart, Dexter, I can't believe you would ever be guilty of murder."

"I'm guilty of many things, Jolene. I deceived you. I wanted you even though I knew you would have to go through widowhood again." His voice trailed off and he was silent.

She waited for him to continue, and could hear the uneven pumping of his heart. She half rose in fear that she was losing him before she could tell him all the things that needed to be said.

He took a shaky breath, and coughed slightly. "Kitten, I did not have John killed."

She let out her breath slowly. She could endure almost anything now that she knew that.

He took his arm away from her shoulders and without opening his eyes he said so softly she could hardly hear him, "Go get the Reverend."

She realized she must have looked a little wild when she tore into the waiting room and motioned to Reverend Taylor. When he realized Dexter wanted to talk to him, he went immediately into his room. Whatever was said between the two men would never be told, but they both acknowledged that Dexter had placed his faith and trust in the Lord and had confessed and repented of his sins. For those in the waiting room, the news was a tremendous relief.

Jolene was prepared to stay at the hospital around the clock, but surprisingly the next afternoon the doctor made the decision to let Dexter go home. He looked at Jolene bluntly and asked if she was any kind of a nurse. She replied, "Probably not, but I think I can take care of my man."

He smiled at that, and told both of them that Dexter may as well be at home because it was plain to see that having Jolene with him was doing more good than any of their medicine.

Patrick came to get them, and he was so delighted that he gave his Aunt Betty a bone-crushing hug. The family wondered if the doctor was right to let Dexter return home, yet when they looked in on Dexter, they said there was no denying the news that he was going home with Jolene had brought a brighter look to his face.

When they arrived at the penthouse Mrs. Runski greeted them at the door with both smiles and tears. She had fixed a light lunch for everyone and they gathered around the table with gratefulness. Reverend Taylor asked the blessing and then Dexter made a point to thank everyone for all the help and reminded Mrs. Runski that she was the best cook in the world.

Jolene thought he looked exhausted and came and stood by his chair. "Ready to head out?" she asked him softly, and when he nodded she helped him up. Together, with his arm draped over her shoulder, they went to their bedroom.

Dexter sat on the edge of the bed and looked to be wondering if he had the strength to turn around and lie down. Jolene took off his shoes and somehow managed to turn him so all he had to do was slump down on the pillows. He smiled at her and called her a big bully. She kicked off her own shoes, and with a huge sigh lay down beside him. He slid his arm around her shoulders and she snuggled up to him. He murmured in her ear that maybe they should have a blanket and instantly she was up and found one in the closet. She spread it over him and once again crawled in beside him. There was contentment with the knowledge that they were together again in their own bed. His arm was around her and soon they both fell asleep.

The last rays of the setting sun were filtering in their bedroom when Jolene woke up. She had slept soundly, exhausted by all the emotions of the past hours and days.

Life without Dexter was looming ahead of her, and it brought instant grief to her very being. Yet while she still had him, she was determined that their days would be filled with joy, especially now that she knew they would be together for eternity. "The joy of the Lord is my strength" crept into her mind. She would need a very close walk with her Lord during this time. Dexter was extremely weak, and she knew that she needed physical strength as well as spiritual. She had made phone calls to her family asking for their prayers and was renewed by their concern. She had even dashed off a quick note to Mr. Sullivan, thanking him for his kindness and telling him about Dexter's heart attack.

She looked up at Dexter, and the usual thrill went through her as she met his eyes. He was looking at her with a tender expression on his face, and then he brought her even closer to himself, and murmured with a catch in his voice, "I don't know how I can leave you, Jolene."

She searched his face and ran a light finger across his lips. "Couldn't we try to find some medical technology or doctors who could reverse this?"

He shook his head, "No, darling." With a sigh he added, "I've had to tell Patrick the same thing. I inherited this from my father. It's a bunch of medical mumbo jumbo, and there's no use in wasting time with doctors. I've already seen quite a list of them."

He kissed her forehead. "I'm so thankful you came back to me. Having you here now is," he stopped to regain control of his voice, "the best thing that I could hope for." Both his arms wrapped around her, and he buried his face in her hair.

She was fighting a losing battle with her tears, and finally she gave up, and laying her head in the hollow of his throat she sobbed and felt his tears mingling with hers.

For several minutes they gave way to their grief, and then Jolene resolutely sat up, and wiping her eyes she looked at him sternly.

"OK, Dexter, now we have that out of our system. From now on, you and I are going to laugh and give thanks for whatever time we have left. This is not going to be a house of mourning. People are not going to come here and tiptoe away and say 'poor Dexter and Jolene.' No, absolutely not. They are going to go away laughing and saying 'those two!'" She looked at him earnestly. "We can do this, Dexter. It will be our witness that the Lord is good, He is in control, and even death cannot overwhelm us because the joy of the Lord is our strength!"

He was looking at her with tear-brimmed eyes, and she realized he knew that what she was saying was true. He gave her a small smile and said, "Amen, Sister Jolene." She nodded her head in satisfaction, and bounded off the bed.

Jolene's plan set the tone for the days that followed. They quickly established a routine of breakfasts on the balcony with Jolene reading devotions to him, lots of resting, and then in mid-afternoon when the balcony was shaded he would sit there again and watch her swim in the pool below. Usually Miss Grey would come to visit about that time, and as Jolene predicted, she would leave shaking her head and saying, "Those two!"

Dexter pondered the verse that said, "The truth will set you free." His regret was that he didn't tell Jolene the truth about his heart to begin with. He found that he and Jolene could make light of his declining strength, and it would bring a smile to his face when he remembered how they solved his showering dilemma.

He had sat on a bench in the bathroom, wondering how he was going to gather enough strength to stand up long enough to take his accustomed shower. He had taken off his shirt and was mulling it over when Jolene walked in.

"Turn the shower on, Jolene, and strip down."

She looked at him in mock horror. "Mr. DeLange!" With a saucy look she started the water running, gathered towels, and did as he said. Within seconds she was helping him into the shower, and that little routine quickly became the highlight of their days.

It was after one such episode that he was resting on the edge of their bed. She fussed over drying his hair, kissed him repeatedly, rubbed lotion on him, and asked him which cologne he wanted to use that day. When he told her the one he wanted she brought it over to him and gently patted it on his face. He smiled indulgently and mildly remarked, "You make dying rather interesting, Jolene." She swatted him lightly on the arm and reminded him that it was her sworn duty to keep him happy at all times. He laughed at that and stretched out on the bed, watching her like a lazy, contented cat as she bustled around. Occasionally he mentioned that he loved her and was rewarded with another kiss. Finally she crawled onto the bed with him and snuggled into his side. He felt like purring when she did.

It was finally raining and the air had cooled down considerably. Instead of her usual afternoon swim, Jolene was doing some floor exercises in the living room. Dexter was watching her as he reclined against the cushions on the couch.

"What are you getting in shape for, Jolene?" he asked mildly.

"One of us has to be strong," she puffed back.

He raised an eyebrow at that. "If you make yourself too strong it'll be a long time before you join me in heaven."

"Time will fly up there, Dexter. You'll hardly know it, and I'll be right there with you." She was beginning to get winded.

"What'll I say to John while I'm waiting?"

"You'll think of something, darling."

"Which one of us is going to be your husband for all eternity?"

Jolene had switched from leg bends to sit-ups, and her voice came and went as she bobbed up and down. "The gospels say that we're not given in marriage but we are like the angels."

"Good grief, Jolene, what am I going to do with an angel?"

"Fix her hair, Dexter. You can fix her hair and John can adjust her wings. You'll get along like a house afire." Jolene lay panting on the floor.

Dexter had a mental picture of Jolene with long flowing hair, sitting in a celestial salon chair while he primped and curled her hair and John added oil to her wings. It amused him so much he broke into loud guffaws.

Miss Grey coming in at that moment thought she had never heard Dexter laugh so hard. She walked into the living room to see Jolene lying on the floor watching him with sparkling eyes and Dexter chortling on the couch.

"Sit down, Edna," he said without moving from his comfortable position. Miss Grey was so surprised that he called her by her first name that she sank into the first chair she could find. Jolene grinned at her and bounced up to get all three of them some coffee. When Patrick wandered in, she made it four cups of coffee, and Mrs. Runski added some of her chocolate chip cookies to the tray.

It was a moment that Edna Grey fondly remembered afterwards. The rain coursing down the windows made the setting cozy while the conversation flowed. Dexter was in an excellent mood, adding dry humor to their talk. He and Jolene laughed easily, and as she sat beside him, he laced his fingers through hers, teasing her, baiting her. Their banter was full of good-natured fun. It was how both Miss Grey and Patrick remembered them in the following weeks.

The next morning Dexter asked Jolene to read Psalm 51 at their devotions. It was one he often requested, and it always made Jolene somber when she read it. It was the prayer of repentance that King David had written after the prophet Nathan came to him about his conduct with Bathsheba.

"Have mercy upon me, Oh God, According to Your loving kindness," Jolene began, "According to the multitude of Your tender mercies, Blot out my transgressions. Wash me thoroughly from my iniquity, And cleanse me from my sin." She continued reading through verse eight. "Make me hear joy and gladness, That the bones You have broken may rejoice."

"Jolene," Dexter interrupted, and she glanced up at him. He was looking at her with tenderness. "Jolene, when you read that verse I think of you and me these past days. We've had joy and gladness."

She nodded her head.

"Can you forgive me for what happened in Sturgis?"

"You know I already have."

"But I need to hear you say it, Jolene. I put us both through hell. If I had told you the truth about my health, we would have had more time together. I—I don't know that I'll ever forgive myself for being so stupid."

"You were understandably stupid, darling. It is a very rare occasion when Dexter DeLange is stupid."

"Jolene, darling, be serious."

She walked around the table and hugged him. "Even when I was accusing you of terrible things, I loved you; even when I said I would never forgive you, I knew I would. I have completely forgiven you, because I love you, and I want you to forgive yourself also."

He seemed satisfied with that. After she sat back down he continued. "I've done a lot of thinking lately. I have been spoiled all my life. I've taken what I wanted. I wanted you, and not only wanted, I needed you. I strongly believe that God wove you into my life so I would come to Him." He noted the tears coursing down her cheeks. "Sweetheart, are you going to be able to finish reading?"

"Probably not," she mumbled, getting up to find a tissue. She brought a box of them and set them on the table, poured more coffee for each of them, and picked up the Bible again, but Dexter had more to say.

"Let me tell you some other things. That red-haired woman in Sturgis was an actress I hired."

"I noticed she seemed quite experienced smooching with you," Jolene muttered, while a little wave of jealousy flowed over her.

His eyes crinkled with a brief smile. "The two men were hired to help you when I became incapacitated." There was irony in Dexter's voice. "Instead, they had to help me. They are trained EMT's and also professional bodyguards." He looked at her intently. "Where did you disappear to, Jolene? They looked all over for you."

"I ran away to the prairie—and the prairie sent me back to you."

She could tell he was getting tired, but he wanted to tell her more.

"Jolene, what I can't understand is why God has allowed you to go through so much grieving. For my part, it's wonderful to have you here, taking care of me, making me laugh, guiding me through this time. But what about you, Jolene, what about you? What's going to happen to you after I'm gone?" Deep concern for her was reflected on his face.

She took a deep breath. "I don't know about tomorrow, about any of my tomorrows. I just know that today we're together, and God will take care of the rest."

She glanced down at where she had been reading. "Listen to this, Dexter. Verse twelve: 'Restore to me the joy of Your salvation and uphold me by Your generous Spirit. Then I will teach transgressors Your ways, And sinners shall be converted to You.'"

She took a swallow of coffee to help ease the lump in her throat. With tear-filled eyes she looked at him and added, "Dexter, my joy for the rest of my life is knowing that you have been converted to Christ, and we will have eternity together."

CHAPTER 19

Alone Again

*H*E LEFT QUIETLY that night. When she woke up she knew instantly that he was gone. For several seconds she held him, not wanting to let him go, and her sobs echoed throughout the room. Finally she got up and called Patrick and Miss Grey, and when they hurriedly arrived, she was dressed and composed.

That evening Bob and Helen came over, and after an emotional greeting, they offered their help for anything that needed to be done. Bob handed her a DVD, and with his voice breaking told her that Dexter and he had put it together before the trip to South Dakota, and it was to be shown at the service. Dexter had wanted her to see it first. Once again Bob's voice cracked. "It's beautiful, Jolene." He couldn't say more.

After they left, Jolene put Dexter's black silk pajamas on, the ones that still had his scent of cologne, and watched it. She cried until there were no more tears.

He had already made his own funeral arrangements, and they carried out his wishes. One of the songs he had requested was the beautiful hymn "I Surrender All," and Jolene broke down and cried when she heard it.

Bob gave a tribute to the man he had worked with so many years. He said he had learned early in their friendship that there was more to Dexter DeLange than what he ever wanted anyone to know. He said he was going to show a video that Dexter and he had made. It wasn't so much to capture the life of Dexter DeLange, but to show the love he had for his wife, Jolene.

It started with a fading shot of Jolene in the red dress at Rachel's wedding, and then it showed some of the footage of the video that Helen had taken with the iced pitcher episode. It caught the expression Dexter had on his face after she had jumped into the pool. There were shots of their wedding, then it was pictures of their honeymoon in Hawaii and different still shots of them together at so many places. Countless times the emotion on Dexter's face showed as he looked at her, and the love she had for him seemed to beam out of every picture. The last picture was in the penthouse, with the two of them cuddled together on the couch. She didn't even know that it had been taken. When it was over there wasn't a dry eye in the church, except for Jolene's.

She greeted her family at the burial service and noted that even Florence was very subdued. Dexter was widely known and respected as a businessman, and there were many people who shook her hand and offered their sympathies. Carl Harris was one of them, and he looked at her with sad eyes and said she shouldn't have to be a widow twice. She appreciated his coming and asked quickly about his parents and David. Before he moved on in the line he said that David and Shannon were expecting another baby.

That evening the Taylors, Patrick, Marcella, and the children lingered at the penthouse. They looked at cards, told Dexter stories, and finally reluctantly left Jolene alone. She was too tired to cry that night.

She and Miss Grey started immediately with the thank-you notes, and all the rest of the many things that needed to be done. The will had been read, and Jolene had been left very comfortable financially. She was glad Patrick and Marcella would be moving into the penthouse. She knew she couldn't emotionally stand to live there.

It was mid October before she loaded up the Navigator and started back to the little stone house. It had been an emotional farewell the night before, and Jolene thought she had never felt so drained in all her life. Losing Dexter was the hardest blow she had ever been dealt, she decided, driving in the autumn countryside toward the sand hills.

She took her time and when she came to an especially scenic area, she pulled off the road and hiked up the hill to the top. The view was beautiful, and Jolene did something she had never done in all her life. She looked up to heaven and stomped her foot.

"Why, God?" She stomped her foot again even more angrily. "Why do I have to keep on losing everyone I love? And let me tell You something, this last one was a real doozy! I know what I said about it all being worth it to have him in eternity, but I want You to know that I can't quit crying over losing him. And I'll tell You something else. I don't know what to do! I don't want to go back to that little stone house. I don't want to live in Denver. I have no place to go, and nothing to do, and I'm lonesome, and not even the prairie can make me feel happy. Is this fair, God?"

For some reason, she felt a little better. "God, this isn't good. Nothing right now feels good." She sat on the ground for a while, not wanting to go to the ranch and have to endure all the condolences of her family for the second time, for the second husband. "Look, Lord, I'm only twenty-five, and I've already lost two men. No one will even want to marry me. I'm a jinx. Marry Jolene and die." She grimaced and continued, "Yes, indeed, this is a pity party, Lord. Just You and me. So far I've done all the talking, and now what do You have to say?"

She looked out across the prairie that had already turned brown and could see a riot of autumn leaves on the river below. A slight breeze whispered through the grass as she sat there, and a lone fly droned somewhere behind her.

Chauncey Sullivan needs you.

"No siree Bob, I have no emotions left for him."

Chauncey needs you.

"Listen, Lord. I tell you that my heart is drained of all feeling. I gave all I could give to Dexter. There's nothing left. Chauncey doesn't need someone who can't love him because she can't get over husband number two."

Let Me take care of that.

"Oh forevermore." Jolene sat for quite a while in silence. Finally she gave a disgruntled little snort, got up, and dusted herself off. She had one last thing to tell the Lord. "Even if he does need me, I can't just pack my bags and head to South Dakota."

She wished with all her heart she could be glad to be back at the ranch, but she wasn't. She was there because she didn't know where else to go. And she wasn't there very long before she knew she would have to leave. The little stone house had memories of Dexter. Sitting in the house with Walt and Arlene brought memories of him talking to their grandchildren. Walking outside reminded her of how he had strolled over to Arlene's flower beds and admired them.

Walt and Arlene and family could tell by her restlessness that she would be leaving again, and that bothered her. It seemed that she had upset their lives constantly with her comings and goings.

It was in one of these unsettled moments that Arlene's phone had rung, and with a surprised look on her face, she handed the phone to Jolene.

"Hello," she said questioningly.

"Jolene, this is Chauncey Sullivan."

After his condolences he came right to the point. They were short-handed working cattle because his brother, Chase, had gotten hurt. He was wondering if she would be the tiniest bit interested in coming to South Dakota for a couple of weeks to lend a hand. He would be willing to pay her.

No, Lord, I don't want to do this!

"Well, actually, well, I guess I could. When would you want me?"

It was decided she could come the next day.

When she hung up the phone she wondered what on earth her family would think of her charging off to be with still another man. *Look what You've gotten me into now, Lord!*

Arlene poured herself and Jolene a cup of coffee. She was going to have a visit with her niece, and she sincerely hoped no grandkids or men folk came in while they were talking.

"Want to tell me about it?" she asked kindly.

Jolene plopped down on the kitchen chair and gazed at her plump, good-natured aunt and wailed, "Aunt Arlene, I'm a mess."

Arlene patted her hand and reassured her she most definitely was not.

"I just keep losing people. And finding people. I've just told this rancher in South Dakota that I'll come and spend a couple of weeks with him to work cattle, and for heaven's sake, Dexter has only been gone a little over six weeks! What am I thinking of?"

"I can't think that helping someone means you'll be marrying them in the next breath," Arlene said.

Jolene put her chin on her hand. "Arlene, I just can't stay here anymore. I love all of you to bits and pieces, but somehow, it isn't right for me anymore."

"I know, dear. You're unsettled right now. I have a suggestion."

Jolene's eyebrows shot up.

"The forest service at Chadron has sent you a letter and I opened it by mistake. They need some office help, and they remembered you helped there when you went to college." Arlene got up and went to her desk and pulled out the opened letter. She handed it to Jolene and sat back down. She looked earnestly at Jolene and continued, "Things change, Jolene, people change. You don't need to feel bad that you need to move on."

The words hit home. Jolene nodded her head slowly, and then she looked at the application the forest service had sent her. A job, different people, new memories, maybe an apartment or house in Chadron, something different. She looked at Arlene and smiled. "Maybe you're right. Maybe I'll fill out the application and drop it off on my way to South Dakota."

CHAPTER 20

South Dakota Cowboys

CHAUNCEY KNEW AS soon as he saw her that he had made a mistake asking her to come. It was too soon after her husband's death, and he could see the "don't touch me" signs over every square inch of her body. She was reaching into her Lincoln Navigator for her purse when he had walked up behind her from the barn. She was thinner than he had remembered her, and when she turned to him he was surprised to see she was much more attractive. He supposed the bruises on her face in August had something to do with that. But it was the haunting sadness that permeated her person that made him realize this might have been a bad idea.

"Hello, there." He smiled down at her.

"Hello, Chauncey," she answered, and didn't offer him her hand. He put his in his pockets, and leaned against the Lincoln before saying any more.

"I was just wondering if …" He paused and looked toward the barn, "If you had a good trip up here."

"Well, I didn't get lost," she said and then added, "the scenery is beautiful."

Some mournful barking came from the garage and she looked at Chauncey questioningly.

"Buzz got sprayed by a skunk this morning and I locked him up before you came."

She smiled and shook her head over that.

"I can carry your bags in, unless you would rather stay at my folks' place."

She looked at him a little surprised. "Would you rather I stay there?"

"Well, actually no, Jolene," and he gave a wry grin and shook his head. "This is a small community and people talk. Just wanted to give you a choice."

She shrugged. "It doesn't bother me if it doesn't bother you."

Chauncey wondered if it wasn't time to admit he made a mistake asking her here.

"Jolene, I want to say again that I'm sorry about your husband. I don't have any experience in these type of matters, and I'm … ah, probably going to say all the wrong things to you." He took a deep breath and continued. "I thought as two friends we could help each other out. I needed a rider, and I thought maybe you needed a little diversion. There's nothing more to it than that, but I may have rushed you a little."

She was looking at the cottonwood tree when he was talking, and when he finished she kept her eyes focused there. Finally she turned to look at him and said, "Thank you, Chauncey, I needed to hear that. And I needed to come. I've had too much time on my hands these past weeks. My aunt may have found a job for me in Chadron, which I suppose would be good."

She searched his face for a moment then gave a short bitter laugh. "I will admit this to you, Chauncey, because we are friends. This has been the hardest thing I've ever gone through and I'm mentally worn out. Being here is good. The work will be good for me, and I hope," she looked away for a second before turning her eyes back to his, "I hope I won't be too much of a drain on your good humor."

He opened the back door of the Navigator and brought out her bags to carry them in. "My good humor will survive this, my lady." His eyes twinkled down at her.

Jolene noticed as soon as she walked in the door that Chauncey had done some serious house cleaning, and said as much.

"I always clean house when I know I'm having company," he exhorted himself. "It's the drop-ins that take pot luck."

"Remind me to call you next time I'm running away from somebody," she replied dryly.

She looked around the galley kitchen while he was taking her bags down the hallway. It was an older kitchen, with white metal cupboards silhouetted against sunny yellow walls, a sink with double drain boards on each side, and a double nine-over-nine window above it. It had appealed to her the first time she saw it. The window looked south toward the barn and the cottonwood tree was framed in it. There was a Hoosier cupboard between the counters and the breakfast nook, and the eating area had windows all around so that it usually provided a sunny spot to sit. She ran her fingers lightly over the table before turning around and seeing him leaning in the doorway, one arm braced against the doorframe.

"Your home was a sanctuary for me, Chauncey. I have fond memories of it."

"Did I ever give you the guided tour?"

"No, but I'd love to see it."

He told her how he had always enjoyed his home, even if it was old, and from the kitchen he led the way into the dining room that she had already seen. Then he opened a door that she wasn't aware of that led to an upstairs. There were two bedrooms there. One was small, and one was quite large. The larger one had dormer windows on the south side and had a beautiful view of the river. Neither one was completely finished, but they had potential.

Back downstairs he told her that the living room had been an addition. He pointed out the cathedral ceiling, fireplace, bookcases, and hardwood floor. He knew it needed freshening up, or at least that's what his sister and mother told him, but he liked it. There was an open porch that faced the east and was accessed through the dining room.

The house had nooks and crannies that added interest, and he said he knew how it had looked in the beginning and how the former owners had added on. Altogether it was a comfortable home. He showed her the room down the hallway that was his office, and she wondered aloud how he ever found anything there. He grinned self-consciously and admitted his bookkeeping methods were unorthodox. The door to the mudroom was across the hall from his office, and there, Jolene knew from before, was also a laundry room and a basement door. Something she hadn't noticed when she was there the first time was the big pantry. It was tucked between the mudroom and laundry room, and was designed to hold large items and lots of groceries.

They went back to the kitchen, and he began to add water to the coffee maker. She remembered where the cups were and put them on the table.

"Chauncey, you really have a nice house. A big dining room for family get-togethers, the all important fireplace for cold weather, a mudroom for heavy coats and boots, several bedrooms ... it's a great home for the country."

He quirked an eyebrow at her. "What would you change?"

Her elbow was on the table with her chin resting on her closed hand. She pondered his question for a while. "Structurally, nothing. It has good flow; it's a comfortable house. Women always decorate differently than men, so that's where I'd make changes."

He poured their coffee and sat across from her. "Tessa, the ex, was always whining about this house. Didn't like it. Too old." He shook his head bitterly. "That's mainly what Tessa was about. Whining."

"How long were you together?"

"She lived here a year, and we were married for two years."

"No children, I take it."

"No children."

They sat together while the sun started going down, drinking their coffee and watching the slanted rays light up the western windows in the house and cast a burnished glow into the south windows of the kitchen. The prairie stretched out around them, the grasses moving in the sunset breeze.

Jolene looked around her as she took another swallow of her coffee. It was the most peaceful moment she had experienced for quite a while.

Chad Sullivan watched the woman in the saddle work his son's cattle with expertise. She seemed to have an instinct for the right place to be at the right time. She was a quiet woman, following Chauncey's instructions without a word.

There was a small crew to pregnancy test the cows and give them their fall shots. The day before, just Chauncey and this woman had brought in the whole herd, and when the men came that morning, Chauncey and she were already sorting the calves from the cows. Chad decided that even if Chauncey hadn't told his family she was a recent widow, he would have known something had happened in her life.

They ran the cows into another pen where the preg-testing chute was situated at the end of the alley. The pens broke down into a series of smaller pens until finally the cows went one by one into a narrow alley and the chute. Each cow was tested to see if she was expecting a calf. If she wasn't, she was marked, and would probably be sold.

Dennis, the neighbor doing the testing, donned his coveralls and stretched his arm into the plastic glove that extended to his shoulder. Chad worked the gates that allowed the cows into the chute, Chauncey gave them their shots and encouraged them along, and Jolene used Fox Trot to bring the cattle into the smaller pens.

Chase came along to aid where he could. He had his arm in a sling, and walked with a pronounced limp, but was still trying to open gates for Jolene.

Chad noticed when they finished the job that she put her horse in the barn and headed up to the house. When the four men came in for dinner, she had the table set and the food ready. She seemed comfortable with the group, and when Chauncey introduced her finally, she made gracious acknowledgements and kept putting food on the table.

They gathered around the dining room table, and Chauncey as usual asked the blessing. The "amen" was hardly said when Chad started passing food around. He was always a little embarrassed by Chauncey's enthusiasm for the Lord, but then, he reflected, Chauncey always had a way of being a little different from him, and he supposed that was one of the many reasons he branched off by himself.

Chase gave the attractive gal a few compliments, and Chad could see Dennis wondering to himself about where this young woman had come from. Everyone was shy of asking too many questions, and she wasn't overloading them with information.

Finally dessert was served and Chauncey poured the last round of coffee. Chad tipped back in his chair with the idea of finding out a little about this woman. She was listening to Dennis tell of one of his kids' escapades, and when he was done and everyone had chuckled over the story, Chad was ready with his question.

"Where did you say you were from?"

She turned toward him and answered quietly, "The sand hills of Nebraska."

"You and your husband had a ranch there?"

"No, that's where my family, the O'Neils, have lived since about 1888."

Chase was impressed. "The same ranch is still in your family?"

"Yes, actually my Uncle Walt lives in the same house my great grandparents did."

"What is your dad's name?" Chad wanted to know.

Jolene hesitated, then said, "His name was Spencer."

"Oh, your father has passed away. For some reason I thought it was your husband."

His comment was met with silence.

Jolene didn't want to embarrass anyone, and usually found when she mentioned her parents' deaths that people didn't know what to say or where to look. She generally avoided saying anything in a group. She was thinking how to answer when Chauncey broke into the conversation.

"Jolene's husband and Jolene's father have both passed away, isn't that right?" he asked, looking at her.

"That's right, and I might add, my mother was killed in the same accident that took my father's life. My Uncle Walt and Aunt Arlene finished raising me, so I know quite a lot about my great grandparents' home." She thought if she ended it on that note they might ask more about the ranch than her life. Wrong again.

Chad brought down his chair with a thump. "Why, that's terrible! What kind of accident did your folks have?"

"The trailer they were pulling came unhooked down a steep hill, and it tipped the pickup over. They were killed instantly." She looked at Chauncey with a silent plea to end this conversation.

Chad was about to ask more when Chauncey stood up and announced they'd better get those calves in and give them their shots so Dennis could get back home. They all scraped back their chairs, picked up their plates and silverware, and headed out to the kitchen.

Jolene stayed behind to put away the leftovers, and slowly cleared off the rest of the table. At least, she mused, she didn't have to break the news to Chad that not only was she an orphan, but also a widow, twice.

By the time she returned to the corrals, Dennis had already left. She tightened the cinch on Fox Trot and rode on out to help bring in the bawling calves.

Chauncey was quiet that evening. After supper, they cleared off the table together, and she started washing the few items that wouldn't fit into the dishwasher. He stood with his back against the counter and a frown on his face.

"I believe I'm having trouble figuring out how many people in your life are gone," he muttered at last.

She sighed. "Sometimes it seems like all of them are."

He grabbed a dishtowel and started wiping vigorously. She continued, "It's hard to explain to people, and they begin to look at me like I'm somehow to blame. It's just easier not to mention it."

"Well, you didn't mention your folks to me. Today was the first I knew about that part of your life. I guess," he looked a little uncomfortable, "that it isn't exactly my business to know any part of your life."

"That's true, Chauncey." She smiled and threw soap bubbles at him.

The next morning they took the hungry and bawling cows back to another fresh pasture. It was a fast ride, because the cows wanted grass and seemed to understand as Chauncey and Jolene were pushing them that it was waiting for them at the end of the trail. Buzz worked his skunk-drenched tail off, and when they were done and coming home, he found numerous spots in which to bathe.

Jolene had volunteered to give him a tomato bath, but Chauncey thought by the time he rolled in the dirt and found all the spots of water he would eventually wear the smell out.

The weaned calves were crying for their mothers, and yet some were already finding their feed and water. The corral would be their home for a couple of days, and then they would be chased to a smaller pasture where they would stay until spring.

In the afternoon Chauncey and Jolene trailered their horses over to Chauncey's parents' ranch and helped bring in the larger herd of cattle to start the whole process all over again. This time there were more riders, as both his mother and sister were helping round up. They had come up to Jolene in the pasture and introduced themselves, saying they sure appreciated her help, and after the work was done, Char, Chauncey's mother, wanted them all to come to the house for something to drink.

The house was a ranch style, very clean and very nicely decorated, and the Sullivans were gracious people. Jolene wanted to get their names straight, so she started down the list. "Chad, Char, Chase, Cheyenne, Chauncey. Now what about your name," she asked Chase's very pregnant wife.

"I broke the chain. My name is Alice," she laughed.

"And my husband's name is Alec," Cheyenne chimed in. "We always told Chauncey he needed an Alicia or Allison, but of course Chauncey never listens to any of us," she quickly hastened to add.

Later in the week when she and Alice were visiting alone, Jolene heard more about Chauncey and his ex-wife. Chase had been at Chauncey's when Tessa came home with the news that her father had bought them a house in town. She was overjoyed to think that now she could be working with a short commute and Chauncey could drive back and forth to the ranch.

Chase had said Chauncey's eyes grew cold, and he told Chase to clean out the horse trailer and back it up to the house. Chase didn't dare refuse. When he got to the house he saw a subdued Tessa being led around the house by a very quiet and determined Chauncey. He was helping her pack. He had grabbed boxes and sacks and anything that would hold household and clothing articles. He and Chase carried out any furniture that belonged to Tessa, and she was making little comments about moving so quickly.

Chase decided he had better ride into town with Chauncey in the pickup because he was worried that his younger brother might do something he would regret later. He had never seen Chauncey so angry, and it scared him whenever he looked into his ice-blue eyes.

They had unloaded everything at the new house, and Tessa's jovial father had joined them. However, one look at Chauncey's grim face told him he might have overstepped his bounds.

When everything was out of the trailer, Chauncey had looked at father and daughter. In a quiet voice that held no humor he had informed them that this was Tessa's new home. She was not to come back to his. The father started to protest but quickly stopped when Chauncey's eyes bored two holes in him.

He had walked into the lawyer's office on the way out of town. In moments he had arranged for the divorce papers to be drawn up. The lawyer knew Chauncey well, and one look at his determined face convinced him not to joke around or waste time.

For a year afterward Chauncey had remained angry and bitter, and his family was wondering if the twinkle and humor would ever come back. Amazingly, one day he appeared with the smiling Irish eyes, and he bounced back, enjoying life once more.

The Sullivans were a hard-working, happy bunch of people, similar, Jolene thought, to her family in Nebraska. She felt comfortable with them, and as they worked together she listened to their lighthearted banter with a smile on her face.

CHAPTER 21

Miss Grey's Wisdom

THE SNOW WAS falling in Chadron as Jolene drove down the holiday-decorated streets to her furnished apartment. When she let herself into the darkened room, the phone was ringing, and she made a dash to answer it before the caller hung up.

It was Patrick, and he and Marcella wanted her to spend Christmas Eve with them and the children. She readily agreed. A few moments later Miss Grey called and invited her to stay at her apartment while she was visiting in Denver. Jolene gratefully accepted her kind offer.

She fixed herself a light supper, eating it in front of the TV, and knew the evening was going to be long. After a couple hours of television, she shut off the set in disgust. Brewing a cup of tea, she let her mind wander. The office work was not challenging, but it was something to keep her from dwelling on her own thoughts. There was talk of needing someone to transfer to the Wall office in South Dakota, and she had applied for it, not really knowing why she did.

She added some honey to the cup of tea and carried it back to her tiny living room. Her throat felt scratchy, and this was one of Arlene's home remedies. She let her thoughts drift back to South Dakota, and Chauncey and his family.

She had worked there for ten days, and Chauncey had kept her entertained with his lighthearted comments. They had ridden a lot, and he had complimented her one afternoon as they were unsaddling their horses by saying she was the best help he had ever had. It pleased her. It seemed like the two of them worked well together. Two friends, he had said, and that also pleased her. He was likeable, and with his blue eyes and black hair, quite a handsome man.

She noticed he never touched her if he could help it. She appreciated that. And yet … and yet when she saw him cradle Cheyenne's little toddler against his big shoulder, she had thought how nice it would be to put her head down against that solid warmth and let the world go on without her for a while.

When she left they said casual goodbyes, and she felt unsettled the minute the Navigator headed out the driveway. She had looked back to wave, but he had already turned and was walking back into the house. Dumb Tessa, she thought, who had had it all and wanted to move to town. If Jolene had met a man like Chauncey in the very beginning, she sure as the world wouldn't be sitting here now, alone and feeling sorry for herself.

Now that you've met him, what are you doing sitting here alone and feeling sorry for yourself? She burned her mouth on her tea after that thought ricocheted through her mind.

She almost called him on the phone, and several times picked it up, but each time she replaced it on the cradle. She didn't know what she would say after she had dialed him.

Jolene stopped to visit Florence on her way to Denver for Christmas. She had brought her a gift, and she doubted Florence would like it, but she remembered Dexter's kindness, and thought she would do it for love of him.

She was surprised that she was greeted warmly, and immediately Florence put the coffee pot on. She seemed eager to talk and chatted on about many things. Then with a quivering mouth she mentioned the video at Dexter's funeral. "How are you going to go on without him, Jolene?" she asked tearfully.

Jolene fought her own tears down, and said softly, "I really don't know, Florence, but I must. I guess the Lord will give me the strength I need."

"I knew he loved you, but I never realized how much until that darn video. It made me cry, and you know how I hate to do that."

She quickly went on about her own affairs and the affairs of the town, and of Dale and his wife, and when Jolene got ready to leave she walked her to the door and surprised Jolene with a little hug. "But you shouldn't have gotten me anything. I never got you a present."

Jolene was several miles down the road before she laughed softly and said out loud, "So what else is new?" Yet she was glad she had stopped. It was the right thing to do.

When she and Miss Grey entered the penthouse Jolene thought she was going to lose her control immediately. It had changed, in the fact that it was now a home to a young couple with children, and yet she could feel Dexter all around her. Miss Grey looked at her with compassion and whispered, "Quick, Jolene, no one is using the powder room."

When she returned, she hoped no one but Edna Grey knew how upset she was. The same group that was there last Christmas Eve had gathered again, but no matter how hard they tried, it wasn't the same without Dexter. Somehow, no one could bear to bring up his name, and yet his presence was so missed that everything seemed to fall flat.

Finally, Jolene gave up. "I hope you don't mind, but I would like to share a few things about Dexter with you." She looked around the table and saw a few nods. "This isn't a new revelation to you, but he loved being in control." There were a few chuckles. She continued with a smile, "Most mornings we would lie in bed and Dexter would plan out our day, and then he would decide what he wanted me to wear. After that I would see him lost in thought and would know that he was planning how to fix my hair."

She laughed a little self-consciously and Patrick added that he wasn't surprised about that. She continued, "But somehow, even though I'm a little stubborn myself, I never minded because he had such good taste in clothes and he so enjoyed figuring out hairstyles, and wherever we went, we had a good time." She looked at her coffee cup. "He was the most fascinating man I ever met. The last weeks of his life were a testimony of his trust in God. I'm grateful that we had those days together." She stopped there. She had more to say, but she wondered if someone else would like to speak a few words.

Bob said softly, "You were like a kitten with an old cat, Jolene, and Dexter enjoyed that immensely. I knew him when we were just two young cats out of college, and decided to pool our resources together to get DeLange Designs started. He was a good, honest partner, and he and Helen and I had quite a few escapades with models and pictures and hair."

They all had stories to tell, and the more they talked about him, the better they began to feel. They missed him. He was an important part of their lives, and they all felt they were richer having known him. His dry humor, his good looks, even his arrogant ways added a dimension to their lives. Yet, it was time to move on. They all said so. Patrick acknowledged he was going to make a few changes in the salon. Edna Grey had some new thoughts in the bookkeeping department. Bob and Helen were slowing down and letting their son come in with the photography. And Jolene? They looked at her with concern. What would she be doing? She said she guessed she would be moving on also.

Later that evening when Edna Grey and Jolene were lounging in their pajamas and robes in the well-decorated and handsome apartment Edna had, Edna brought up Dexter again.

"I want to say this, Jolene, and I don't want you to take it wrong." Miss Grey took another swallow of cocoa. "You and Dexter were the talk of the salon. People still come in and look at your pictures, shake their heads, shed a few tears ... Oh, yes, dear, that's a fact," she said to Jolene's startled response. "Patrick is going to start removing some of the pictures, but he has several that will be framed."

She continued, "But I was concerned for you. Dexter dominated you. I think he was so possessive of you that even had he had his health, he would have wanted you all to himself forever. It worked for the duration of your short marriage, because you gave him everything he wanted. But what about children? I know he always was concerned that he would pass on his family history of heart problems and I worried about that because I knew you loved children. And what of your other interests? I worried about that too. The age difference would have mattered in later years." She stopped and looked at Jolene to see how she was reacting.

"I don't mean to be saying things that are out of line, Jolene. I've always admired you immensely. You took a very difficult man, loved him through a tumultuous experience, and gave him hope for eternity. And yes, dear, I know he gave you a lot also. There is no doubt in my mind that he loved you with a passion few men have."

For a while on that Christmas Eve, Jolene stared into the gas fireplace, forgetting where she was, forgetting her cocoa, forgetting Miss Grey. Dexter would always be an exciting chapter in her life that changed it forever, yet Edna Grey put her finger on the very page that had bothered Jolene the most.

A week later, on New Year's Eve, alone and in the little stone house, Jolene sat down and looked through the scrapbook the Lewises and Miss Grey had given her for Christmas. They had done an amazing amount of work and included many photos, newspaper articles, and modeling pictures from the catalogs and magazines. She had a box of tissue and a cup of coffee beside her and had told herself this was going to be her night to remember and grieve. She did both. She pored over each picture, remembering the events that led up to it, how Dexter had looked at her with his smoldering eyes that always thrilled her and how his slender and talented hands would work through her hair. She remembered how he looked in his black silk shirts, his firm build, his warmth. When she was through with the album, she went to the closet and admired the clothes he had bought for her, then on to the jewelry, and the perfumes, and then to his own colognes. She fingered through his Bible, and noted again how many places he had underlined.

The hours ticked away while she dwelt on the ways their lives had intertwined. He had continually dealt with his poor health without ever revealing the seriousness of it. He had tried to keep fit, he had developed a stroll that worked his heart as little as possible, and had made it his trademark, complete with an indifferent attitude. He had a vocation that made him relatively famous and yet was not strenuous on his heart. All these things he had done with a certain arrogance that made him attractive to her.

That same pride led him to marry her without revealing that their time together would be very short. She could be bitter about it and his lack of honesty, or she could thank God that for a brief time she had known his love. Edna Grey was right in saying he dominated her, and the issues she had mentioned, including not having children, had troubled Jolene. Their marriage had been like a beautiful fairytale, and she had felt like a pampered princess. Yet a small part of her knew that in time she would have wanted to live in the real world, complete with babies and puppies and matters important to her.

She had cried off and on throughout the evening. Then she had showered and put Dexter's pajamas on. It was almost midnight, and soon a new year would be starting. She would move on now. She had had her evening of remembering, and the rawness was healing. Tomorrow would be a new beginning. With God, she remembered, all things are possible.

CHAPTER 22

Dakota Blizzard

$\mathcal{I}$T WAS A cold and bleak January morning, and Arlene watched Walt and their sons stomp into the warm ranch house with cold feet and even colder hands. More problems had cropped up with the tractor they had supposedly fixed in the fall, which meant they had to fix them in the shop, which was heated, yet it was no match for the zero weather outside. It had also meant a delay in getting the cattle fed, which in Arlene's mind, was in close conjunction with the bombing of Pearl Harbor, if one were to judge from Walt's attitude.

She had learned that cinnamon rolls and coffee often were a great mood enhancer, and a sympathetic listener added to her husband's and sons' well being. With patience she listened to their report about each nut and bolt that needed replacing, but finally she interrupted with some news of her own.

"Jolene is being transferred to South Dakota."

"Where at?" Danny wanted to know.

"A little town on Interstate 90 called Wall." Arlene added, "I think it sort of sits on the Badlands Wall, and is where that big drug store is that so many people talk about."

Ben and Danny both had been there, they recalled, and said it seemed like a nice place. The drug store was fascinating, and the people were friendly. They couldn't seem to remember any Forest Service building, but then again, they hadn't been looking for it.

Walt ate his second cinnamon roll and looked unhappy. "With all the money Dexter left her, she sure wouldn't need to be working in an office."

Arlene noticed Danny and Ben look at each other. Their dad's worry about Jolene was an oft talked about subject, and his insistence that she was an O'Neil and had all the qualities of the O'Neil women when it came to horsemanship and cattle savvy often irked their wives, neither of whom enjoyed riding or working cattle.

Walt continued on with his grumblings. "I wonder why she doesn't go visit that Chauncey fellow again. They seemed to have a lot in common. Doggone it, if she lets the only fellow who is suited to her get away, I'm gonna sit down and have a heart to heart talk with her."

"It's a little too soon to be talking about her and any other fellow," sniffed Arlene in defense.

"Well, maybe not. I was at the little stone house when she left, and she told me she was going to have to put the year behind her and move on." Walt took another swallow of steaming coffee. "I told her then that she'd better find a rancher."

"Yeah," countered Ben. "My wife says there is no one like us ranchers to be married to." His droll comment was met by a hoot from his brother.

"My wife says the same thing. She says the ranch is a jealous mistress that no woman can compete with," Danny added.

Walt looked a little sourly at both young men. "That's just it. An O'Neil woman accepts all that and works hand and fist right there alongside." After an intense glare from Arlene he hastily added, "But I wouldn't trade my two beautiful daughters-in-law for anything or anybody. They have contributed many wonderful things to this ranch!" Arlene decided her husband had almost pacified everyone.

Walt would have had mixed feelings if he had known that very afternoon, with only a couple hours of daylight left and an increasing wind and snowy weather advisory predicted, Jolene was leaving Chadron and heading toward South Dakota and Chauncey's ranch.

Several times Jolene wondered if she should turn back, as she observed the heavy skies and spitting snowflakes, and watched the winds ruffling the snow-covered prairies, but then she would rationalize that she was packed and had warm clothes and a Thermos of hot coffee. The Lincoln Navigator was well equipped, and she was grateful Dexter had given it to her. She placed a lot of confidence that it would get her where she wanted to go.

She had finally called Chauncey the night before and had told him to beware, because she would be moving to South Dakota soon because of her job. She had said it lightly, hoping that he would respond enthusiastically. She was somewhat deflated that he didn't. When she asked him what he was doing, he claimed to be in mortal danger of a brain overload because he was trying to figure out how to install a computer he had just bought. He wondered if she knew about such things, and when she said she was somewhat computer literate, he wondered if she would like to come and help him. He mentioned that with Martin Luther King Jr. Day she would have a three-day weekend, and he would even fix her some chili and cinnamon rolls and let her pet Buzz.

She had responded that it would definitely be worth the trip to be able to pet the dog, and they had discussed other details, such as when she would be arriving there. After she hung up, she flew into a frenzy of packing so she could leave directly from work.

Now she had been on the road for an hour, and the conditions were worsening. Still, the visibility was at least a quarter of mile, and she hoped that maybe it would be better once she reached Rapid City. However, by the time she reached the hill that looked over the north country she would be traveling, her heart sank. It was almost dusk, and the lights of the truck stop below were blurry from the snowy conditions. She tried to call Chauncey on her cell phone, but when she didn't get an answer, she decided to keep on going.

At least, she consoled herself, she would be on gravel roads where the traffic would be at a minimum. She decided if she kept a slow, steady pace and kept on the road she shouldn't have any trouble.

The wind was beginning to pick up, and sometimes when she crested a hill she could hardly see the road in front of her. She knew how long it would normally take to get from the truck stop to where the turn off to Chauncey's ranch was, but now she was uncertain because of the darkness and the obliterated landmarks. To make matters worse, she was afraid she was lost. She worried she might have taken a wrong turn, although she was quite certain she had been staying on the main road. She had sent several prayerful requests for help and wondered if it ever bothered God that people like her were always wanting things. Just when she knew for a certainty that she was in trouble, she saw lights up ahead. She kept her slow, careful pace, and realized when she came abreast of the lights that she was at Chauncey's mailbox and he was waiting for her in his pickup.

She turned in and rolled down her window as he got out of his outfit.

"I'm so glad to see you!" she almost shouted.

"Not half as glad as I am to see you," he answered rather grimly. "I'll turn around and you can follow me home."

Carefully she followed him back to the ranch, and when he opened the shop doors and indicated she was to drive in, she breathed a sigh of gratitude. Getting out of the Navigator in the shop and out of the storm was more of a relief than she imagined possible.

"How long were you waiting for me?" she asked him as he came around to where she was standing.

"Long enough to start getting worried." He smiled down at her.

"I tried to call you but when I couldn't get you I decided to keep coming," she said, reaching into the Navigator to get her bags out. "I was beginning to think I was lost, and you, sir, will never know how relieved I was to see your lights!"

"It probably equals the relief I felt when I saw your lights," he said quietly. "I was really worried, Jolene."

They braved the wind and snow and hurried into the warmth of the house carrying Jolene's bags and other things. The mouth-watering smell of chili cooking in the Crock Pot permeated the air, and after Chauncey had taken her things back to the spare bedroom and she had shed her coat, she realized that she was not only hungry, but also overjoyed to be back in Chauncey's house.

"Look at you," he said softly, coming back into the kitchen. "You look like you stepped out of a designer catalog, and not like someone driving in bad weather for several hours."

She had on the same black slacks and dark green sweater she had worn to the office, plus some jewelry. She smiled at him. "Thank you, very kind sir, but I feel like I'm in knots!"

His eyes traveled slowly down her slim frame, from the sparkling pendant necklace she wore to the warm boots on her feet, and by the time he made the journey down her person he was shaking his head and smiling.

"Every time I see you, you get prettier. I just don't understand it."

"Maybe it's like the song, 'The girls all get prettier at closing time.' Have you been out much lately?"

"Haven't been out at all."

"That explains it. Compared to a cow or chicken, a woman probably looks pretty to you."

He grinned at her and seemed ready to say something more, but then he asked her if she was hungry.

They ate in the alcove off the kitchen and listened to the wind and snow beating against the windows. Jolene told him she never had eaten such delicious chili, and he reminded her that being hungry makes anything taste good. For a long time they visited about each other's news. He discovered she really didn't care that much for her job but needed something to do. She found out that his loan payment was due pretty quick, and that the interest was eating him up. They talked over coffee for another hour, and then amiably cleaned up the kitchen together.

Afterwards he put his hand lightly on her back and guided her into the living room, where the fireplace was snapping with a log fire. She commented on his furniture arrangement, and he laughed and told her that he had a summer and winter style, and now that it was winter, the furniture was grouped around the fireplace.

She gratefully sank into the rocker closest to the fireplace, and for a while relished in its comfort and the warmth of the wood fire.

Chauncey took the wing-back chair opposite her, and put his feet up on the huge old leather ottoman.

For a while he studied her then asked, "What happened, Jolene?"

She was a little confused by what he meant, and her raised eyebrows indicated that confusion.

"You're different than when you were here in October. What happened to make you change?" His blue eyes were serious.

She thought for a while, then smiled at him and shook her head. "I guess I'm moving on, Chauncey." She looked at him lounging in the chair with his denim shirt unbuttoned at the neck exposing a black winter tee underneath, his black hair with the unruly curl sweeping over his forehead, and his worn jeans and boots. She thought a more good-looking cowboy would be hard to find.

"Does that mean I can touch you now?" he asked, still serious.

She smiled again. "Did I have a 'Do not touch me' sign on in October?"

"Yes, ma'am, you did. I was scared to death I would accidentally brush up against you and take a whopping back hand."

"I noticed you acted frightened around me," she commented dryly.

He grinned at her lazily and studied her closely for several minutes without speaking. Finally he said in a soft voice, "I'm glad you're here, Jolene. I missed you."

She looked down at her hands in her lap. "I missed everything about your place, Chauncey. I missed Buzz, the house, the girls in the coop," she grinned at him, "and you, Mr. Sullivan."

"I'm grateful that I'm right up there with the chickens," he muttered, but there was a small glint in his eyes.

"Actually, you rate quite highly with me. I've sung your praises to my Uncle Walt so much that he thinks you must be the best cattleman in South Dakota."

"Well, well." Chauncey's blue eyes twinkled even more. "Coming from the best cattleman in Nebraska, that must be high praise." He added on a more humble note, "I might fall from your ratings after we put that blasted computer together."

Their subject changed then, and their talk centered upon their upcoming project. They decided to check out the boxes in the den, and Chauncey gave her his hand to help her up. She took it, and was hauled gently up to a standing position, and then his strong arms were around her, and he was looking into her eyes with questions in his own. She laid her head on his broad chest and sighed. Never had she felt so completely safe and peaceful as when Chauncey Sullivan put his arms around her in the middle of a South Dakota storm.

"To be quite truthful, I think before we put this together we should find you a different desk," Jolene informed Chauncey the next morning.

They had already fed the cattle, and it had involved taking the tractor and scoop and clearing out some snow so they could get to the pasture. The prairie looked white and fresh with all the new snow, and there were still light flakes sifting out of the low-lying clouds. She had enjoyed going with him and had brought her insulated coveralls and sturdy snow boots for just that reason. They had visited with the girls in the hen house, gathered fresh eggs, fed the cats and horses, and with Buzz dancing all around them had finally finished all the chores and headed into the house.

After some coffee and cinnamon rolls, they rolled up their sleeves to tackle the computer. Chauncey gave her remark some thought, and finally remembered an old oak desk in the basement.

When they went to look at it, Jolene pronounced it just the ticket. It was a huge desk, with many drawers and a pullout tray. Their only problem was going to be getting it upstairs. It was too wide to get through the doors, and after trying it several different ways, Chauncey decided he would have to take it apart. While he was on that mission, Jolene started clearing out a space for it in the den. She opted to place it on the wall where the telephone jack was, and that involved moving more things around. Because the room was so crowded, she started putting excess items in the hallway and soon had as much there as was in the den.

When they carted the desk up and placed it where she wanted it, the small room seemed full of desk. Nevertheless, when she cleaned it with lemon oil, it gave a good, solid look to the room, and they began un-boxing the computer. Soon there were cords and cables running every which way, and Jolene sat in the middle of it with the instructions, trying to figure out what to plug in where.

Chauncey looked baffled and decided to take the empty boxes out to make more room. Jolene heard the phone ring, but was absorbed by the directions. When Chauncey poked his head in the door twenty minutes later, she had everything hooked up and was feeling quite proud of herself.

They started putting things away, only to discover they had different ideas on filing. Jolene immediately informed him that he had no filing sense, and he looked at her with quirked eyebrow and said of course he did.

He proceeded to show her that opened bills were tossed on the desk; unopened ones were tossed on the floor. Bank statements were unopened until needed. She was horrified.

"It works perfectly fine. When the opened ones are paid, they get tossed into this box. Now tell me, what could be more simple than that?"

"What are all these other papers in boxes and on the floor?

"Beats me."

"But Chauncey, how do you find anything?"

"Most of the time I don't," he admitted cheerfully.

She stewed about that for a while and decided she needed another cup of coffee.

"Mr. Sullivan," she said primly when she returned to the messy den with two steaming mugs, "would you allow me to put your bookwork in order?"

"My lady," he replied gallantly, and bowed slightly, "I realize of course that I should protest your working so hard in my humble abode, but then I might offend your delicate sense of duty and cause you great distress. Therefore," he paused in his ramblings to take the proffered mug, "therefore, my fine lady, feel free to do what you want, and I, of course, will be more than happy to assist you in any way you deem appropriate." He looked at her with twinkling eyes as she started shaking her head at him and chortling at his Irish blarney.

Chauncey soon discovered she meant to take him at his word, and to his obvious chagrin, he was sorting through papers he hadn't bothered with in years. At the end of the day they were drained, but his den was in proper order with labeled files, a working computer, and bagfuls of unnecessary papers removed.

He escaped to do his evening chores, and Jolene wandered into the kitchen to brew more coffee. Looking out the south window she could see the wind was still whipping through the trees, blowing drifts of snow around. She ambled into the living room where the fireplace crackled and the aroma of fresh coffee filled the air, then on to the den to admire their work all over again. She sighed with contentment. What a great day this had been.

During the night the wind began to blow harder, and when the light of day came, it was to a world of white. More snow was falling and blizzard conditions were reported in western South Dakota.

Once again Jolene went out with Chauncey, but this time it was a more frightening experience. She stuck close to him for fear of getting lost in the blowing winds, and he soon realized that his cattle would have to go without their customary hay. He fought his way to where his yearling calves were wintering and was able to feed them, because it was a more sheltered area, but coming back to the barns was an ordeal. Several times he knew he drove the tractor off the road, but with zero visibility he had no true idea of where to go. They were glad to put the tractor in the barn and scramble to the house.

Jolene thought they looked like two snowmen walking in. Chauncey helped her out of her coat and coveralls, and soon her reddened cheeks were burning from the warmth of the house. She walked stiffly with cold legs to the counter where the coffee was, and pouring two mugs full, she took them into the living room where Chauncey was putting his wet gloves to dry by the fireplace.

Fluffing out her flattened hair she sank into the couch and put her stocking feet on the coffee table. Chauncey sat beside her and they silently drank their coffee while enjoying the heat from the fire.

"I just had a thought," he mused, still staring into the flames.

"Is it important?"

"Actually, it's a pretty good thought."

"But is it important?"

He reached over and ruffled her hair. "I don't think you're going to be able to leave for a few days. The roads will be blocked."

"Can we pay the county not to come out and clear them?"

"I'm scandalized that you would want to bribe county officials."

She smiled at him sheepishly and leaned closer to his warmth. He put his hand on her cold knee encased in denim, and gave it a gentle squeeze.

"I just had another thought," he mused again.

"Is it important?"

"Yes, ma'am, it is." He took a last swallow of coffee and set his empty cup on the coffee table. He turned to look at her, and his eyes were both twinkling and serious.

"Why don't you quit your job and just come and live with me?"

She looked at him over the rim of her mug. "But of course you are not serious, Mr. Sullivan."

"Yes, ma'am, I am serious." His eyes looked naughty as he put his arm on the back of the couch.

She reflected for a moment and set her cup down. "Out of the question, Mr. Sullivan. You would immediately discover I snore at night."

His arm was trailing down on her shoulders and his hand had discovered her arm sheathed in flannel. "Interestingly enough, ma'am, I have already discovered you snore, and I still want you to live here."

She grabbed a pillow and hit him with it. "I do not snore, Chauncey Sullivan, and you know it!"

He grabbed her laughing body, started giving her a good tickling, and pushed her into the cushions. They were both out of breath when he kissed her.

The ringing of the phone went unnoticed for a while, and when Chauncey raised his head, he took a deep breath before he slowly got up to answer it. Jolene stayed where she was, waiting for her heart to settle down to its normal pace.

She peeked over the back of the couch only to meet two piercing blue eyes watching her while he listened to the other end of the conversation. Sinking back down into the cushions, she muttered to herself that only an Irishman could kiss passionately one minute and gab the next.

Finally she went into the kitchen and started peeling carrots and potatoes to add to their roast beef dinner. Finishing that, she decided to start Chauncey's computer and get some data entered into the bookkeeping program. She had realized the day before that Chauncey operated on a shoestring budget, and he was telling the truth when he said the interest was taking a heavy toll on the ranch. He had been brutally honest with her about his financial affairs, and then in self-deprecation had admitted that while he loved everything about ranching, the bookwork was something he hated. She had volunteered to get the money program set up for him on the computer and he had agreed, but it was clear that he was not enthusiastic about it.

He came into the den bringing another chair and sat down beside her to watch what she was doing. She explained as she went along, and gradually he seemed to grasp the concept. He started rustling through some papers to give her more information. For an hour they worked together in compatibility until the aroma of their dinner began to make their stomachs growl.

"Dad said to tell you hello," Chauncey informed her while they were putting food on the table.

"I didn't know if you would tell them I was here or not," she worried out loud. "Do you think they approve of my staying here?"

Chauncey waited until she sat down before he said, "They all like you a lot, Jolene. They've been asking me since October to call you and invite you over; they know after my episode with what's her name I will be a moral young man."

He bowed his head to pray, and it touched a tender part of Jolene's heart to hear him ask the Lord for protection of the animals during the storm.

That evening when they were sitting on the comfortable chairs in front of the fireplace, Chauncey told her they should play the "What If" game. He had stretched his legs out on the ottoman again, and this time Jolene had placed hers there also. They were enjoying one final cup of coffee before unplugging the coffee maker for the day.

"I never heard of that before," Jolene countered, wondering if Chauncey had made it up.

"Everybody plays that game. What if I had done this or what if I had done that? I'll start." He looked at Jolene in half seriousness. "What if I said I love you?"

Jolene quickly took the challenge and replied, "What if I said I love you too?'

"What if I asked you to marry me?"

"What if I said yes?"

He grinned lazily at her and scrunched to get a more comfortable position in his chair. "What if I said when?"

Jolene squinted at him through the steam of her upraised coffee cup. "What if I said is this an actual proposal or a bunch of Irish poppycock?"

He laughed aloud, clearly enjoying himself. "What if I said this is an actual proposal?"

Jolene couldn't help smirking. "What if I said this is the strangest proposal I've ever gotten, and remember, I have had experience along this line?"

He looked into the fireplace with his eyes twinkling, then back at her. "What if I said you still haven't answered when we would get married?"

Jolene rocked a little faster. "What if I said when would you like to get married?"

He sat his cup down with a thud and in all seriousness said, "Soon."

"What happened to the 'What If' game?" Jolene wanted to know.

"Jolene," he said, reaching down to tweak her stocking foot, "we have a strange dilemma here." She nodded her head at him as he settled back into his chair. "You and I are about as perfect for each other as two people can be. I'd marry you tomorrow if I could, but ..." He looked at her intently, "Are you ready for another marriage?"

She rocked for several minutes and gazed into the fire. Finally she looked at him and said softly, "If this morning's couch episode is any indication, I'm almost ready."

They sat across from each other remembering the passion they shared and would have continued if Chad hadn't interrupted them with his phone call. Neither moved from the chairs, but their minds held their own conclusions.

The storm moved in an easterly direction during the night and by morning the western sky was clearing. The cold was intense, and when Chauncey looked at the thermometer it barely registered zero. He made a quick trip out to the barn to make sure his tractor heater was plugged in and then took care of his girls in the chicken house. They were grousing at each other but enjoyed their corn and wheat with their usual gusto.

After breakfast he headed out again. Jolene stayed behind to call the Chadron office and tell them she was snowbound in South Dakota. She quickly donned her coveralls and warmest mittens and pulled a green Scotch cap low over her ears and went outside. Even though the western sky was clearing, it was still cloudy where the morning sun rose, and with a stiff little breeze, the air was like ice crystals. For a moment she enjoyed the white beauty of the landscape. Drifts were everywhere, some as high as four feet or more. The wind had blown a lot of the snow into the draws, but there was still a foot or more covering most of the prairie.

She could hear Chauncey's tractor running and headed toward the sound. The drifts made walking difficult, and she was puffing by the time she found him. Together they fit into the tractor cab and headed toward the yearling's pasture. While he was checking the calves' water supply, she started scooping snow out of the feed bunks.

Chauncey watched Jolene working industriously as he dumped the chopped hay into the cleared bunks, and knew if he didn't keep his mind on his work she would invade every thought he had. With hungry cattle to feed it was important to be alert, he scolded himself. The prairie sometimes offered only one chance to do things right.

From the yearling pasture they took the tractor to the farther winter pasture for the cattle. Once the hungry cows heard them coming, they started making a beeline to the feeding grounds. Jolene popped out of the cab and opened the gate for Chauncey to drive into the hay yard. She stayed there to keep the cows out of the stacks while Chauncey went back and forth with the tractor and loader, dispersing the hay around in circles for the cattle to eat. He fed them extra to make up for the day before, and then grabbing a sack of cattle cubes from the cab, he walked through them and slowly poured them on the snow-covered ground. Within minutes the cows were milling around him trying to eat the mineral-packed cubes.

It was while he was walking through them that he noticed one of the cows breathing hard, and upon closer inspection he realized that she needed a shot of antibiotics. It would mean coming back with a horse and chasing her home. He could take better care of her if she was in the corral by the barn. She was one of his prize black cows, so he decided right after dinner he would be back for her. He noted that even if she was one of his better ones, she was also the orneriest, and even though she wasn't feeling well, she would still probably give him trouble chasing her.

Jolene convinced Chauncey that two riders would make it an easier job, so after dinner they saddled the horses and slowly made their way back to the pasture. Fox Trot was walking carefully, but Chauncey's horse was snorting and stomping.

"Tango!" Chauncey spoke sharply, "Straighten up."

Jolene looked at him with her mouth in a surprised "o." "Is your horse named Tango?" At his brief nod, she looked at him incredulously. "All this time I've never bothered to ask you what his name was. Do you know that my horse in Nebraska was named Tango?"

"Two Tangos?" he asked, wondering what the odds were that both of them had horses with the same name.

"My Tango is old. I've had him since I was a little kid. Now he mostly takes Walt's grandkids for short rides. Whoops!" she exclaimed as Fox Trot slid a little on the frozen ground.

Chauncey frowned. "It's slippery under that snow. We'll have to be careful chasing number forty-two."

He explained how they would drive the sick cow home, what gates they would be going through, and what corral they would put her in, and Jolene appreciated his instructions. They quickly picked out Forty-two, and even though she was sick, as Chauncey predicted, she was difficult to chase. Finally she headed toward home with her rattling breath, and in the cold air it looked like she was smoking.

They were almost to the corral when Forty-two gave a snort and spun to the side to escape. Fox Trot immediately swung to turn her, and in the process lost his footing. Before Jolene could jerk her foot out of the stirrup, horse and rider slammed down on the frozen ground.

Fox Trot scrambled to get up but kept sliding, and in one of those slides, Jolene was able to get her foot out of the stirrup and rolled over to the side, away from his hooves. She had the wind knocked out of her and couldn't answer Chauncey when he came tearing over to her hollering her name.

He knelt on the snow and gently cradled her in his arms. "Jolene, Jolene, answer me!" she heard him say, and slowly opened her eyes to stare into his pale face.

"I'm OK," she whispered.

He held her while she got her breath back, and when she struggled to sit up he looked at her with flashing blue eyes and told her to lie still.

"Chauncey," she gasped, "it's darn cold lying on this snow."

He looked a little wild. Finally taking a deep breath he asked her if anything was broken.

She moved her feet and legs, and shook her head. He slowly stood up and helped her to her feet, then he put his arms around her and held her against him for several minutes. She could feel his heart pounding even through the layers of clothes they both had on.

"We'd better get that cow before she gets clear back to the pasture," Jolene muttered into his chest.

"Fiddle with her. She can die for all I care," he spat out, and gathering the reins of the two horses with one hand and holding on to her with the other, he slowly took the little procession to the barn.

"I really am OK, Chauncey, just a little shook. We could go back and get her," Jolene suggested. He shook his head and unsaddled the horses while she sat on a bale of hay.

"You might be a little shook, but I'm almost a basket case," he stated flatly as they walked toward the house. When they got to the mudroom he peeled off her coveralls and continued, "I never want to see you underneath a horse again, Jolene." He started pulling off her boots while she leaned against him. "I don't know how you ever kicked free. I had visions of Fox Trot dragging you all over the snow." He ran his hands through her tousled hair, and then pulled her close to him again. "My lady, you scared me half to death," he whispered a bit raggedly.

She sighed and wrapped her arms around his solid waist. Laying her head on his chest she murmured, "I scared myself. It happened so fast that I was on the ground before I knew what happened." She looked up at him, "But I really am fine, Chauncey. It could have been so much worse."

The phone started ringing and he exploded. "That miserable phone! I should jerk it out!" He stomped over to where it shrilled, and barked a hello into the receiver. He listened with irritation written all over his face and snapped, "No, we don't need any help." He paused and listened with growing impatience and spat out, "Yes, sir, I am a bit touchy. Fox Trot fell with Jolene, and no, she's not hurt but if you would ever get off this phone I could see what damage has been done, and yes I'll call if we need help. Goodbye." He ran the last sentence all together and slammed the phone down.

"Good grief, I moved out of there so I wouldn't have to have all his advice and what does he do but call me every time there's a change in the weather," he muttered while turning around. He met Jolene's dancing green eyes as her shoulders twitched with suppressed laughter. Shaking his head, he walked over and swatted her gently.

He insisted she stay in the house the rest of the afternoon, and while he was out finishing chores, she snuggled into the cushions on the couch and slept. When she woke up it was twilight, and the soft light of the fireplace cast shadows in the room. She groaned as she sat up, flexing sore muscles, and then jerked with surprise to see Chauncey in the wing chair watching her.

"Hello," she croaked with her still-sleepy voice. He nodded, but didn't say anything. She yawned and eased back into the cushions. "Did you get everything done?"

Once again he nodded, then got up and went into the kitchen and brought back two mugs of coffee. Handing her one, he sat back down in his chair.

"Jolene," he said softly, "I've been thinking."

"Is it important?" she croaked again and cleared her throat.

"Yes, my lady, very important."

She took several swallows of very good coffee while she waited for him to continue. He sat musing silently while watching her, his blue eyes serious.

"I'm probably getting the cart before the horse, but I want you to consider this." He paused again. "It isn't good for you to be here, sleeping in the room next to mine." He shook his head. "It's like a time bomb, Jolene. Either we get married soon, and I mean soon, or we'll have to stop being together like this."

She took another swallow of coffee and didn't trust herself to say anything for a while. Then she slowly nodded her head and whispered, "I know."

"The trouble with being a rancher is that we're tied to the place. Cattle to feed in the winter, then calving in the spring, then haying, and finally in July or August a little break. I just do not want to wait until then to get married, do you?"

She shook her head and sensed her heart revving up.

"Tell me what you think, Jolene," he asked her softly.

She uncurled herself from the couch and stood up. She walked around the living room and then back to the fireplace where he sat, and then she eased herself on his lap and kissed him. "What if you tell me first what you're thinking?" she whispered.

"I can't think clearly when you're this close to me." He nuzzled the hollow of her throat. When she started to get up he pulled her back down and she curled herself into his shoulder. For a while they sat in silence listening to the crackling of the logs. Then he began again.

"I'll tell you what I think. I want you to give Chadron their two-week notice that you're quitting. I want you to go back to Walt's and start packing, and I'll come and get you. We could get married in February, before calving starts."

She mulled that over and had a question. "Are you sure you love me enough to take all my emotional baggage?"

"What baggage, Jolene? You're one of the most sensible women I know."

"I go through husbands rather fast."

He tousled her hair. "You'd better love this one a lot because he's not going anywhere, and you'll be stuck with him for life."

"Chauncey," she draped one long leg over the side of the chair, "does it seem strange to you that I could love again so soon?"

"I think the Lord led you to me. As I said before, we're a perfect match."

She sat up and looked at him. "It is strange how I came here, almost like God was saying to me that He had a grand plan in the weaving of my life. He gave me a little glimpse of the ranch and you, and then took me back to Dexter. When I hit rock bottom and complained, He reminded me about you." She sat on his lap with the light of the fireplace reflecting on their faces.

"This is where I belong, Chauncey. I feel it every time I come here." She looked at him with questioning eyes. "But what will people think of me?"

He brought her closer to him and said softly, "It only matters what God thinks. Why don't you ask Him?"

CHAPTER 23

Rainbow of Promise

*A*RLENE SAT ON her kitchen chair with flour on her cheeks and a stunned expression on her face. Walt looked at her in alarm when he came into the room. When he asked what was wrong, she could only shake her head in disbelief. He asked her again with worry in his voice and she squeaked one word. "Jolene."

Walt loved his two sons as only a father could, but Jolene had held a soft spot in his heart since the day she was born. He knew he raved about her O'Neil blood until everyone was tired of it, but he justified it to himself every time he saw her on a horse or working with cattle. He wasn't happy when she married John, but he tried to be gracious for her sake. Dexter was a complete surprise, and even though he liked him, he thought he was all wrong for his niece. He grieved for her sorrow and continually prayed God would grant her some happiness with a rancher. His first reaction over Arlene's demeanor was horror that Jolene had been in an accident. He spoke sharply to Arlene and demanded to know what was wrong.

She roused herself with difficulty. "I just got off the phone with Jolene." Walt knew instant relief. "You will not believe what she told me. You will not believe it. I can hardly—I just can't see—what is the girl thinking of?"

"What? What? Tell me something for heaven's sake!"

Arlene's eyes snapped. "Well, first of all, she's quitting her job."

"Is that a big deal? It's meager pay for someone who has the money Jolene has."

"And," Arlene stressed the word with indignation, and repeated it louder, "and she is going to get married, again, in February." She shook her head. "What is she thinking about?"

Walt was beginning to feel quite satisfied. "Who's the lucky fellow?"

"That Chauncey fellow from South Dakota." Arlene slapped the table with her hand.

"Aha! Aha! Finally she listened to Uncle Walt!" He did an awkward little jig over to Arlene. "This time she is right where she belongs! This time, I tell you, this time Jolene will be happier than she's ever been in her life! This time …" He was interrupted by Arlene's sharp rejoinder.

"This time she is only waiting five months! Five months, for heaven's sake, Walt! What are people going to say?"

"Well," said Walt defensively, "what's the use of waiting any longer to be happy, for crying out loud? The girl has had nothing but one heartache after another. She deserves to have a rainbow, Arlene O'Neil, and why should she wait to enjoy it?" He started rummaging thru a drawer until he found what he was looking for. Holding up a tattered page from the devotional *Our Daily Bread,* he read the words with a flourish. "When the sunshine of God's love meets the showers of our sorrow, the rainbow of promise appears."

He put his hand on Arlene's shoulder. "I'd say that just about sums up the situation for Jolene, Mrs. O'Neil."

Arlene stopped fretting and sat still for a minute. Then she stood up and planted a flour-smacked kiss on his leathery cheek. "I guess that's true, but it still seems too soon."

Jolene drove into Walt and Arlene's yard the first week of February and bounded out of her vehicle with a bounce. She hugged her aunt, and when Walt heard her voice he came beaming out the door and gave her a bear hug that almost crushed her ribs.

"Finally listened to your Uncle Walt, didn't you," he gloated unabashedly, and Arlene swatted his shoulder.

"He's been carrying on like this since he heard the news," she groused.

Jolene grinned at both of them and said, "He's coming to get me and my things in a week, so you'll get to meet him. I know you'll like him ... after all, he's Irish!"

"But best of all, he's a rancher," Walt beamed. "Tell me about that place, Jolene."

For the next hour Jolene filled them in on all the details she could think of, then waving goodbye, she went down to the little stone house. It was cozy warm, thanks to Walt's consideration, and she walked through thinking of what she would take and what she would leave. She had left most of her parents' furniture in their house, and when Ben and Sarah moved in, they kept what they wanted and stored the rest in Arlene's basement. She decided she would see what was there, and then for Arlene's sake, she would get rid of what she didn't want.

The day flew by as she went through closets and emptied them out. She found the flag that was presented to her at John's funeral and quickly went outside to the Navigator to get the box she wanted for it.

She wrote a note to the Harris family, telling them that she was getting remarried, and that she was emptying out her little home on the ranch. She wanted them to have John's flag and the wooden box she was sending with it. She said that some American Legions across the country were putting up the flags in the boxes as memorials to the veterans, and she was including his military pins and ribbons and his picture. She ended by wishing them all well and added the note to the package. "There," she sighed. She felt like she had tied up a loose end.

That evening after her shower, she put Dexter's pajamas on for the last time. She remembered Chauncey's face when he had seen her in them. It was when she and Fox Trot had their mishap, and she had showered that evening and was preparing to go to bed early. As usual, she had put Dexter's pajamas on and was heading down the hall to her room. She didn't know Chauncey was standing in his doorway until he stopped her to ask if she had any black and blue marks. She raised up one pajama leg to show him, and in the light he looked her up and down and said when she was his wife, she would wear different pajamas. Even though it was a reasonable statement, she had bristled slightly. She informed him that she intended to, but she didn't bring any others along, and they weren't married yet. He reached out to touch her then drew his hand back. "My lady," he said softly, "I just can't cuddle a woman who wears another man's pajamas." He had gone into his room and shut the door in her startled face.

She had tossed and turned all that night and wanted to blame it on her hurting body, but wondered if it could partly be what he had said to her. They were both quiet the next morning, and while they were out doing chores, they had seen the snowplow coming through. She wondered if she should leave that afternoon, but the realization that there were still unresolved issues between them made her hesitate.

At noon he wanted to see her leg again, and when she rolled up her pant leg she was surprised to see how black and blue it was. He was horrified, and wondered if she was bruised elsewhere. She told him she hadn't paid much attention when she was getting dressed. He brusquely raised her sweater and swore when he saw her side and back. He would not let her leave, he said, until she was in better shape. She reminded him that driving down the road wasn't exactly hard work. He had looked at her rather sadly and had asked her if she wanted to leave, and she had wrapped her arms around his neck and sobbed that she never wanted to leave, and then she rambled on about not having any other pajamas and she didn't want him to be mad at her, and by the time they comforted each other the afternoon was far spent, and it was too late for her to leave.

The following morning their decision had been made, and in her purse was the resignation letter to the Chadron office. She thought the next two weeks would never end.

After she crawled into her bed at the little stone house that night she lay awake thinking of all the things she wanted to do the next few days. Then she thought of Chauncey, and how hard it was to say goodbye to him the morning she left for Chadron. She thought of the ranch and the house she would be living in, and her mind couldn't stop redecorating the rooms. She remembered she hadn't prayed yet, and with good intentions started telling the Lord how thankful she was for His wonderful planning of her life. She was asleep in minutes.

For the next couple of days she was busy loading the Navigator with articles she would need right away at Chauncey's. She was amazed at what she had collected in the little house, and had a hard time deciding what to take and what to throw away.

Arlene went with her to the basement, and she was surprised to see her dad's desk there. Arlene looked at her and said softly, "Ben thought you might want this, and it's been down here for quite a while." Jolene ran her fingers over the top of it and nodded her head.

Another find that she had overlooked before was the box of her mother's dishes. She was elated, and soon there was a pile that would go to South Dakota, and another pile that would be thrown away.

"Hurray, Arlene! You will finally get your basement back!" She hugged her plump and smiling aunt.

Arlene and her daughters-in-law had a conspiracy among them, and it was hard for Arlene to be around Jolene and not give it away.

They had consorted with Chauncey, and were planning Jolene's wedding to be right there at the ranch with the immediate family present. They were busy with the details and many times wondered why Jolene didn't tumble on to the fact.

But Jolene was thinking of other things. She could hardly wait to see Chauncey, and counted the days, then the hours, until he came. She heard his diesel pickup before she saw it and was waiting outside the stone house when he drove up. He stepped out with his blue eyes twinkling and she was in his arms in seconds.

"I missed you!" she murmured to him in between kisses.

"Good. I was afraid you might tell me you missed the ranch first, then me," he teased her.

He had gotten a very early start, so it was still mid-morning when they started loading things up.

Both Ben and Danny came over to the stone house to help with the bigger things, and they sized up Chauncey Sullivan in a hurry and liked what they saw.

Walt didn't meet Chauncey until they drove up to his house to load the furniture there. Walt shook his hand and noticed it was hard and strong. He could see the broad shoulders knew how to work, and he liked the honesty that smiled from Chauncey's eyes. They talked cattle and weather, and Walt approved heartily of this young man.

Jolene thought Arlene looked a little flustered as she was fixing the midday meal and she thought with a pang that this was extra work again for her aunt. She was surprised when Danny and his wife showed up with toddlers in tow, and even more so when Ben and Sarah and little ones came trailing in. She thought it was no wonder that Arlene looked a little frazzled, and then her astonishment grew as Arlene herded them all into the dining room and the local minister was sitting there visiting with Chauncey. It wasn't until she saw him in a white shirt and black denim jeans that she realized something was going on. Sarah was pulling her out of the room and guiding her upstairs, and when they reached Jolene's old room, she saw the outfit she had described to Sarah and Danny's wife as the one she would be married in.

"You schemers, you!" She fondly scolded them, and listened to their laughing confession of how they arranged everything with Chauncey's help over the phone. Quickly she put on the taupe-colored straight skirt with it's matching taupe and white sweater that she had bought in Chadron. The girls had thought of everything, even to the perfume, and Chauncey had brought a pearl necklace he wanted her to wear. It took very little time to style her casual hairdo, and in less than fifteen minutes they were back downstairs.

Chauncey thought Jolene had never looked as beautiful as when she came downstairs. In front of the rock fireplace with it's hewn mantle decorated in red and white roses, Jolene and Chauncey exchanged their vows, and Chauncey slipped the plain gold band that Jolene had requested on her slender finger. Then he took her into his arms and kissed her without a bashful thought about her family watching. Her green eyes sparkled with happiness as she held out her hand to him, and they couldn't stop looking at each other during the minister's short ceremony.

Afterwards they all gathered around the big dining room table and there was delightful fellowship among them that would stay in their memories for many months. After the roast beef dinner, Arlene came in with a wedding cake she had baked, and Jolene and the daughters-in-law helped serve it.

All too soon the party had to end, and soon the pickup and horse trailer, and the Navigator, were ready to hit the road. While they were standing outside, Walt motioned for them to come to the back of Walt's pickup. He said he had a little something for them, and his family looked at one another curiously.

He uncovered two saddles that had been meticulously cleaned. They had belonged to Jolene's parents, and Walt wanted her to have them. He also had cleaned their bridles, and even had her dad's spurs and his rope. It was a tearful moment, and Jolene hugged him and thanked him over and over. Chauncey looked them over carefully, commenting on the leatherwork, the make of the saddles, and in general, endearing himself to everyone with his tactfulness. They were loaded with extreme care in the back seat of Chauncey's pickup.

It would be a long drive home with each driving their own vehicle, so once again goodbyes were said. Jolene told them they had made her wedding day perfect, and she could never thank them enough. As she was leaving the yard she took another look at the familiar barns, the old ranch house, and her waving family. She tapped the horn several times and put her arm out the open window for a farewell salute. She heard Chauncey's horse trailer rattling over the auto gate, saw the brim of his hat reflected in the side mirror, and settled more comfortably in the seat as she followed him to South Dakota.

CHAPTER 24

Settling In

THE AFTERNOON SUN highlighted the prairies, and Jolene enjoyed the familiar countryside she was passing through. As she drove she began to pray. *Heavenly Father, You have taken me through the highest mountaintops and into the deepest valleys. But You have always been with me. I appreciate that, Lord. I ask Your guidance in this marriage. I know there will be problems, but with You guiding both Chauncey and me, we should be able to work through them. I know that by myself I make wrong choices, say the wrong things, think the wrong thoughts. It's only when You guide me that I am able to do what is best.* Her eyes blurred for a second with the sincerity of those words.

Her thoughts rambled back to their wedding and she continued, *Lord, bless Aunt Arlene and Sarah and Tina for putting that beautiful wedding together. They really went the extra mile, and I appreciate it so much. And bless the minister for coming to the ranch and gracing us with his words of advice. Bless Uncle Walt for giving me my parents' saddles and tack. He couldn't have done one other thing that would have pleased me as much. I remember Mom and Dad riding through the pastures on those saddles and enjoying the ranch. Thank You for my parents, Lord. They gave me a good foundation in knowing You.*

Chauncey's pickup and horse trailer ate up the miles ahead of her, and once he hit the highway he consistently drove the top of the speed limit. There was limited traffic so it was an easy drive over the Nebraska highways. She thought of Chauncey and how easily he fit into the family. They had liked him, she knew that right away.

Lord, You have given me everything I ever wanted with Chauncey. He is so easy to love, with his gentle manner, good looks, humorous ways. Most importantly, though, he loves You. It's amazing, Father God, how You brought us together. Lord, Chauncey has a beautiful ranch, and no money. I have money because of all those who loved me and are now with You. This is a tricky situation, Lord. Chauncey is a proud man, and probably won't want any help from me. I pray You will guide me with Your wisdom and help me do Your perfect will.

The miles clicked away while she thought of others she wanted to pray for. Before she realized it, they were in South Dakota, and Chauncey was pulling off the road by a café near Hot Springs.

As she drove beside his pickup and horse trailer, she noticed he was checking to make sure everything was in proper order. She appreciated his caution and attention to details, and also appreciated the way her husband looked in his denim jacket, jeans, and boots.

Chauncey had pulled away from the O'Neils knowing that he was blessed to be a part of their family. The saddles that he had in the back of his cab touched his tender heart, and he wanted to make sure they were always taken care of properly. He looked in the side mirrors and saw Jolene following him and counted her as one of his richest blessings. *Lord, she is beautiful. I've loved her since the moment I laid eyes on her, even when I didn't have any right to. Even when she was battered and bruised and her heart was breaking. She's a feisty gal, tough, and yet warm-hearted.*

Lord, thank You for reminding me that I made a promise to You after my disaster with Tessa that I would never take another woman into my bed unless we were married. Thank You for not letting me sleep with Jolene until she was my wife. You know how hard it was to shut the door in her face that night. Even when she was in his pajamas, I still wanted her. I could not have carried that promise through unless You had helped me.

He thought of their wedding, and knew he owed the O'Neils a big thanks for putting it together. He thought of when they would get to the ranch, and how he and Jolene would share his home. He had bought flowers for the occasion, and had felt like a darn fool at that, but he thought it would add a special touch, and she was worth anything extra he could do for her.

But Lord, there will be hard times ahead, when this or that will remind her of him, and I won't know how to handle it. I'll need Your help, Your wisdom. I hope she realizes that I can't spend money on her like he did. It looks like he gave her the moon and stars. Like that Lincoln Navigator. One thing we've never talked about is her money. She doesn't bring it up, I don't ask. Help us to work through these problems, Lord.

Chauncey checked his mirror again and Jolene was still following.

Lord, I asked that You give us an unsettling spirit if we were rushing things too fast. We both felt comfortable with going ahead at breakneck speed. I so wanted her there with me all the time, and she was at loose ends, wanting a home. I see her, Lord, loving my old house, wanting to fix it up, and I can't wait to have her begin. Maybe in a way I should be grateful to Tessa for showing me that women like Jolene are a rare prize. Chauncey chuckled to himself over that thought. He never thought he would be grateful to Tessa for anything.

He thought if they ate at the café by Hot Springs it would be about the halfway point. He made sure she was following him and when they were both out of their vehicles he watched her walk towards him with her blond hair blowing slightly in the breeze. He was positive he was the luckiest man in the world.

They pulled into the ranch in the late evening, and Chauncey put the loaded trailer and pickup in the shop. He and Jolene started unloading the Navigator in the crisp air, and both had suitcases in tow as they walked up to the door.

Jolene was about to enter when she heard Chauncey's voice.

"Put your suitcase down, Jolene," he ordered, and she looked at him with a frown.

"Put it down," he insisted, and stood abreast of her. His eyes were laughing, and he reached over to open the door. "Don't look so grumpy, my lady. This is the customary thing to do." And in so saying he swooped her into his arms and carried her over the threshold.

She laughed with him and kissed those tantalizing lips. Then he dropped her with a thud and told her now she could bring the suitcases in. She swatted him for that and was still chuckling when she came back in. She followed him down the hallway and stood a second before she entered his bedroom. She had only glanced in before, but now she looked the room over carefully. When he saw her standing there he came over to take the luggage and usher her on in.

"It's not fancy, Jolene," he wrapped his arms around her, "but it's ours."

She laid her head on his chest and felt her eyes sting with unshed tears. She took a shuddering breath. He quickly raised her chin with one hand. "What is it?" he asked softly, his face etched with concern.

"It's ours, Chauncey. It seems like I've wandered from place to place for so many years. Now you've given me a home." She looked at him with brimming eyes. "I'm so happy, darling," she whispered. He kissed her tear-filled eyes, her cheeks, her trembling lips, and held her close to him.

Chad Sullivan was on a mission, and he was in a hurry. Telling Char to hurry up, he bolted out the door and into his waiting pickup, expecting her to follow closely, which she did.

"What's the hurry and where are we going?" she asked a little breathlessly as they bounced down the road.

"We're going to Chauncey's so I can borrow Molly for the grandkids, and I want to catch him before he leaves to feed his cattle."

"But why am I coming along?" Char almost wailed. She hadn't had her morning coffee yet and couldn't see the point of coming along just for the ride.

"I want you to talk some sense into him about that Jolene woman. He won't talk to me except to tell me to mind my own business, but he might listen to you." Chad was still irritated that Jolene had come and gone before he got to talk to her again.

"Chad," Char said sternly, "I know you want Chauncey settled and you think she's the one for him, but you've got to stay out of his affairs. He's told you that enough times."

"Yeah, bites my head off every time I call over there," Chad muttered.

"Have you talked to him about Molly?" Char wanted to know.

"Well, no, couldn't get a hold of him yesterday. Don't know where he went."

"For heaven's sakes, Chad," Char sounded exasperated. "Why didn't you call this morning to at least ask him?"

"Well, I'll ask him when we get there," Chad said belligerently, and to him it made perfect sense.

When they pulled up to Chauncey's house, they couldn't see any vehicle, but Buzz was excited to see them. "Chauncey must still be inside, if Buzz is here," Chad decided. "Let's go in, and you can talk to him while I get Molly."

Char said maybe she could talk Chauncey out of a cup of coffee and followed Chad up the sidewalk. He didn't bother to knock, which made Char chastise him, and seeing Chauncey's work coat still hanging in the mudroom, he loped down the hall to "get that boy up."

When he burst into the bedroom, he had no idea he was going to see "that boy" in bed kissing a blonde-haired woman in a passionate embrace with the covers strewn in complete disarray around them. He gasped and then yelled, "What's going on here!"

Chauncey jerked some blankets over Jolene and glaring at his dad he yelled back, "Can't you stay out of married people's bedrooms?"

Chad spun on his heel and hurried back down the hallway, sputtering and mumbling all the way, and when he got to the kitchen where Char was making coffee, he hollered at her to follow him.

Char made it clear she had had enough. "Sit your miserable tail down here, Chad Sullivan. You go around like a chicken with its head cut off. Sit down and cool your heels and let Chauncey have his say to you."

To her great surprise he slumped into a chair without saying a word.

It didn't take long to hear Chauncey stomping down the hall. When he rounded the corner he hadn't bothered to button his shirt, his black hair was tousled, and he had war in his eyes. He zeroed in on his dad.

Chauncey wanted to give his father a piece of his mind. He wanted to yell and stomp and vent his grievances, yet Jolene's whispered words, "Take it easy on him, Chauncey," were on his mind, and when he saw the whipped look on Chad's face, he cooled down a little.

He looked at both of them with irritation, and kept his voice to a quiet shout. "What are you doing here? You never," and he stressed the word *never*, "come into my house. Good grief, the first morning I'm married, here you come, and into my bedroom no less."

Char tiptoed over to him and kissed his whiskered cheek. "Congratulations, Chauncey, we're happy for you … and extremely embarrassed." She looked over her shoulder, "Aren't we, Chad?"

Probably to salvage his wounded dignity, Chad muttered, "You could have told us you were getting married. Man, we didn't know anything about it."

Chauncey was ready to retort when Jolene came gliding in with bare feet, wearing jeans and a tee. Her hair was tousled, but her eyes were dancing. She walked over to the flustered Chad and gave him a kiss on the cheek.

"Hello, Dad." She grinned and then walked over to Char and hugged her. "I think we have some doughnuts here someplace, and Chauncey can get us some cups."

There was stunned silence for a couple of seconds. Then Char burst out laughing and so did Jolene. It took the two men considerably longer to see the humor of the situation.

Sitting around the table eating doughnuts and drinking coffee, Chauncey and Jolene filled his parents in on the details of their wedding and her move to the ranch. Chad told her how sorry he was to burst into their bedroom like that, and Jolene accepted his apology with graciousness. Chauncey would have liked to say more to his dad, but wondered if finally Chad had learned a little lesson in tactfulness.

Before the men left to load up Molly, Chad stood before Jolene and said with all the sincerity he possessed, "Welcome to the family, Jolene. We're honored you joined us." Chauncey forgave his dad for a lot of things after that remark.

After everyone had left and the house had settled into quietness, Jolene took her coffee cup and wandered through the rooms,

251

deciding where to put her household items. She didn't have a lot of things, but what she did have she treasured. She planned to put her dad's desk in the living room where the morning sun would make an inviting spot for her own bookwork. Her mother's mission oak china cupboard would go in the dining room and would hold her dishes. The hall tree that had belonged to Great-Grandmother O'Neil would also go in the dining room beside the entry door. She also had an antique dresser that she would put in the guest room, and several other smaller pieces of furniture that held memories for her that she would find places for later.

She walked back into the sunny kitchen, and mentally rearranged the cupboards. The cookware she and John had received for a wedding gift would replace some of Chauncey's battered kettles, and she decided to replace his mismatched table settings with her complete set of Fiestaware. She thought the dishes would complement the sunny yellow of the kitchen.

While she was waiting for Chauncey to back up the trailer she started clearing out the cupboards and putting things in boxes. She hoped he wouldn't think she was presumptuous to begin without consulting him. Finishing that, she started cleaning and sweeping the mudroom, then went back into the bedroom to unpack her clothes. She admired again the lovely roses that Chauncey had put there, and then stood and looked at this room they would share.

She thought of the look on his face when he asked her when she first knew she loved him. She had told him that he had been on her mind since October, but probably realized it when he pulled her up from the chair the first evening she was there in January. She leaned over the bed to pull up the covers and giggled a little thinking of Chad's face this morning. She and Chauncey had been so preoccupied with each other that they hadn't heard a thing until he hollered at them. Chauncey had moved like lightning to drag a cover over her bare shoulders, and she barely had time to turn her head and see the shocked look on Chad's face before he pivoted out of the doorway. She shook her head. It looked like life would be interesting!

By evening the house had a different look. Its barebones bachelor décor had given way to a softer decorated style, and Jolene had taken great delight in adding those touches. Chauncey admired everything she had done, and he especially appreciated coming in from chores and seeing his contented wife cooking supper.

To Chauncey's chagrin his family hosted a neighborhood reception for them a couple of weeks later at the Sullivans' ranch house. They had put a picture of Chauncey and Jolene in the paper, and on a chilly Sunday in late February cars started gathering and the house became more and more crowded as well wishers came to greet them.

They stood together at the entry way and greeted each one as they came in, Chauncey in jeans and a blue shirt that made his eyes vividly blue, and Jolene in black dress pants and a green and white checked sweater that decidedly accented her eyes. People were happy that Chauncey had found his bride and as he introduced her to each one there was no mistaking the pride in his voice. When it seemed like there would be no more newcomers, they had mingled with the guests and were standing side by side with his arm around her when one of the ladies looked at Jolene and said she looked so familiar that she felt she knew her.

Jolene was sure she had never met her before, but the lady was insistent that she knew her. Finally she wondered what her maiden name was, but O'Neil didn't ring any bells with her. Then she wondered what Jolene's married name was, and when Jolene said DeLange, the lady gasped and said, "You were Dexter DeLange's wife!"

It wasn't a question. It was a statement of fact, and when Jolene asked her how she knew that, she got a long, detailed explanation of how the woman's sister lived in Denver and one of the times she had visited her they had made appointments at DeLange Designs, and she had seen the pictures of Dexter and his wife, Jolene, on the salon walls.

She knew about the modeling Jolene had done and loudly promised all those around that she would show them the pictures, and then she tapped Chauncey on the arm and said he had brought quite a Denver celebrity among them. Jolene saw the questions in the eyes of the community and groaned inwardly.

Chauncey had tightened his arm around Jolene, but suddenly he relaxed it, and giving her a squeeze on the shoulder, he laughed lightly. "She was a beautiful model," he said, turning to look at her, "and she looks good on a horse too." Jolene stood on tiptoe and kissed his cheek, which brought an "ah" and laughter from those standing close by.

They were both grateful to Char for announcing lunch was ready.

Jolene had gone into their house after helping with the morning chores and was glad for its warmth. It was the middle of March, and snow mixed with rain had made for a chilly ride. They had brought in thirty or more cows that were getting close to calving and put them in a small pasture closer to the barns. Chauncey had decided there was one more he wanted to look at and was riding back to the larger pasture to find her. He had looked at Jolene's wind-teared eyes and red cheeks and had her unsaddle and go to the house. He had changed horses and taken the fresher Fox Trot in case the cow gave him some trouble.

She had been watching for him out the window anxiously for a couple of hours and gave a sigh of relief when she saw him walking toward the house. As soon as he stepped into the mudroom she knew he had had trouble. His jeans were wet and stiff, and his boots looked sodden. She quickly helped him off with his coat and peppered him with questions. He was chilled to the bone, and after taking off his boots, took a hot shower and sat down by the fireplace with a cup of hot coffee.

He had been giving Fox Trot a drink by the Belle when the horse plunged into the deeper water and wanted to roll. He quickly brought him out of it, but not before getting doused. He had cussed himself for ever giving the horse the opportunity to do such a thing, and had finished his ride, but he was so cold his hand shook when he was taking a drink.

A couple of days later he developed a cold from the incident, and it quickly became a concern for Jolene. She watched as he stubbornly kept the calving schedule of checking cattle during the night, and then finally made him stay in bed while she went. She knew he was totally miserable, or he would not have let her go. For a couple of days she worried as he seemed to get worse, and finally one night after she had checked to see if any heifers were calving, she crawled into bed to feel him hot and clammy, and made up her mind she would take him to the doctor the next day. He was diagnosed as having pneumonia, and told to go to the hospital, but he refused. Jolene filled his prescription and they came back home.

She looked at him with fire in her eyes and said he was going to stay in the house until he was well, and she would not hear of anything different. She reminded him she was twice a widow, and wasn't about to make it thrice. He looked startled at that and meekly went to bed.

For five days she handled all the workload outside, from the feeding, to the checking of the cattle, to marking the newborn calves, plus getting up at night. She fell asleep on the couch as soon as she came in and nursed him besides. He was a grouchy patient and she was a grouchier nurse, and one day when she came in with her hair plastered to her head from the Scotch cap and weariness in her walk, he croaked that she didn't look like much of a Denver celebrity to him. She threw a potholder at him, and said he looked like a pretty sorry Irish sop himself. They gave each other a grim smile. They were both relieved when he started feeling better.

Chauncey hated being sick and confined to the house, but he hated his financial outlook even more. When he was back outside doing his work he worried about what the figures were telling him, and when he was inside he worried about his cattle.

One rainy afternoon he sat before his computer and stared at the figures that bothered him so much. His loan payment was due in two weeks and there just was not enough money to cover it.

Jolene came in with an extra chair and sat down beside him.

"I just had a thought," she said.

"Is it important?" His voice was still slightly hoarse.

She grinned at their reversals in the conversation. "Yes, sir, Mr. Sullivan, it's important."

He wasn't in the mood for games, but she had worked so hard he felt he owed her a little consideration. "This had better be good," he muttered with a slight smile.

"Chauncey," her voice became serious, "I know what the figures say, I know the loan is coming up, and I know how to help."

He wasn't looking at her. She continued, "We've never talked about pooling resources, but you have let me consider this my home, and I have what we need to get out from under this debt."

"Jolene," he said softly, finally looking at her, "you're wounding my pride."

"I know, darling, that's why I haven't brought it up before. Wounded pride is hard to deal with."

"Maybe ..." He swiveled his chair around to face her. "Maybe we should talk about how much money you have."

She took a deep breath. "I actually have quite a lot, Chauncey. After my folks died, Walt was meticulous in keeping my finances in order. When John died, he had a life insurance policy that took care of our debts, and left a little besides. When Dexter's will was read, I learned for the first time that he had taken out a life insurance policy several years before he died, and I was the beneficiary. I have over six hundred thousand dollars."

Chauncey looked at her incredulously. She went to the kitchen to get a couple of mugs of coffee and to let the amount sink into his mind. When she came back he was still sitting with the same look on his face.

"Chauncey," she said rather timidly, "I didn't mention it before because I ... well, because it wasn't that important to me."

She didn't know if she liked the look he was giving her. "Why didn't you just go and buy your own ranch?" he wondered.

She looked startled. "I never even thought of that."

He stood up and paced around the room. "I don't know that I like my wife having that much money."

"Well," she answered practically, "we could pay off the debt and I would have a lot less."

He looked out the north window and then back at her. "I don't know that I want my wife to pay off my debt with her money."

"We could put the ranch in both of our names and then I would be paying off my debt with the money," she offered helpfully.

"I don't know that I want my ranch to become your ranch," he countered flatly.

"Well, forevermore, Chauncey, what do you want?" she yelled at him.

He slammed his coffee mug down on the desk and shouted back, "I want ... I want ..." His expression softened. "I want you, Jolene."

She looked at him so surprised that he burst out laughing and came over to wrap his arms around her. "Silly goose," she sputtered into his shoulder.

"I know, Jolene," he said softly into her hair. "This hasn't been much fun lately, has it." He kissed the top of her head. "I can't get over a woman who has that much money working her tail off to help me. You know, Jolene, you could have hired someone to come in here and do the work."

"I guess I never thought of that either," she admitted, enjoying his arms around her.

"We have some thinking to do," he said, turning her around to head out the door, "but maybe not in here."

Epilogue

A HAWK CIRCLED LAZILY over the high ridge that overlooked the Belle Fourche River on a soft spring evening in June. All around the prairie the wildflowers were blooming in abundant profusion and the meadowlark's song could be heard trilling over the hills.

Jolene and Chauncey were parked in the midst of this with their four-wheeler, enjoying all the sights and sounds of the high plains. The gentle breeze was lifting her hair and resettling it, and it softly caressed both of their faces. They had been out to the pasture to put salt blocks out for their cattle, and had decided to watch the sunset from this spectacular vantage point.

They were excited about their future. With one huge payment, they became debt free. Chauncey could hardly believe after seven years of struggling to make ends meet he was now in the position to improve equipment and barns, and as Jolene reminded him, a few tweaks on the house. She had taken her money and merged it with his in the bank, and he had taken the deed to his ranch and added her name to it.

But even more exciting to both of them was the baby they were expecting in January. The first, they hoped, of their four children, and Jolene and Chauncey didn't even care if their baby had mottled hair, as Jolene had predicted last summer.

Chauncey had taken his bride to Colorado Springs on Memorial Day, and they laid flowers beside the grave of the young captain and visited for a brief time at the cemetery with his family. David had shaken their hands haltingly and had looked away when he said he had been informed that the two suspected mechanics were actually inspectors who were investigating a faulty system installed in several planes, David's included. John's crash had pinpointed the problem.

Traveling back to Denver they detoured and stopped at Dexter's grave to add flowers there. For a while Jolene gazed over the mountains and tears brimmed her eyes. Chauncey drew her close and she rested her head on his shoulder. She took his hand and gave a farewell look at the tombstone, and slowly they had walked away.

The sun was slowly sinking behind the Black Hills, and its rays were sending the clouds into radiant colors of purples and pinks. Beyond them the prairie was bathed in golden light, and the hushed sounds of birds settling in for the night echoed over the hills. The rich smell of the prairie—the sages and wildflowers mixed with the scent of earth—wafted over them.

While the earth remains, seedtime and harvest, cold and heat, winter and summer, and day and night shall not cease.

The Weaver continues on. His plans and His ways are not always understood, but His love never ceases.

CPSIA information can be obtained at www.ICGtesting.com
230736LV00001B/5/P